Sweet, Sweet Wine

BY

JAIME CLEVENGER

Bella
BOOKS

2014

Bella Books, Inc.
P.O. Box 10543
Tallahassee, FL 32302

Printed in the United States of America on acid-free paper.

First Bella Books Edition 2014

Editor: Medora MacDougall
Cover Designer: Judith Fellows

ISBN: 978-1-59493-431-5

Acknowledgements

Thank you to my editor. Your patience and tender loving care pushed me to make this little story shine a bit brighter. Thank you also to my first-pass readers, Corina and Carla. I made the sexy parts sexier because of you.

About the Author

Jaime Clevenger lives with her wife and two kids in Colorado. She spends her days working as a veterinarian and playing with her family. Her dog and cats would all like a little more attention but every evening, much to their dismay, she settles in at the computer to write.

PART ONE

Rebound

Riley dropped her backpack on the nightstand and sank down on the bed. The red plaid blanket was rough against her hands and smelled of wood smoke but was thick enough to keep out the chill. Sharon had pulled back the curtains to show off the view of the courtyard. There was a gazebo painted dark purple with white trim, wicker chairs pulled out onto the grass to catch the last of the afternoon sun and, beyond this, a flagstone path leading to the hot tub and the main house. Aspen were grouped at the edge of the manicured grass and these held their green leaves but the maples were already beginning to turn a golden yellow.

A man came out of the back door of the main house. He stepped off the porch and lit up a cigarette, then strode down the path, eyeing the hot tub and the cottage. He tried one of the wicker chairs positioned with the best view of the garden, but the chair wobbled under his weight or, more likely, wobbled because the seats had all been arranged on the slanting hillside. He changed seats twice before settling on one with the least wobble.

Riley kicked off her shoes and leaned back on the bed. She had left Denver at rush hour and then sat in traffic for over an hour before even reaching the highway to the mountains. It was too late for a hike and she had no plans for dinner. She glanced at her watch. Lisa's plane was due to leave in twenty minutes. Jen was likely already seated next to her, in the seat Riley had reserved for herself. Riley pulled the blanket up to her chin and closed her eyes.

The sound of rushing water awoke Riley with a start. She was certain a pipe had burst behind her head, but as soon as she realized she was dry, she recalled Sharon's warning about the loud plumbing. She rubbed her head and fell back on the overstuffed pillow. She was in the same clothes she'd worn to work. She thought of changing but made no move to get out of bed. After some time, Riley realized the water in the pipes was battling with the noise of rain pattering on the shingles overhead. She stared at the sliver of light beneath the bathroom doorway, waiting for it to disappear.

Several minutes passed, possibly more, but there was no clock in the room. Riley wondered if the other guest had already left the bathroom and had accidentally left the light on or if it now served as a nightlight. She tried unsuccessfully to close her eyes and ignore it, but the light seemed to draw her attention like a beacon. Time dragged with only the sound of the rain to occupy her thoughts. After what seemed close to an hour had passed, she threw back the wool blanket and crossed the three steps from the bed to the bathroom door. She knocked lightly. No one answered. The door was unlocked and the fluorescent light within was blaringly bright. Her reflection in the mirror was that of a squinting stranger with wrinkled clothing and short, tousled hair. Cursing, she slapped the switch and hurried back to the warmth of the wool blanket.

* * *

"Go early, if you're hiking today," Sharon began, setting a steaming mug of coffee on the counter in front of Riley. "Last night was only a taste of the rain we're due. Do you want one or two slices of French toast?"

"One slice, thank you."

Sharon passed her a plate with a single piece on which a pat of butter was melting. "Enjoy. There's more syrup in the dining room if you want it."

"You've got a full crowd out there. Want help serving?"

"No, this is the best part of my job." Sharon pointed to a stool. "Sit down and enjoy your breakfast. There's milk in the fridge for the coffee." Sharon placed two pieces of French toast on each of three plates, garnished them with fat slabs of butter and a smattering of powdered sugar and then sliced orange slices onto the side. Balancing all three plates, she smiled at Riley and scooted through the swinging door into the dining room.

Riley found the milk, pulled the stool over to the counter and sat down with her mug. Sharon had left the newspaper open to the section on local news, and Riley flipped the pages until she found the world news. After scanning the first few headlines and being hit with a wave of gloom, she folded the paper and resolved to ignore the news for the next several days. She ate the French toast, thinking she should have had two slices when the first disappeared quickly. She took her plate over to the sink, already half full with other plates. The window above the sink framed a view of the mountains, which were cloaked this morning with mist so thick that the highest peaks were entirely concealed.

Sharon reappeared with empty hands. "They like the toast."

"It was delicious." Riley held up her empty plate. "You really do enjoy this, don't you?"

"Amazing, isn't it, considering this whole thing never was my idea? In fact, I distinctly remember standing right here in this kitchen and telling Cherie she was crazy if she thought I'd be able to cook breakfast for a dozen guests—or more—seven days a week. But, yes, I really do. Tomorrow I'm making breakfast frittatas from my favorite cookbook. I make it even better than the book with a little green chile sauce on the side."

"You won't mind if I help with the cleanup? I want to do something in exchange for room and board if you won't let me pay you." Riley rinsed off her plate and set it in the dishwasher.

"Deal. But sit down and finish your coffee first. I'll have that sink filled in a half hour and then you can really get to work. Sometimes I dream that I've made enough money to hire a year-round kitchen elf. I barely break even as it is through the slow winter months, though, so it doesn't make sense to have another hand. Still, I wish I could…Meredith comes at noon to clean the rooms, but I don't pay her enough to do the kitchen as well. In the busy summer season, I pay her daughter to help with the cleanup, but then she goes back to school and I'm left with all of this." She sighed and found a towel to wipe a puddle of spilled orange juice off the counter tiles. "But you can't beat September in the mountains. You've picked the best time to visit."

An attractive woman pushed the door halfway open and glanced from Sharon to Riley and then back to Sharon. Sharon quickly motioned her into the kitchen. "What is it, sweetie?"

"Any more coffee? We're empty out here."

Riley guessed that the woman in the doorway was in her early thirties, but she showed no sign that she minded being called sweetie. Only a grandmother could get away with calling their customers terms of endearment like "sweetie," Riley thought. Sharon had three grandchildren, in fact. Riley had seen all of their baby pictures. Sharon had been married once, years ago, but she never talked about the marriage except to say that the one good thing she got out of it was her son, Max. Max was twenty-nine, same as Riley, but he had already managed to father three kids.

"Of course." Sharon reached for the carafe she'd filled earlier and then set another pot on to brew. As she filled the woman's cup, she said, "Ana, meet Riley. You two are sharing the cottage."

Ana held up her hand. She had manicured nails and a gold bracelet that caught the light when she moved her hand. "She might not actually want to meet me this morning," she said, this time pointedly looking at Riley, "I think I may have woken you up last night. I needed a shower and forgot I was sharing the cottage."

Sharon shook her head. "Don't worry about Riley. She's a sound sleeper. Her ex was a snorer."

Riley laughed. "How'd you know Lisa was a snorer?"

"Oh, I know more secrets than that, honey." Sharon winked. She excused herself and went out to serve the coffee.

Ana set her mug down and opened the fridge door to get the milk. She had a trim but curvy figure that was noticeably attractive even in loose pants and a sweatshirt. The rest of her was easy to appreciate as well, Riley thought. Ana seemed to know her way around the place. Riley guessed this wasn't her first time staying at Sharon's.

"Mind if I join you? I like the kitchen seating better than the dining room. It's stuffy out there." Ana pulled the second stool up to the counter. "I had an ex who snored. I always tried to convince him to stay up late so I could get to bed first."

"I used that trick once or twice," Riley agreed.

"But it's hell if you wake up in the middle of the night to go pee, right? And earplugs drove me crazy. The sound of my own breathing isn't something I ever want to hear in stereo." She shook her head. "Anyway, that relationship lasted too long."

"Yeah? So did mine," Riley said. Ana flashed a smile, and Riley felt her heart skip a beat. She nearly laughed at her body's eager response. *Easy does it*, she thought.

"Here on business?" Ana asked.

"No, this is my week of vacation," Riley said. "I decided it was time for me to climb a mountain. I came here when my Alaska plans didn't pan out."

"Too bad. Alaska has some nice mountains."

"And I bet my ex is enjoying the view."

"Newly ex?"

"It's a long story…Let's just say I'm done with snorers." Riley took a sip of her coffee, which had cooled to lukewarm, and felt her stomach grumble. Sharon had come back and started another batch of French toast, and the smell of it was intoxicating. She thought of helping herself to another slice. "It does feel good to be here alone. I think I need some time to climb mountains and forget about girlfriend issues. I've been talking about climbing one of the fourteeners for two years now. Decided I should either shut up or do it. What about you? Business or vacation?"

"Business." Ana glanced at her watch. "In fact, I've got my first meeting this morning. But I am going to fit in a jog beforehand. Do you run? Want to join me?"

Riley considered the offer. She didn't ever really feel like running, but with Ana's company she thought it might be more entertaining than a solo jog. She glanced over at Sharon, who, she realized, was carefully listening in on their conversation despite her apparent concentration on the grill. "No, I think I'm hell-bent on climbing straight up a rock slab to get a good view."

"You know, you can drive to the top of Pikes Peak. You don't have spend all that time hiking," Sharon said, lifting slices of golden brown toast off the grill. "Anyway, I think you should start with the Grade. It's a nice trail and a good test of your oxygen levels at elevation."

"I live in Denver, Sharon. I think I'll be fine."

Sharon shook her head. "You'd be surprised."

"Your day is going to be more interesting than mine no matter which hike you pick," Ana said, carrying her mug over to the sink. "Thanks for breakfast, Sharon. Delicious as usual." She left through the back door, glancing back once at Riley.

Riley followed her with her eyes until the cottage door closed behind her. "I know she said her ex was a guy, but she doesn't seem all that straight to me."

"I won't remind you that you just broke up with Lisa this past week."

"I'm just saying."

"You're 'just saying'…uh, huh. I've heard that tone in your voice before and no one is ever, 'just saying,' when they say things that way. I don't think you're ready, Riley."

"She was the one who came over to sit down with me. I was just sitting here drinking my coffee and she invited herself over."

"What's wrong with you butch women?" Sharon waved her spatula. "She's friendly and talked to you for two minutes. That doesn't mean she's interested."

"Well, not always. But in this case, I think she is." Riley held up her hands when she saw Sharon's skeptical gaze. "Look, I'm on vacation and could use a distraction. And she's cute. Besides, you know everything with Lisa was a long time coming. If I'm not mistaken, I broke up with her in December and then again in April. I'm not freshly bruised."

"And she still lives with you. 'If I'm not mistaken,'" Sharon said, mimicking Riley's tone, "a month ago when you were going to break up with her for the third or fourth time, you decided to work things out. What if that happens again?"

"It won't," Riley said. "Not after she and Jen have been to Alaska together."

"Not 'after Alaska'? How about 'not after realizing that she'd been sleeping with her ex for months despite telling you and everyone otherwise'?" Sharon paused, then waved her spatula again at Riley, adding, "You deserve better."

"Everyone says that. What you really mean, is, 'you deserve someone who will be monogamous,' right? But the thing is, Jen wasn't the problem with our relationship."

"No, the problem was that you decided to pretend the thing with Lisa and Jen wasn't really happening," Sharon broke in, raising a hand and cutting Riley off when she tried to speak. "You knew. You knew Jen was her girl on the side whenever you two had a fight. But you didn't want to be alone, so you let her hang on long after you should have locked the door."

"I didn't know the half of it," Riley defended. "Not for a long time, anyway. She said nothing was going on and I believed her."

Sharon picked up two French toast platters and a pitcher of water. "Lisa and Jen were more than just friends from the very beginning. I warned you last Christmas…You may have thought that she was going to forget about Jen eventually, but it never happened. And I think you still aren't convinced that the relationship is over. You are still holding on."

"Trust me, I am *done*. I'm done with all of the games, and Lisa knows it. And I don't need an 'I told you so' right at the moment." Riley's stomach had tightened into a hard ball. She didn't want to hash out the details of her breakup with anyone, even someone as well-intentioned as Sharon. And she had already admitted that Sharon had been right about more than a few things with Lisa.

"You are still letting her stay at your condo."

"Should I have kicked her out the same day I broke up with her?"

"Yes. She could stay with Jen. Or go live with her mom."

Sharon was close friends with Lisa's mother, Jeanette. In fact, Riley had first met Sharon at Jeanette's Christmas party two years ago. They didn't see each other again until Jeanette's next Christmas party, which was the same night Riley broke up with Lisa the first time. Jeanette was also the owner of the clinic where Riley worked, which had made the whole situation with Lisa muddy right from the start.

For some reason, Sharon and Riley had formed an unlikely friendship. Unlikely not because of the difference in their ages, but because most of their conversations had involved Sharon trying to convince Riley to forget Lisa and move home to Washington. Sharon had been a stranger at the time and Riley had decided to trust Lisa instead.

Riley downed the last of her coffee and stood up, reconsidering the idea of going for a run. "It really doesn't matter at this point, does it?"

"I think it does. You aren't ready to start something with anyone, straight or otherwise."

"There's no harm in flirting."

Sharon shook her head and pushed open the door. She paused, balancing the platters and water pitcher with practiced ease. "I think you need to be alone. Try it for a little while anyway. The last thing you need is to get involved with another woman. And stick to the easy hike today. The rains might pick up this afternoon. I don't want to worry about you up on the Peak."

Riley stuck around in the kitchen long enough to clear the sink. By the time she returned to the cottage, there was no sign of Ana. She thought of waiting until she returned from her run, but she couldn't come up with an excuse to have another conversation. She stood in the doorway of her side of the cottage, pondering what to do next. The room was cramped and made her long to be outside. There was a narrow walkway between the double bed and the dresser and an old woodstove stood in one corner while the nightstand took up the other corner. The door to the shared bathroom was on the same wall as the bed, and Riley now understood why Sharon had warned her that the plumbing was in the wall behind the headboard. She doubted anyone could sleep through the noise of the shower.

She considered her options. For the first time in months, she had no real agenda. If she'd had more time to plan, she would likely have jumped on a plane headed for France or maybe Costa Rica. Instead, with only two days' notice, she'd called Sharon. The last vacation she'd taken alone was in college. Since then, she'd always had a girlfriend's company when she traveled.

Riley pulled out the trail map that Sharon had given her and glanced at the circled hikes. She recognized the Grade, easily visible from the cottage window and marked by the brown gouge cutting in a straight line up the side of the mountain. Dark evergreens covered the terrain on either side, giving the trail the look of an abandoned ski run even though it was clearly much too steep to be one. She changed into her hiking boots and tucked the map into her cargo pants' pocket along with her wallet and phone.

Riley took the winding main road through downtown Catori, testing her Honda's old brakes frequently for a good number of tourists. The entire downtown took up only four or five blocks. Storefronts filled with mountain resort kitsch and tie-dye apparel fought for space among pubs and restaurants, none of which seemed to target a local crowd.

When she got to the trailhead parking lot, Riley found it poorly marked but filled to near capacity. She pulled her Seattle Seahawks ball cap over her short hair and felt a twinge in her shoulder. She owed the sore muscles to the crush she had developed on the woman who led the group lifting class at her gym. For the past few months, she had managed to shift her work schedule to start appointments an hour later to fit in morning workouts. Mostly she had used the class as an excuse to leave the house early. Lisa wasn't a morning person, and since Riley had finally come to terms with the fact that Jen was more than Lisa's friend, she could hardly face Lisa at all, let alone in the morning. The weight class had, however, done good things for her abs and back, something that was useful in her line of work. Over the past few weeks, though, she'd pushed her limits. The coach had finally noticed and intervened. By then, however, Riley had lost the desire to flirt with her. Convincing Lisa that their relationship was over had taken too much energy. The weight routine was a good outlet for stress and had helped her fit into her favorite pair of 501s, but that was all.

Sharon had claimed that rain was predicted for every evening that week, but there was only a weak breeze, and a cloudless sky framed the mountains in a blue that left the eyes to wander in search of something more interesting. Pikes Peak, a grayish-purple rock slab that was too large to appreciate in the lens of her iPhone when she snapped a shot, loomed close and cold. Most of the surrounding mountains were softened with evergreens, juniper and a gravelly red soil that crunched underfoot. On the northern edge of the vista, ridges of dusty brown claimed the skyline. A fire the year before had left scarred hills thousands of acres wide. Riley trained her gaze on the Peak, not the burned hills in the distance or the closer green slopes.

The Grade was aptly named, if nothing else. There was little else to consider about the trail other than the grade itself. Railroad ties were arranged into stairs reaching upward to the summit in a number that seemed never-ending. A seasick feeling rose in her stomach when she turned to get a look at the view about halfway up. The range stretched out in a flat line of fading browns and darker blues as far as the eye could trace the horizon, disrupted only by a cluster of red rocks jutting skyward. Riley had walked arm in arm with Lisa along the paved paths between those red rocks a year ago. She even recalled bits of their conversation: they'd discussed the name of the place—Garden of the Gods—and wondered if the plural had been intended, if whoever had named it had believed in more than one omniscient being. Somehow, that discussion and the entire day, in fact, had ended without a fight. So much had changed since then.

Riley shifted to the edge of the path to make passing space for a stream of joggers. She had already caught her breath, but she wasn't going to let herself race to the top. Some in the group grinned or even nodded their heads in a greeting, others grimaced or had the same set gaze as the determined faces on folks struggling on Stairmasters back in the gym. One couple came up clad in matching yellow road bike racing uniforms, chatting all the while. As they neared her spot, Riley noticed the woman hesitating as she placed weight on her left knee. She wasn't limping, but she was clearly uncomfortable. Riley guessed she had an old injury to her meniscus or her ACL, or both. As soon as this thought passed her mind, she chuckled. She couldn't make it even one day out of the clinic without work thoughts springing up to distract her. She let the bikers get some distance up the hill before she fell in line behind them. Row after row of railroad ties, each cased in soil with the same texture and crunch as Grape-Nuts, drew her attention back to the trail.

* * *

"I volunteered us both for a work crew up in Williams Canyon. You can save the Peak for a clear day." Sharon said the next morning. She handed Riley a plate holding chunks of cantaloupe. "You know, you missed my frittatas. They ate every last bit. Tomorrow is omelet day. You really don't want to miss my omelets."

"You make a mean omelet too?"

Sharon nodded.

"So you signed us up for a work crew?"

"The work crew helps with flood mitigation work on the burn scar. And don't worry, you'll get plenty of exercise. Besides that, the view is amazing."

Riley sat down at the center island in the kitchen. She took a bite of the fruit. "It barely rained last night."

"But tonight it is supposed to pour. You won't have time to make it all the way up and back without getting caught in the storm. I doubt you even thought to pack a jacket."

"Sometimes you sound like my mom, Sharon." Riley wanted to ask about Ana. She hadn't seen her since yesterday's breakfast. Somehow, despite their sharing the cottage, she had missed her coming and going and there had been no late-night shower.

"You missed Ana," Sharon said, guessing Riley's thoughts. "She liked my frittata. She also asked about you. I told her you were lazy and were probably going to sleep through breakfast." Sharon finished loading the dishwasher and then went to work on the pans in the sink. "We need to leave in an hour to make it to the meeting site. Mind picking us up sandwiches at Cheddar's?"

Riley wanted to ask if Ana had said anything more, but Sharon didn't seem to be in the mood to chat. Cheddar's was the café down the road. "There's no arguing out of this work crew thing is there?"

Sharon shook her head. "It's possible I don't want you getting yourself in over your head climbing the Peak alone. The weather isn't right for it, Riley. Not today. Save that for another day."

Cheddar's was on the main drag through town, three blocks down from Sharon's bed-and-breakfast. As Riley walked there, she saw that the clouds had cleared and the sun had burned off the morning's mist. From this vantage point, the Grade was easily visible on the nearest green mountain slope and, behind it, Pikes Peak. North of this were the burned mountains. To the south, all of the mountains were green. The canyon where the town lay seemed to be the dividing line between the two sets of mountains. Squinting, Riley could make out hundreds of blackened tree trunks stabbing the charred land. Now that Sharon had suggested it, the idea of working on the mountain slope on a beautiful sunny day was appealing.

The previous summer had been inexplicably hot and dry. When the fire started, Sharon had been evacuated along with the rest of the town. She'd stayed in Denver with Jeanette for a few days and had been glued to the news. Though the fire had spared the town, it had decimated thousands of acres and burned with such heat that only scarred trunks remained. The burned area was something Sharon talked about often. The fire had scarred more than the hills.

Riley entered the café and the man at the counter waved and nodded as if they were old friends. Sharon had talked about the owners of the café enough that Riley felt as if she knew them.

"Weathermen are about as likely to get it right as a coin toss," a customer was saying to him.

"And I think it's fifty-fifty with that river any time it rains." The man at the counter was short and balding, like his partner, who was at the sink cleaning dishes. Sharon was friends with the pair and recommended the café to all of her guests, she'd told Riley, on the sole premise that the owners were gay. "It depends on whether the clouds get stuck over the burn scar."

The customer nodded vigorously. "All of the sandbags in the world won't help if a storm really opens up on the canyon."

Earlier in the summer, before the grass had reseeded the burned land, monsoon rains had started. Sharon said that the rains had been a daily occurrence since then, mostly falling as a light rain for an hour or two every evening. One night, however, the rains had pelted down on the burn scar, and the creek, which usually flowed like a lazy snake through the center of town, had swelled to a rushing river. When it overflowed its banks, several homes and businesses flooded. Less than a month later, though, there was no evidence of that flood. The damage had been minimal, and the town had been quick to clean up the debris. But every new rainstorm was a possible disaster in the making. Sandbags were still propped up in doorways in the downtown section near the creek, and Sharon had said that there was a general fear of a repeat flood whenever clouds collected over the mountains. Sharon's place was well above the flood zone, but she knew every business owner near the creek by name.

Riley ordered two sandwiches and chips to go and dropped her change in the jar labeled "Catori Flood Relief."

The man at the counter nodded his thanks, handed over two tightly wrapped sandwiches and pointed at the rack of chips. She tucked the sandwiches and chips in her backpack.

"You're staying with Sharon, aren't you?" the man asked.

Riley had never lived in a place where everyone knew everyone else and found it a bit unnerving. She nodded.

"I'm Scott." He smiled. "Sharon called earlier and said she was sending you. Riley, right? I forgot to tell her that I've got a new cookie recipe. She buys two dozen from me every day and passes the cookies off as her own to the guests." He paused to point to the cookies lined up on the cookie sheets behind him. "Anyway, I'm calling these cookies Firemen's Oatmeal Chunk Cookies. Can you ask her if she minds if I send these instead of the usual chocolate chip this afternoon?"

"I'll ask. I doubt Sharon will mind." She held the door open for a customer and then stepped outside, waving to Scott as she left. His returning smile made her realize why Sharon had stayed in Catori after Cherie's death. There was something to be said about living in a small town.

A group of twenty or so volunteers were standing in the parking lot outside the fire department when she arrived. Riley approached the woman who appeared to be in charge. She was in her late fifties and had short, spiky gray hair. She wore a green forest ranger uniform and was holding a clipboard.

"First-time volunteer?"

Riley nodded.

"Waiver forms," the ranger said, handing over two forms and a pen. "In case a log rolls down the hill and crushes your leg."

"How optimistic."

"I used to say, 'in case a log rolls down and kills you,' but my boss asked me to soften the verbiage."

Riley grinned and took the offered forms. "I'm Riley Robinson. Sharon McBee wasn't able to make it."

The woman glanced at her list and then looked up at Riley. "Sharon isn't on my list today. But I do have a Robinson." She jabbed her finger at the name and squinted at Riley. "That's you?"

"Yeah, that's me. I guess there was a mix-up with Sharon's name not getting on the list. Anyway, she isn't coming, so it doesn't matter." Sharon had told Riley that she'd had one guest shorten his trip by a day and then a last-minute reservation call that morning so she had to stay home to clean. Now Riley wondered if she'd ever planned on going at all.

"Sharon's already put in three days on this project. As much as I like to have her on my crew, she's done her time. It's nice of her to send an able body in her place."

Riley wondered if the ranger was hinting that Sharon was more than an occasional volunteer interest of hers. The women were about the same age, and she knew Sharon liked the rugged mountaineer look. She could easily imagine a mutual attraction. "What exactly are we going to be doing?"

"Pick out a hard hat and finish up with those forms. We'll give everyone a briefing on the drive up." The ranger pointed to one of the two vans in the parking lot. "Find a seat on that one. Half of the group is going with me and the other half is going with Andrew. I'm Deb." She stuck out her hand. "Sharon's told me some about you already, but I won't pretend to know any secrets."

Riley followed the group when the time came to load onto the van. She watched Deb closely, wondering what level of relationship Sharon had with her. It was just like Sharon to not mention anything. They drove on the highway a few miles north of town and then turned off the road at a sign marking a closed trailhead. The hills were steep and scorched trees stuck out of the soil indiscriminately. In a few areas grass grew, but most of the soil was barren. The ranger hopped out of the van and unlocked a chain securing a barricade. She got back in the van and then continued driving up a windy gravel road for a half mile or so. She parked the van and then stood in the aisle to address the volunteers.

"The other crew is going to spend the next two hours raking debris and reseeding. But you lucky folks get to drag logs. We're going to plan out an erosion barrier on this hillside"—she paused to point out the front window—"and then we'll drag the logs that were cut over there"—she pointed to another hill—"into position. We've got a ditch that the crew from last week dug that has to be sandbagged in case you're interested in that job as well. After two hours, we'll switch with the other crew and you can tell them how much fun it is to drag a log up the side of an unstable hillside. Take breaks to drink plenty of water and watch your footing. I don't want to deal with any broken limbs today, all right, folks? Now, let's have some fun."

When Deb finally called for a lunch break, Riley sank right down on the log she'd been dragging. Scott, the guy from the café, laughed out loud. "What the hell are you doing?"

"I'm exhausted."

"You're sitting on a log perched halfway up the side of a ravine on a slope with nothing but rocks to slow you down if that thing takes off."

"But I've got a good view."

"Your eyes are closed," he countered.

Riley opened her eyes and smiled over at Scott. She'd been paired up with him for the past two hours and had learned more of the town's juicy gossip from him than she'd ever heard from Sharon. Scott was convinced that people viewed him as a therapist who also happened to own a café. His partner, Oliver, was keeping the café open at the moment so Scott could work on the flood mitigation.

"Hey, I bought two sandwiches from this awesome café and my friend bailed on me. Want one?"

Scott smiled. "I brought three-day-old cookies that were too old to sell and bruised apples. Sounds like a picnic."

"What about your new recipe? Those firemen cookies. I want one of those."

Scott shook his head. "I brought an old batch. Ginger snaps."

After a short rest to catch their breaths, they trudged over to the van, found Riley's backpack and Scott's bag of cookies and ate together without a word. Deb passed out donated bottles of Gatorade and radioed the other ranger to discuss the details of the planned job switch. A few minutes later, she clapped her hands and scooted everyone back out on the hillside. "The other crew is running behind and hasn't stopped for their lunch break yet, so we'll keep working on the erosion barrier for another half hour and then make the switch."

By the time Deb signaled the end of their workday, Riley was thoroughly covered in dirt and soot. Her blue jeans were a blackish gray from mid-thigh down and her white T-shirt was a filthy brown. She followed Scott into the van and closed her eyes as soon as she sat down. Scott jostled her awake when they reached the fire station. Dark rain clouds had collected over the past hour, and a light rain spotted the van's windshield. Deb was shaking hands with the volunteers as they filed out of the van.

"Come by the café tomorrow and I'll pay you back for the sandwich. I'm making gumbo for lunch tomorrow."

"I'm so tired, Scott, I don't think I'm going to move tomorrow."

"Sharon's got a hot tub. Have a soak tonight."

Riley watched Scott hop out of the van and then realized she was the only person remaining. She stood and stretched.

"Robinson, you all right?" Deb hollered.

"No. I'm sore as hell."

"Just wait till tomorrow." Deb laughed. "Scott is short, but that man is all muscle. And you're more of a lean colt. But somehow the two of you pulled as many logs as the boys from the National Guard."

"That might be comforting tomorrow."

Deb smiled. "Want me to give you a lift over to Sharon's?"

"No, I better walk this out. Unless, of course, you're looking for an excuse to see Sharon."

Deb blushed and looked down at her boots. "No, no. I don't think I…Well, maybe, tell her I said hello."

Riley nodded. "So you two aren't seeing each other?"

Deb shook her head. "Well, so far it's only been a complicated friendship. I'm giving her time."

"Sharon will take too much time if you let her, Deb." Riley picked up her backpack and shuffled out of the van. Despite the heavy cloud cover, the air was still pleasantly warm and the rain felt light and refreshing. Riley took the alley to bypass the main house, noting Sharon on the front porch greeting a newly arrived guest. The back gate was jammed. Riley worked the rusted latch until she realized the rain had swollen the wood in place. She gave the gate a hard kick and it finally budged loose with a groan.

Steam rose off the hot tub, where one of the guests was just climbing out. In the rain, the thought of the hot tub was even more appealing. She unlocked the cottage door, kicked her dirt-encrusted shoes off and immediately stripped. The shower took a long while to warm up, and she kept her eyes closed all the while. Her only thought was whether she wanted dinner before or after a soak in the hot tub.

* * *

The rumbling of pipes startled Riley awake. It was dark, but there were noises in the courtyard outside. She fumbled for her phone on the nightstand and read the time in disbelief. It was after nine. She'd laid down after her shower and managed to sleep through dinner. Her belly growled in confirmation. She searched her backpack and found the bruised apple that Scott had given her earlier and a baggy of trail mix, an emergency ration that she'd packed for the Grade. She ate this and the apple that Scott had given her. Both tasted better than expected. She pulled on a clean shirt and a pair of shorts and headed outside.

A light rain was misting the courtyard. The hot tub was covered now. She debated asking Sharon for food or venturing out alone, then decided to raid Sharon's kitchen and tell her in the morning. She glanced at the front half of the cottage and noticed that the light was on in the bedroom. The shades were drawn, but she could see the shadow of someone moving about the room. Without thinking, she knocked on the door.

Ana opened the door, eyed Riley for a moment and then smiled. "What happened to you? Rough day on the mountain?"

Riley immediately reached for her head. Going directly from the shower to bed had produced predictable results. She could feel the disheveled strands and wished that she'd taken a moment to glance in the mirror. It was too late now to turn around and she didn't have the energy to offer up an excuse. "I was thinking of going in the hot tub later, but I wanted company."

"And this was the first door you tried?"

"Kind of."

"Anyone's company might do?"

Riley grinned. "It was either you or that bald guy who's managed to wear the same Hawaiian shirt for the past two days."

"He overdoes it on the aftershave."

"Yeah, I was hoping you'd say yes. But I need food first." Riley glanced over at the main house. "I'm going to raid Sharon's kitchen. And I didn't want you to go to bed."

Ana laughed. "You didn't want me to go to bed?"

"Well, not without asking you about the hot tub first. I was going to ask you yesterday, but I didn't see you after breakfast." Riley paused. She had the urge to reach out for Ana's hand. She was feeling like an awkward middle schooler in search of a dance partner. Ana continued to stare at her with the same playful expression she'd had at breakfast the day before. Riley started again. "Of course, if you want to go to bed, that's fine, but I wanted to ask before you did. And it's raining so I didn't know if you'd go to bed early because of that."

"It is raining, but I don't see how that changes when I go to bed. Anyway, I'm hungry too. I had my last meeting tonight at a steak house and I don't eat meat. Literally, the only vegetarian thing on the menu was an iceberg lettuce salad. The tomatoes were terrible."

"Welcome to cattle country."

"Think Sharon will mind if we both raid her kitchen?"

"No. Well, probably." Riley shrugged. "But I can't bring myself to put on real clothes and go to a restaurant. I'll wake up early and run to the store to replace whatever we eat."

Ana grabbed her keys, locked the cottage door and followed Riley down the path to the main house. Riley flipped on the kitchen lights and saw a plate of oatmeal cookies on the island. She picked up a note that had her name written on it and handed a cookie to Ana. "They're from Scott. He's the sweetie I spent the day with and the reason I'm so sore."

Ana arched her eyebrows. "Scott?"

"We drug logs up the side of one of the burned hills in a drainage canyon. The idea is that the logs will slow down the water flow. They've also built these big ditches to try and catch the debris before it finds its way to the river. If they control erosion up there, they're hoping the town won't get bathed in mud when a big rainstorm hits."

"Let's hope it works. I spent all day in one of the buildings by the river. It's beautiful down there." Ana took a bite of the cookie and nodded approvingly. "You know what this dinner needs? A glass of milk." She went over to the cupboard and found two glasses, then pulled the milk out of the fridge. "Judging by the way you looked, I thought maybe you had climbed Pikes Peak after all."

"Saving it for another day, I guess. I actually had a good day, despite appearances."

"Well, aside from my run this morning, the rest of my day was shitty. I would rather have been dragging logs with you." Ana filled the glasses and then handed one to Riley.

"What was your meeting about?" Riley asked.

"I'm trying to help someone make a tough decision. The corporate folks want us to buy out the franchise owners for the location here and orchestrate a change in management or close the place." Ana paused. She reached over the plate of cookies to touch Riley's hair. She ran her fingers through the short strands and then pulled her hand away. "I'm sorry. It's just hard to have a serious conversation with you right now."

"My hair's crazy?"

Ana smiled in return. She leaned closer and tried again to press Riley's hair into place. "Unless you were trying for that bedhead look."

"Nope. Without gel, this is the real deal." Riley found the strands that were standing on end and pressed them down, doubting anything short of a shower would have any effect. She didn't mind that she'd given Ana an excuse to touch her, however.

Ana pulled Riley's hand away from the hair and laughed. "It's a lost cause. But I kind of like it."

Riley smiled. "You were telling me about your meeting."

Ana nodded. "Anyway, of course, the owners want to hold on to the winery, but they don't know how to do it. I consult for multiple wineries, but this corporate work makes up most of my paycheck so I need to somehow make everyone happy. Boutique wineries have a narrow margin. With last year's fire and then the drop in tourists, this place had a rough start." She paused and then said, "You know, I don't really want to talk about work right now. Do you mind if I take a pass on the rest of this?"

"Yeah, I understand. I'm trying to see if I can spend an entire week without talking about my work too."

"Well, I already know what you do in the real world, so I won't ask," Ana confided.

"How's that?"

"Sharon." Ana finished her cookie and sipped the milk. "I asked her about you this morning. She doesn't skimp on details."

"Why'd you ask her about me?"

Ana blushed. "Why do you think?"

"I'm not entirely sure." Riley was testing her and watched her expression for some hint that she was wrong. "Should I think that you…"

She hesitated. What was the right way to ask what she needed to know? Gay or bi, it didn't really matter. The important question was if she was interested in Riley, not if she was interested in women in general.

Then again, that mattered too.

Ana nodded. "You should."

"That doesn't really answer my question."

"You weren't specific." Ana smiled.

Riley finished her cookie and the milk, eyeing Ana all the while. She went over to the sink and rinsed out their glasses. Ana leaned against the counter watching her. Riley wiped her hands on the kitchen towel. "I really want to ask you something, but…" Riley couldn't bring herself to finish the sentence.

"What do you want to ask me?"

Riley didn't answer. Ana arched her eyebrow and crossed her arms. A minute passed with Ana only staring at her. Somehow, even this felt suggestive. "You wanna go sit in the hot tub with me?"

Ana slipped her arm through Riley's as soon as they stepped outside. The closeness of Ana's body ignited Riley's senses. Her perfume was faint but appealing. Riley was a few inches taller than Ana and averted her eyes when she realized she was able to glance down at the low neckline of Ana's blouse. They parted without words at Ana's doorstep. Riley went into her side of the cottage and changed into her bathing suit. She thought of grabbing a towel, but Ana was in the bathroom. She went outside, tiptoeing quickly over the cold stones, raised the hot tub cover and slipped her hand in the water. The temperature was perfect. The rain had finally stopped, but the air was misty and heavy clouds concealed the stars.

Ana's hands settled on Riley's hips. Riley glanced over her shoulder and smiled. Ana had changed into a black bikini. She let go of Riley, letting her hands brush across Riley's midsection as she did, and climbed into the hot tub. She sank into the water slowly. "Okay, this day isn't a total loss after all. Damn, this feels good." She sank lower and sighed. "Sometimes I think I should get a hot tub. But there's no point, really, since I'm never home."

Riley eased into the water. She picked a spot opposite Ana. "Where do you live?"

"Airport hotels, mostly. But I've got a condo in Napa. I call that home." Ana crossed the distance between them. She floated in front of Riley for a moment, then steadied herself with one hand on the step nearest Riley. "You know, I've been distracted all day."

"Really? Why's that?"

Ana put one hand on either side of Riley. She rose up from the water, their faces only inches apart, and then she hesitated. The next moment, she turned abruptly and dropped under the water's surface. She swam back to the other side of the hot tub and reemerged. The water cascaded off her smooth shoulders. They stared at each other for a long moment before Ana finally looked away. Ten minutes passed with neither of them speaking.

Riley closed her eyes. She thought of the last time she had been in a hot tub. It was early summer and Lisa's friend, Elle, had invited them over for a barbeque. Elle was obsessed with baseball. Most everyone was inside watching the last inning of the game on her big-screen TV. But Riley had been out in the hot tub with Lisa and Jen. Lisa had been distant all evening. Riley had tried to think of something she'd done to piss her off, a common occurrence, but had come up empty. Work had been busy that day and her thoughts had drifted to the patients she'd seen. At some point, someone had come outside, likely Elle, and switched on the hot tub lights. In a brief moment, Riley saw Jen's hand on Lisa's leg, then the two moved away from each other. She was nauseous and furious, and yet she couldn't form a single word.

Now, months later and with too many wounds to bother recounting, she wondered what Lisa and Jen were doing at the moment. She imagined them in a narrow ship's cabin, curled about each other in bed. Shaking off this thought, she exhaled slowly. This tub was a perfect ending to the day. She didn't want to ruin it with thoughts of Lisa. Riley opened her eyes when she heard Ana stepping out of the hot tub.

"I've got an early meeting tomorrow."

Riley nodded. She watched her reach for a towel and, wrapped in this, tiptoe across the flagstones to the cottage. At the cottage door, she hesitated and glanced back at Riley. Riley knew she was once much better at flirting, better at initiating the first kiss, better at convincing a woman to spend the night talking even if there was an early meeting. But she'd lost her footing in this realm. She watched as Ana went inside and closed the door. Riley sank low in the water, letting it envelop her aching shoulders.

* * *

A loud knocked wrestled Riley away from her dream. It was near dawn, judging by the faint glow in the sky. Sharon was dressed in a dark blue robe and puffy pink slippers. "Are those yours?" Riley wondered aloud.

Sharon glanced down at the slippers as if seeing them for the first time. "Max gave them to me last Christmas. They're comfortable," she added. "I need you to run an errand. One of the guests has a head cold. He's one of my regulars and a real sweetie."

Riley combed her hand through her hair. It was still a mess. "You want me to go pick up a decongestant?"

"I'd do it, but I've got to get dressed. Apparently no one should see me in these slippers."

Riley shrugged. "They give you a grandma look."

"I *am* a grandma," Sharon riposted. "And I've got a full house for breakfast this morning."

"No problem. I'll shower and be out the door in five minutes." Riley was in the habit of getting out of the house quickly. For the past three months she'd made a habit of avoiding Lisa by dodging out the door before she'd woke each morning and then staying at work late. "And you're making omelets."

Sharon nodded. "Hungry?"

"I somehow slept through dinner."

"But you had milk and cookies with someone. Tell me what happened when you get back from the store. Oh, and bring me a receipt so I can pay you back."

Riley checked the time and then headed for the shower. Ana opened her door to the bathroom at the same moment that Riley opened hers. Riley stepped back into her room, closing the door with an apology. The shared bathroom only made sense, she decided, when a family had rented out the entire cottage. Otherwise it was just awkward, especially if the person who had nearly kissed you the night before was in the opposite room.

A minute passed and the lights flicked off. Riley slipped into the bathroom and quickly showered. She dressed and grabbed her keys. A knock sounded again on the front door. She opened it, expecting Sharon. Ana was dressed in a tailored navy business suit with a skirt. She opened her mouth and then closed it again. She turned to leave and then paused. She turned back and said, "I'm not sure what happened last night."

Riley felt her stomach sink. A straight girl was about to tell her how much she really liked men. She had never had this particular conversation and never thought she'd have to hear it. Fortunately, she'd always been attracted to women who were interested in women. Riley held up her hand to stop Ana's next sentence. "You know, don't worry about it at all. We ate cookies together, nothing more." Riley started past her. "I've got to run an errand for Sharon. See you around."

Riley jogged to her car, trying to push away the image of Ana in the navy blue suit. She couldn't help her attraction to her, but Ana's quick exit from the hot tub and the brush-off this morning made Riley wish she had no feelings toward her at all. Riley turned the key in the ignition and the Honda's old engine sputtered to life. She concentrated on the errand, content with this distraction, and drove until she found a convenience store.

Riley bought two different decongestants and an orange juice vitamin drink, thinking it would be a nice touch. Sharon was clearly interested in impressing this guest. She got back to the main house in time to see Ana leaving. The business suit fit her like it had been made to accentuate her curves exactly. Ana climbed into a red rental car. Riley wondered what type of car she had parked at the condo in Napa. A midsized American-made red sedan just didn't fit her. Riley sighed. Sharon was right. She needed this trip to be about clearing her mind, not about filling it with thoughts of an unattainable, beautiful woman.

Sharon had changed out of the robe but still wore the pink slippers. She took the bag from Riley and handed her a bell pepper and a knife. "Thank you. Can you chop?"

While Sharon delivered the juice and medicine, Riley chopped peppers, onions and mushrooms. Sharon returned and took over the cooking, setting Riley to the task of making coffee and toast. Except for the guest with the cold, everyone else wanted an early breakfast. The omelets disappeared quickly. Eight guests later, Riley was finally given a plate. She wolfed down the food. Sharon shook her head when she set her plate in the dishwasher.

"Did you even taste it?"

"Delicious."

"Make yourself another piece of toast. I want company when I eat." Sharon finished cooking her own omelet and then sat down on the stool next to Riley. The dining room had been cleared, and over the next hour, the guests would file out to enjoy the day of sunshine. No one was checking out or arriving, so only the kitchen cleaning had to be done and Sharon was in a good mood.

Riley let Sharon finish her omelet and then asked, "So, what's going on with you and Deb?"

"Nothing."

"Okay, how about this: Want to talk about why you aren't seeing Deb?"

Sharon shook her head. "You know why."

"It's been a long time, Sharon."

"Three years. I'm not ready for Deb—or anyone else for that matter—to move into my life."

"I don't think Deb is looking to move in. I think she would be happy taking it easy. You could just get to know her. Have her over some evening and play cards."

Sharon sneered. "Did you meet the same Deb? Taking it easy isn't her thing. And I don't think she wants to play cards with me." She pushed her plate away from her and tossed her crumpled napkin onto it. "Yes, I like her, but I don't think it would work out. She wants a commitment and I feel like I've used up all of my commitments."

"I don't think that's how it works."

"I was with Cherie for twenty years. Did you know that we weren't always monogamous?"

"What?" Riley shook her head. "Don't tell me this. I've had the idea in my head that you two must have had the perfect relationship. I don't want the story tarnished."

"Well, you didn't know Cherie."

Cherie had passed away from cancer the year before Riley had met Sharon. From the stories Sharon had told her, they'd had their ups and downs. Somehow, in Riley's mind these ups and downs did not include sleeping with other people, however.

"In fact, Deb and I were close, for a while. Cherie knew it then. But Deb was the sort of woman that every dyke in town had kissed at least once. I'm certain Cherie and she had a fling, though we never talked about it. I knew it didn't mean anything, really, even at the time. Deb was with Rhonda then. They had an open relationship, but it was all on Rhonda's insisting. Deb was in love with Rhonda and only pretending with everyone else. One day Rhonda decided she was sick of the mountains, sick of small towns, and before we knew it, she'd moved back to New York. She didn't want Deb to come with her." Sharon's eyes were distant, remembering. "Anyway, if Deb doesn't want to wait for me, so be it. But I know that woman well enough. If I tell her I need to go slow, she'll be over every night."

"Would it be awful to have company every night? She's good-looking and has a sense of humor. Why not see where things go?"

"I like my alone time. It gives me space to remember."

Riley stopped at this. Sharon's eyes were moist, and it was clear she didn't want to share any more. Cherie had been the reason that Sharon's marriage had broken up. She'd married early and had her son, Max, by the time she was twenty-three. Not long after Max had been born, she'd moved to Colorado and met Cherie. Shortly thereafter, she was divorced. But there were many pieces of the puzzle that Riley had yet to learn. Sharon was a great one for starting conversations, but as soon as the topic turned serious, she'd get a faraway look and clam up.

"I should have realized…I'm sorry for bringing it up."

"Don't be. Three years does seem like a long time, doesn't it? I probably would tell someone the same thing—time to move on." Sharon had wiped her eyes and forced a smile. "I half sent you up there to work on the burn scar and half to help me feel out this situation with Deb. She knows I'm attracted to her. That's no secret. I've been acting interested in her for years."

"I'm not saying move on. I'm just saying it might be nice to have company."

"And yet it feels like I'm cheating on Cherie whenever I'm around Deb. Ridiculous, isn't it?"

"I don't know. I've never lost someone I loved."

"Deb is a go-getter. And at one point in my life, I wanted her attention nearly enough to slip out on Cherie. Just for one night, I told myself…" Sharon shrugged. "If I could explain it better, I would. But now after years of flirting when we knew we really shouldn't, we're both single and I'm not ready."

"Go figure."

Sharon wiped her eyes again. "Scott makes good cookies, doesn't he?"

Riley noted the change in her voice. She'd changed to the chitchat voice she used with guests. "He's good at dragging logs halfway up a hillside too." Riley rolled her shoulders and neck.

"And Ana liked the cookies?"

"Almost as much as you like asking leading questions." Riley smiled. "By the way, what exactly did you tell Ana about me? She said you didn't skimp on details."

"Oh, I skimped on plenty of details." Sharon stood up and carried her plate over to the dishwasher. It was overfull and it took some jostling to get the last plate in. She turned on the wash cycle and sat back on the stool. "Let me see, I told her about your work. She asked me how long you'd been working as a physical therapist, but I couldn't remember. And I told her about Lisa. I told her that you should have never gotten involved with her and that you probably knew it. I told her you probably wouldn't stay in Colorado."

"You don't think I'll stay?"

"What's holding you here?"

"Work. Friends." Riley had thought about moving back to Seattle too many times to recount.

"Maybe. We'll see. Anyway, I changed my mind about Ana. I don't think she's very straight. And she's definitely interested in you." Sharon finished her cup of tea and cleared her throat. "What happened last night?"

"Nothing. It was almost something too, which I think is worse than nothing. She still thinks she's straight."

"Been there." Sharon gathered the toast crumbs on the counter into a pile with a sweep of her hand. She stood up and went for the broom. "I don't know, though. Maybe it isn't about her at all. Maybe it's about you. It is possible that I insinuated that you weren't ready."

"Thanks a heap, Sharon." Riley sighed. "Well, I wasn't hiding the fact that I was interested in moving forward."

"It's possible that I told her a bit more about what happened with you and Lisa than I really should have, considering." Sharon had her back to Riley, sweeping around the center island. She leaned down with the dustpan and disappeared from view. When she popped up again, she stared at Riley for a moment. "Maybe she doesn't want to get involved with someone who isn't ready."

Riley wondered if Sharon was projecting but decided not to challenge her about this now. "When does she check out?"

"Monday morning."

"I don't think I'll convince her one way or the other in three days." Riley thought of Ana's expression this morning when she'd knocked on her door. She had looked at Riley as if they were merely strangers sharing a cottage. "Anyway, you mentioned that you had some projects you needed help with around here. I'm all yours today. The last thing I want to do is climb any mountains. Or even hills, for that matter."

"How do you feel about climbing ladders? The gutters need to be cleaned."

"On it."

Sharon smiled. "I'm glad you didn't go to Alaska. It's good to have you here."

"I didn't like the idea of being stuck on a boat in a freezing ocean anyway. And the company here is better."

Once the gutters on the main house were cleaned, Riley moved on to the cottage. It was light work compared to the erosion control, but her arms ached when she'd finished. Sharon came out to inspect the job, then set her to the task of mowing the lawn. By lunchtime, Riley had worked up an appetite. She went to Cheddar's and ordered a bowl of Scott's gumbo. Oliver, Scott's partner, served her. He apologized that Scott wasn't there to serve her himself and mentioned that he'd been sore from their work dragging logs. Riley took some comfort in this.

She ate the gumbo with a slice of crusty bread. There was a good-sized lunch crowd and, once again, plenty of talk about the weather. Heavy rains were predicted that evening. The café was buzzing with the debate over whether the mountain pass highway would be closed early in anticipation of mudslides off the burn scar.

Riley listened with more interest now that she'd seen the canyon and had a better idea of the lay of the land. She also had a vested interest in the logs and run-off ditches that would, in theory, curtail the debris running off the hillsides. More work was needed before she wanted to see Deb's erosion control plan tested.

As she was leaving the café, she heard her name and scanned the street. She spotted Scott and waved. He hollered across the two lanes of cars, "How'd you like my gumbo?"

Riley held up her thumb and he smiled. He scanned for a break in the line of cars and jogged over to her. As he did, she saw Ana coming out of the building behind him. She was with three others, a man also dressed in a business suit and an older couple in more casual attire. Ana looked directly at Riley but was clearly in the middle of a conversation; she glanced away quickly. Her group crossed the footbridge that passed over the river and then disappeared behind another building.

Scott approached with a big grin. "Please tell me you are as sore as I am."

"I think I was more sore before Sharon had me up on her roof cleaning gutters."

"Hey, I need my gutters cleaned too. Do you do that?" He looked skeptical, but eager.

"Not normally. Sharon won't let me pay rent for the week I'm going to be here so I asked her to find ways to let me earn my keep."

"She needs company. I know she's got to feel alone in that house full of strangers…Sometimes I wonder if I'd ever want to run this place alone." He gestured to the café and shook his head. "That inn of hers was in Cherie's family for years. Do you know that Cherie died without a single living relative? I didn't think that ever happened, but it's true. Cherie had no one else. Anyway, no one contested the will that she'd written up, so Sharon got the inn."

"I think Sharon would have walked away from it if any of Cherie's relatives had shown up. In some ways, I think she probably should leave."

"But the memories hold her there. And it wouldn't have been the same to have someone else running the place. I knew Cherie's parents. They ran that place until they got too arthritic to climb the staircase to the front porch, then Cherie took over. They passed away not long after. Now Sharon runs the place just the way it has been for years."

Scott paused and looked at his storefront and the café sign that was in need of paint. "Sometimes I wonder, if Oliver left me, would I keep up the business alone, like Sharon's done, or just walk away from it all?" On cue, Oliver appeared in the doorway, gesturing to Scott. His look was urgent. "It's good to be wanted...I'm serious about the gutters, by the way. I'll trade you a week's worth of lunches if you want the job. I hate ladders."

Riley shook her head. Scott sighed and turned to head into the café. Riley watched him enter the café and then, through the window, saw him set down his packet of mail and tie on an apron. Oliver pointed to two tables that needed clearing and a sink full of dishes awaiting his attention.

Riley glanced over at the building she'd seen Ana head toward. Curious, she crossed the street to the footbridge to take a closer look at it. Several storefronts, including the boutique winery and a busy restaurant, were housed in the stone building on the other side. The tables outside the restaurant were all full of diners, but there was no crowd at the winery. A sign outside it disclosed its business hours—they were relatively short—and the wine selection, which looked like a fairly limited offering. It stated that all the wine was made on the premises, but she guessed that the grapes or probably the juice came from California or a state with a better growing season. A winery seemed out of context in Colorado. Beer was the prevailing beverage here and the state's rugged mountain terrain did not conjure up images of grapevines.

Riley went back to the footbridge and stared down at the river. It was a fast-moving mass of water, entirely unwelcoming, with a cloudy brown color and churning with branches and uprooted stumps.

* * *

Black rain clouds gathered on the horizon just after five. They obscured the mountains with hazy streaks and then, moments later, dropped sheets of rain on the town. Riley had come out to sit with Sharon on the covered front porch. They stayed outside for the first part of the storm, both noting that the heaviest clouds were hanging over Williams Canyon.

When the rain increased in intensity, choking the drains on the streets below and spilling over gutters on some of the neighboring houses, Sharon looked over at Riley and said, "Good timing on the gutters, sweetie."

When the flood siren sounded Sharon was inside checking the news, worried about the river. The blaring siren was followed by a man's recorded voice informing everyone to move to higher ground. Sharon's house had the distinct advantage of being a full story level above the street. An old staircase made from red rocks and seamed together with a hundred-year-old cement led down to the sidewalk below. It was treacherous in the rain, though, and the railing swayed when grasped. The entire property was well above the flood risk zone, therefore, but unreachable if the streets below flooded.

From this vantage point, the river appeared now to be nearly level with the street. Another inch of rain up in the higher terrain would likely cause it to overflow its banks. The roads through the pass were almost certainly closed at this point. Fortunately, most of the guests had already returned from their day's adventures.

Riley hadn't seen Ana, though. She squinted, trying to see the buildings on the other side of the river. It was nearing dusk and she could make out little more than the blue pulsing light on the police car blocking the bridge. A television crew had parked its van on the street below just in front of the sign for the B & B. The reporter stood under an umbrella and the cameraman huddled under his poncho. They returned to the comfort of their van after a brief filming, sloshing through several inches of rain as they crossed the street.

She spotted Ana hurrying up the sidewalk under an umbrella shortly after that. She had a bag in one hand and her purse in the other. She tried the back gate, but it was stuck closed. She glanced over the gate at the back path. It snaked around the house to the cottage and the parking lot, but Riley guessed it was already a muddy mess. Finally, she turned and took the treacherous stairs up to the main house. When she reached the landing, she shook out her umbrella, closed it and set it among the others all tipped upside down in a line against the house. She turned to head inside and then startled when she saw Riley.

"What are you doing out here?"

"Watching the rain."

The flood siren sounded again and the recorded voice repeated its speech.

When the recording had finished, Ana said, "The water's level with the footbridge. Any more rain and the river will flood the town. At least, everything lower than us." She shivered. "I thought Colorado had an arid climate."

"Until the monsoons."

She pulled off her heels and stepped over the muddy doormat. The door closed behind her and the porch light snapped on, casting an orange glow on everything. With the light on, Riley couldn't make out the shadowed street below. She headed inside a few minutes later, passing the guests clustered around Sharon's television in the living room and Sharon, who was on the phone and waved at Riley distractedly, and then she slipped out the back door. She hadn't thought to bring an umbrella and the downpour soaked her in seconds. Water pooled on the gravel between each of the flagstones. Riley dodged into the cottage. The pipes were rumbling from Ana's shower. She pulled off her clothes and hung them over the woodstove. The sound of the shower stopped abruptly. She waited for the light to switch off and then took her turn in the shower.

Her last remaining clean shirt happened to be the one nice shirt she'd packed, a dark blue, collared shirt that she'd last worn at Lisa's request. She'd said the color matched Riley's eyes. She pushed this thought away and pulled on her favorite Levis, tucked in her shirt and slid a belt through the loops. She felt like going out for the evening, but there was no way she could drive in this weather and no business in town was open anyway. Aside from that, she had no desire to eat dinner by herself on a Friday night.

She propped open the front door to let in the smell of the rain and the cool breeze. The rain showed no sign of letting up anytime soon. She thought of going over to the main house so she wasn't alone. The lights were on over there, the drapes were pulled open and she could make out Sharon in the kitchen at the stove and people still grouped in the living room. The television screen reflected in flashes of light on the window.

A knock sounded on the bathroom door, and a second later, Ana poked her head inside. "Good. You're dressed."

"What would you have done if I wasn't?"

"I would have closed the door. Maybe I would have apologized." Ana came into the room and looked around. Riley had made the bed out of habit, but her clothes were strewn about drying and her backpack was open on the nightstand. Ana seemed to note all of this, then said, "I've got the nicer room."

"You're paying."

"You got this place for free?"

"Such as it is. The bed's comfortable, though." Seeing Ana's eyebrow arch at this, she added, "I didn't mean anything by that. Just that it's comfortable. It would be small for two, but it's fine for me."

"It took me a while to get used to sleeping in a big bed alone. Hotels always have king-size beds or two queens, and for some reason, getting two queen beds always feels ridiculous so I get the king and then just think about how I have all of that extra room. I've taken to sleeping diagonally so I don't think about how there's room for two and I'm alone." She paused and then added, "I'm fine alone, though. I mean, I'm not super clingy or anything. You get used to eating and sleeping alone when you're traveling all the time."

They stared at one another for a moment, with Riley guessing at Ana's intentions. Was she simply lonely tonight and looking for company or was she actually interested in more?

Ana held up the sack she'd seen her carrying earlier. "Wine and hors d'oeuvres. We each took a few of the open bottles and split what food the chef had already prepared. Everyone thinks the place will flood." Ana glanced around the room, presumably searching for a table to set down the items, then said, "Want to come over to my place tonight?"

Riley followed her through the bathroom to the other side of the cottage. Ana's bed was made with the corner tucked down, so Riley knew that Sharon been in earlier to tidy up. She had the same woodstove in the corner, but next to hers were two high-backed armchairs with a small table for magazines. Ana cleared off the magazines and set out a paper plate. She placed baguette slices with some sort of tomato and cheese topping on the plate and then pulled out two bottles of wine. Each was about two-thirds full, one white and one red.

"Where's your stuff?" Riley asked. "It doesn't even look like anyone is staying in here."

Ana pointed to the closet and then to the dresser. "The only way I stay sane with this traveling schedule is if I unpack as soon as I get to wherever I'm going. I'll unpack even if I'm only staying for two nights. I let it slide when I'm only staying one night, though." She sank down on one of the chairs. "And I always try to stay at the same place when I travel for work. Red or white?"

"Either. I don't have a preference." Riley wasn't going to admit that she didn't like wine to someone who had a career because of it.

"Then we'll start with this one." She uncorked the bottle of white wine and poured two glasses, then handed one to Riley. "Don't tell my boss, but I can't tell most of the wines apart. I've never been much for wine, in fact. But I'm starting to have a few favorites. I only pick the ones that go down easy."

"I thought wine was your business. You don't like it?"

"I'm a business consultant. I happened to fall in with wineries. They're big business in Napa. I always thought I'd like to live in Napa. Getting in on the wine business seemed like a good fit. Funny though, I'm never really *in* Napa. Anyway, the taste has grown on me."

Riley sniffed the glass. It smelled like peaches. She checked the label on the bottle. "This is peach wine?"

"They add peach juice to a sauvignon. Then they can charge more for wine that, on its own, wouldn't be worth the high price."

Riley took a sip. "Not bad." She set the glass down and then checked the label on the red wine. "This one's sweet too?"

"No, that's just the merlot that I like. I figured you'd be one for sweet wine, for some reason, so I grabbed the peach. Their merlot's good, but it does have a bite to it."

"So I was in your plans for the evening?"

"Maybe." She took a bite of the baguette, coated with cheese, and then looked up at Riley. She licked cheese off the edge of her finger. "Are you going to sit down?"

"I'm not sure."

Ana laughed. "Sit down. You'll make me uncomfortable."

"What was up with this morning?" Riley sat down but kept her eyes on Ana. She wondered about the mixed signals Ana had sent earlier.

"Can we forget about it?" Ana stared at Riley. After a moment, she said, "Maybe I changed my mind."

Riley nodded. There seemed to be a tacit understanding that this evening might turn into a late night so long as neither of them said anything to blow it. Riley had no intention of doing so. Ana had changed out of her business suit into a white cotton skirt and a gray tank top. She stretched out her legs, smooth and naked from the edge of her skirt downward, and gazed out the window. Raindrops splattered the glass and made rivulets as they descended. Ana played with the ruby pendant on her necklace and took another sip of wine. Riley decided on the second sip that the wine was quite drinkable. They polished off the pre-topped baguette slices and the first bottle of wine while listening to the rain and the intermittent flood siren.

"I wonder if the lower parts of the town have flooded yet. We put sandbags all around the doors at the winery, but I doubt they'll hold back much of the water. Do you want to turn on the news?"

"Not really. There's nothing we can do at the moment." Riley stood up and went to open the door. If anything, the rain had gained in intensity. The flagstones were now entirely submerged and the patio lights reflected on what had been the path but was now a stream running between the door and the grass.

Ana had come to the door as well. She dimmed the room lights and the porch lights shone brighter. They watched the rain for a moment, and then Riley reached over and took Ana's hand. She lightly traced the lines on Ana's palm and then continued with a fingertip stroke up the underside of her arm. She reached her other arm toward Ana's hip and turned her slightly. Their lips met. The first kiss was tentative. Riley waited, testing Ana's response. Ana didn't move away, but she seemed to be waiting as well. Riley kissed her again, feeling her desire for Ana mount. Ana pressed into her this time, closing the door as they parted.

"I think I should explain what I said earlier," Ana started.

Riley waited, holding Ana's hands in her own. Ana gazed up at her but was silent. Riley kissed her again. "You don't seem to want to explain."

"You're right. I don't feel like talking at all right now."

"Then tell me later."

"I doubt I'll want to tell you later."

Riley ran her hand down the length of Ana's skirt. "If it's important enough to make me stop, you better tell me soon." The cotton was so thin that she could easily feel Ana's curves through the fabric.

Ana pulled off her tank top and started working on Riley's shirt buttons. Riley kissed her again, then moved toward the bed. She wondered how far Ana would want to go. She undid Ana's bra and slipped it off, her hands tracing the shoulders she'd longed to touch in the hot tub. She kissed Ana again. "Should I keep going?"

In response, Ana took Riley's hands and placed them on her breasts. Riley cupped them, the satisfying weight resting in her palms and her skin a muted contrast to Riley's in the dim light. Riley ached to feel more of her. It had been months since she'd done anything more than share a bed with Lisa and longer still since she'd really wanted to be close to her. The desire that choked her now was raw and overwhelming. She leaned down to encircle Ana's dark nipples with her tongue, willing her body to go slow. Ana murmured in response. She sank down on the bed and stared up at Riley, then reached for Riley's belt and pulled her down on top of her.

The Levis and the skirt were off a moment later. Riley moved from Ana's breasts to her soft belly, then lower to her hips and thighs, covering every inch with soft kisses. Ana caressed her back and ran her hands through Riley's hair, tugging on the strands when Riley kissed a sensitive spot. Riley shifted lower to kiss between Ana's legs and heard a murmur of encouragement. Ana pressed her body against Riley's lips, her hands gripping Riley as she rocked her hips into her. Riley couldn't slow her desire any longer. She had little doubt that Ana wanted what was going to come next as much as Riley wanted it.

When Riley slipped her fingers inside, Ana's nails dug into her shoulders. She kept her hands on Riley's shoulders as she climaxed, gripping her legs together and clutching Riley's hand. Riley felt her own body respond. Naked, sweaty skin aroused her every nerve, and her fingers were wet and scented with musk. Even without touching her, Ana had pushed her to the edge. She longed for Ana to reach for her; she knew she wouldn't be able to hold back if she did. But Ana's hands relaxed and lay still on Riley's back. Riley slipped her fingers out finally and pressed her thumb on Ana's swollen clit. She felt a satisfying tremor race through Ana's body. Riley shifted off Ana a moment later. She lay on her side, watching Ana drift to sleep, the sound of the pelting rain on the roof soon overlaying all other sounds. She closed her eyes.

* * *

The morning sun glistened on the lawn chairs and every other surface beaded with water, which was everything, it seemed. Riley had slipped out of Ana's bed in the middle of the night and awoke to Sharon's knocking shortly after dawn. Sharon didn't ask about the night's events. Instead, she handed Riley a shovel. "We've got several inches of mud to clear off the sidewalk so guests can get out front. And the parking lot is full of debris. The river flooded. There's mud and debris all across the road. It's impassable at this point, so I don't know why I care about the debris in the parking lot, seeing as how no one can drive anywhere at the moment, but I do. It's going to be a long day."

Riley ran her hand through her hair, smoothing the tousled parts. "Let me splash water on my face and get dressed."

"I'll be in the kitchen. No matter that the town's flooded, there'll be eight mouths wanting to eat in a couple of hours." She turned to leave, choosing to walk through the wet grass rather than try to pick her way across the flagstone path, which now resembled a streambed more than a path at all. Her pink slippers padded across the grass, leaving a line of bent blades to mark her route.

Riley dressed and used the bathroom. She'd just snapped the light off when Ana opened her side of the door and snapped the light back on. She leaned against the doorframe, staring at Riley. She was wearing a pair of pajama pants but no shirt. Her arms were crossed, barely concealing her breasts.

"I didn't think you'd be the type to leave in the middle of the night."

Riley looked at Ana's reflection in the mirror. "I didn't know how you'd feel about what happened last night by the time morning came round."

"It wasn't like I was drunk. I knew what I was doing."

Riley nodded. "The river flooded. There's standing water everywhere and apparently several inches of mud on the sidewalks and the main road. Sharon's sending me out to clean a path so the guests can get to their cars."

Ana turned and went back to her room, switching off the light as she left. Riley sighed and headed outside. She could spend the rest of the morning second-guessing this conversation...and probably would.

The morning sun was blinding. Rays bent across the water and prisms formed in every direction with no clouds to deflect the light. Riley took the shovel and went to the parking lot behind the yard, keeping clear of the puddles that had sprung up everywhere. She gathered up branches that had fallen in the rainstorm, some of them quite large, and then took the muddy back path that wound around the main house down to the street.

Sharon's description of the sidewalk and street had been accurate. It looked like a mudslide had covered the street. Aside from the mud and branches, there were a number of good-sized boulders littering the road. The river was still high, cresting just under the edge of the rock wall. Logs sped by as she watched, the river's current fast and headstrong. She doubted Deb's erosion control plan had withstood last night's deluge and figured those hours of dragging logs were lost. She picked her way through the mud until she reached the staircase leading up to the porch and then, with determination, slid the shovel into the start of the mud layer.

Within the hour, she had company. Several other business owners and locals were out to survey the results of the rainstorm and many of them had shovels. The sound of metal scraping on concrete echoed through the streets as shovels worked to clear a path. Ana came down the staircase with a mug of coffee in her hand. She offered it to Riley, then glanced down the street toward the wine shop.

"What's your guess?" Riley wondered.

"I already know the building flooded. I got a text ten minutes ago from the owner. He says there's over a foot of mud in the restaurant that shares the same building. One of the glass panes broke and the water must have just ripped through the place. The winery wasn't hit as hard as the restaurant, but I doubt there will be any other bit of good news today. He said he was standing in several inches of water while he was texting. I'm about to go see how bad it is in person."

"I'm close to done here. Give me a minute and I'll go with you." Riley leaned the shovel against the stair railing and went up to tell Sharon that the sidewalk was cleared as far as the end of their block. Sharon was scuttling from one table to the next with maple syrup in one hand and a pitcher of coffee in the other. She went to the kitchen for a sandwich she'd fixed for Riley and then nodded her off to help the ones downriver.

Ana led the way, picking slowly through the muddy parts and climbing over branches the size of small trees that were blocking the sidewalk. Riley, distracted by the view of Ana's backside, reprimanded herself every time she stumbled on a branch or the fist-sized rocks that were strewn everywhere. Finally they reached the footbridge. The news van that had been parked by the bridge the night before had returned to cover the scene. The reporter was interviewing the restaurant owner and already the place had a dozen or more volunteers shoveling mud.

Ana, Riley decided quickly, was much more attractive than the newswoman. She was, in fact, probably too attractive. The idea that their one night together might lead to anything more became a distant thought with every glance she had of Ana in full daylight. Even dressed down in faded blue jeans with mud up to her knees, without a bit of her usual makeup and with her dark brown hair pulled back in a ponytail that Riley longed to grab, she was the most striking woman Riley had ever slept with.

They passed the chaos of the restaurant and met up with the owner of the wine shop, who Ana quickly introduced as Joe. Ana introduced Riley only to say she was a volunteer. Joe wasn't one to mince words. He saw Riley's shovel and pointed her to the entrance of the shop, where mud had piled up against the door. After the mud had been cleared and the door propped open with a log that was lying next to the pile of shattered glass, Joe led her inside the shop. Ana had gone in through the back entrance and was standing ankle-deep in water wielding a push broom.

The wine shop had little furniture and most of that was metal, so the water wasn't immediately a crisis here. They moved the toppled chairs and tables outside to the brick patio to dry in the sun, then swept out the water with big push brooms, one from the wine shop which had a handle shaped like a grape leaf that someone had clearly added to be cute and one that someone from the restaurant had loaned them. After the bulk of the water had been cleared, Ana said, "The real problem, of course, is the wine."

Joe sighed. "You know, I think it would be easier if we were a regular wine bar. All we'd have to deal with would be bottles of wine. What do you think about that idea?"

Ana shook her head. "Well, the business model for the franchise isn't that, you know, Joe."

As it turned out, there were boxes and boxes of bottled wine in the place, but since the shop made the wine on the premises, they also had juice and barrels of wine in different stages of fermentation. Most of the barrels were too large to move, so Riley was set to shoveling the mud and removing debris from around them. After the debris was removed, the place could be power washed. When she'd finished with the shoveling, she helped Joe and Ana move box after box of wine upstairs. He and his wife lived in one of the apartments above the wine shop and the front room of their apartment was soon lined with boxes. Joe's wife helped intermittently with the work but spent most of the morning yelling into her cell phone at their insurance agent.

By lunchtime, Riley was exhausted. She stepped out to the back patio and weaved her way over to the railing to have a look at the river. The water level had dropped to about a foot from the top of the bank. She closed her eyes for a moment, listening to the fast-moving current, and enjoying the sun on her head. She felt a hand on her back and turned to see Sharon.

"Don't look so disappointed! Who were you expecting?" Sharon laughed. She handed Riley a brown paper sack. "I figured you'd be hungry. By the way," she swept a hand across Riley's brow, "you have mud here, and…"—she tapped Riley's cheek—"and here, and…"—she tapped the other cheek—"here too."

"Thanks for lunch." Riley pulled over one of the chairs and sat down within view of the water. "What's the weather report?"

Sharon sighed. "More rain tonight."

"It seems futile, doesn't it? I think they should simply close down the businesses that are this close to the river. Reopen them after the burn scar has had time for some plants to take root and well after the monsoons."

"That would be ten years from now, at least. Maybe twenty. And the view is nice, isn't it? Besides, we wouldn't necessarily need a monsoon. Just a few inches of rain and a slow-moving storm that settled in the canyon..."

"Well, then, close these places indefinitely."

"As their business consultant, I wouldn't advise that," Ana said. She had come up from behind Riley and now pulled a chair over to where Sharon stood. "Have a seat, Sharon." She got herself a chair as well and looked expectantly at the bag that Riley held.

"Yes, there's a sandwich for each of you in there," Sharon said. "I'm heading over to check on a friend. I couldn't get an answer from her on the phone this morning and her house is on the other side of the river with a foundation two feet below where it should be. Did you hear that two people were killed last night? They found the bodies this morning, though far enough downstream to be out of our police officers' jurisdiction."

Riley and Ana ate silently after Sharon had left. The mud and destruction of the buildings were easy enough to get past, but the thought that people had died in the flood made Riley shudder as she gazed again at the river.

Riley returned to the cottage late that afternoon. She'd gone from the winery to Sharon's friend's house, which had indeed also flooded, and then on to another neighbor's place from there. Her muscles were shaky from all of the shoveling and she was splattered from head to toe in a mud that smelled like something from the depths of a swamp. She peeled off her clothes without even going into the cottage, after making certain no one was near enough to see her in only underwear and a bra. Her hiking boots were so disgusting that she considered throwing them straight into the trash. She showered, scrubbing thoroughly, then dried off only enough to manage getting her damp body into the bathing suit.

Ana met her on the path, now a path again with the water miraculously evaporated in the day's heat, and nodded at the hot tub. "I'm on my way there as well."

Ana had already changed out of her mud-encrusted clothes and was wearing the white cotton skirt from last night and a new tank top. Riley wondered how she'd managed to leave Joe and the winery. By the time Riley had left to go help out at Sharon's friend's house, Joe was inconsolable. He'd gone from cussing to crying and back to cussing, with Ana patiently absorbing all of this and intermittently offering suggestions on what could be done while Joe's wife, who had a mouth far worse than her husband's, added her two cents as well. The insurance agent had determined that they had specifically signed a waiver on the flood insurance, and there was no way the agency would cover any of the damages.

Riley sank into the water, feeling her tense muscles release. She exhaled and dropped below the water's surface, then came up for air as her mind slowed enough to consider her next breath instead of all the other thoughts that had been swirling around and around in her head all day. Chief among these thoughts, of course, was Ana. Riley got out of the water and sat on the deck that edged the hot tub. She let her feet dangle in the water and leaned back, looking up at the sky. Clouds had already begun to gather behind the Peak.

Ana appeared a few minutes later. She stepped into the hot tub and found a seat opposite Riley. "What a strange twenty-four hours…"

Riley knew that she was referring to more than the flood. She felt strangely satisfied that Ana had mentioned their night together now. They had worked today as strangers and were really barely more than that. The events of the last night had slipped into backstage and had nearly become something Riley wondered if she'd imagined.

"Are you okay?"

Riley nodded. "I'm exhausted."

Ana climbed out of the hot tub several minutes later. As she left, she brushed her hand over Riley's shoulders. The touch sent a tremor down Riley's spine. "Come to my room when you're finished here," she said as she left.

Riley dropped into the water again. She watched Ana enter the cottage and closed her eyes, imagining the wet bathing suit being tugged off and Ana's naked body underneath. She stood up and climbed out. She covered the hot tub, guessing that no one else would brave the coming storm for a soak tonight. She hadn't thought to bring a towel and the wind chilled her skin.

Riley considered knocking. She stood outside Ana's door, trying to decide if the invitation to come over meant that formalities could be dropped. Ana's door was unlocked. Riley opened it and hesitated in the doorway, thinking she should, in fact, have knocked, but Ana beckoned her forward. She was in bed, her hands folded behind her head and the pillows pushed up against the headboard. The sheets were pulled back, and she was wearing a loose white V-neck T-shirt that was even more enticing than the bikini had been.

Riley noticed a bottle of wine on the nightstand and two wineglasses. "I don't think I've ever drank this much wine."

"Are you suggesting I'm a bad influence? I usually don't drink this much either." Ana said, stretching to reach the bottle. "But Joe sent this one for you. As a thank you for today." She uncorked the bottle and poured. Red wine swirled into the glass.

Riley lifted hers and smelled it. "Berries?"

"Raspberry pinot noir. Joe sent you a few other bottles as well. I think you'll like the apple Riesling, but it didn't seem to fit my mood tonight." Ana took a sip and then set her glass down on the nightstand. "Do you want to shower first?"

"Before what?" Riley asked, grinning. Ana shook her head. She leaned back against the pillows. Riley took another sip and then set down her glass. "Yeah, I'll rinse off."

Before Riley had finished her shower, the door slid open. Ana was naked. She slipped inside and immediately wrapped her arms around Riley. "I've had a hard time not touching you today," she said. She kissed Riley's back and shoulders, then stroked her hands down Riley's thighs. She moved from the back to the front and her caressing kisses continued up and down Riley's back. Riley turned around to meet Ana's lips with her own.

Riley shut off the water as Ana's kisses became more demanding. She followed her out of the bathroom, toweling off as Ana led the way. Ana pushed her onto the bed. Riley looked up at her, waiting. Ana took a sip of wine, watching Riley all the while. The rain had started again, pattering on the roof of the cottage and streaking down the windowpanes. Riley waited for Ana to set down the glass, then reached for her, pulling her down on top of her. Ana's lips were full and warm. She kissed Riley's neck and collarbones, then made her way down Riley's chest. Riley ran her hand through Ana's hair, damp from the shower. She wanted to feel Ana between her legs nearly enough to be willing to beg for it. Ana moved lower, kissing below her belly button, but before she reached the place Riley wanted her, she shifted position so Riley's leg was between hers. She rubbed her thigh into Riley's groin. As she moved faster, Riley heard her begin to climax, and a moment later a wave swept through her own body.

After a while, Ana eased herself off Riley and went to use the bathroom. She came back to bed but didn't lie down. She sat, propped up by overfilled pillows, and ran her fingers through Riley's hair. "Are you asleep?" she asked.

Riley was stretched across the bed, entirely relaxed, without even a sheet to cover her. Her eyelids were half shut. "Mm-hmm," she murmured.

Ana climbed on top of her again. She brushed a fingertip over Riley's eyelids and down her nose and lips. "You're beautiful, you know."

Riley shook her head.

"Yeah, that's why I'm telling you."

"Okay." Riley wanted to drift to sleep, but she could tell Ana was too awake now.

"My mom dated women for a while. I remember her saying how much she hated the fact that so many good-looking dykes didn't think they were attractive. She was drunk when she told me that and probably would deny our conversation ever took place. Of course, she'd deny dating women as well. But to my mom, if a person didn't dress well or didn't act like they thought everyone in the room ought to be noticing them, then clearly they didn't think they were attractive…"

Riley opened her eyes. "Go back a minute. Did you just say your mom dated women for a while?"

"It happens." Ana continued, "She has always claimed to be straight, but at one point, there were several women she cycled through."

"So what does she think about you?"

"If you mean, what does she think about this," she motioned to Riley's body under hers, "she has no clue. She hasn't met anyone I've slept with since my old high school boyfriends. We haven't had the best relationship for the past few years."

"Where does she live?"

"Lodi. I go there for Christmas and Thanksgiving. Easter too if she's in the mood to have a party. My mom throws a pretty good party, but then she drinks too much."

"Lodi's in California, right?"

"Yes. In the middle of nowhere." Ana traced a finger down the center of Riley's chest.

"Is your mom the reason why you don't drink much?"

"I drink when there's a good reason and then only good wine." Ana pulled her hand off Riley's chest. "My mom drinks vodka or anything she can get. And lots of it. She makes good mixed drinks as well. She was a bartender for a while. Why did I get us started talking about my mom? Can we change the subject?"

"Okay. What did you want to be when you grew up?"

Ana raised an eyebrow. "Are you suggesting that a girl can't dream about becoming a business consultant? I happen to be very good at what I do."

"I don't doubt it."

"I wanted to be an actress for a while, then an artist, but I get stage fright and my paintings of alfalfa fields weren't going on anyone's wall. Then I just wanted to be rich. I know, lofty goal, right?" She paused for a long moment before continuing in a softer tone, "My dad left my mom when I was five. She raised my sisters and me alone. We didn't have anything extra, and I remember wanting to always have plenty of money so I wouldn't have to worry about the landlord knocking on the door. My mom wouldn't ever pay the rent until the landlord was ready with the eviction notice. Damn, I'm back to talking about my mom." She paused. "Can you hear the rain?"

Riley nodded. The rain had changed from the early pitter-patter to a loud pounding against the shingles.

"Rainy days make me want to go home."

"Does it rain a lot in Lodi?"

"No. But I always think about going home when it rains. Some sort of primitive impulse to find a cave and take shelter from the storm, you know. I don't really have a cave, though, so I think about my family, I guess. What's your family like?"

"There's only my parents, my brother and me. Pretty normal childhood, I guess. And no one was trying to evict us. My parents both worked good jobs, but they've retired now. My brother is kind of a screw-up. He seems to know how to find trouble. When we were kids, if he wasn't trying to burn down the house or choke the neighbor kid, he was keying someone's car. He got kicked out of more than one school and, eventually, out of more than one sober program. I think I had to be the good kid."

"Your parents know you sleep with women?"

"I told my mom when I was seventeen. She nodded and said, 'Yep, we knew you'd figure it out soon enough.' I had expected her to ask questions or tell me I was crazy or something, but apparently my parents had decided I was probably gay when I was in grade school. Go figure."

"I wish things in my world were that easy." Ana rolled off Riley and pulled the sheet and then the blankets up to cover them. She curled up against Riley. "Don't leave in the middle of the night this time, okay?"

Riley murmured in agreement.

"I was pissed when I woke up. You were just gone. Do you know, you're the first person who's ever done that to me? And then you acted like nothing happened the morning after. Do you know what that does to a person?"

Riley turned to look at her and was relieved to see the teasing expression on her face. "I'm not going anywhere tonight. I promise," Riley said, closing her eyes. Sleep came quickly. She was entirely spent and deliciously warm with Ana wrapped around her body.

* * *

"The highway's open," Ana said. "Looks like last night's rain skipped over the burn scar. The river is the same level it was yesterday morning." She was dressed and holding a mug of coffee. "And there's probably a hundred people already out on the streets with shovels and brooms."

Riley rubbed her eyes and rolled over to look at the clock. It was past nine. "I never sleep in."

Ana sat down on the edge of the bed. "No, *I* never sleep in. You just did."

"Wait, what day is it?"

"Sunday." Ana sipped her coffee. "Sharon's coffee is better than usual."

Riley cringed at the mention of Sharon's name. She'd promised Sharon that she'd pick up pastries at seven on Sunday. "What is she serving for breakfast?"

"Banana pancakes."

"No pastries?"

"What, you don't like pancakes?"

"I love banana pancakes. But I forgot to go pick up the Sunday morning pastries. She must have made the pancakes because I didn't bring the pastries and she probably knocked on my door to remind me and then realized where I was sleeping."

"Wait, are you embarrassed because Sharon knows you were in here with me?"

"No, not at all. But I am going to be embarrassed that I slept in and flaked on her. She'll call me out on it as soon as I see her."

"She definitely gave me a raised eyebrow when she saw me." Ana rested her hand on Riley's arm. "Get out of bed before I decide to climb back under the covers with you."

Riley shook her head.

Ana set her coffee down and crossed her arms. "Come on, there's work to be done out there and you look good pushing a shovel."

"You said there's a hundred people outside already. By noon, this town will be filled with volunteers." Riley pulled back the covers, waiting. Ana sighed and kicked off her shoes. She took off her pants and then paused.

"I'm probably going to get a text from Joe within the hour wondering where I am. And I'm expecting a call from my boss this morning."

"It's Sunday. Turn off your phone," Riley said, reaching for her.

Bleary-eyed, Riley headed for the shower just before eleven. Ana was still in bed, stretched out naked on top of the sheets. Riley smelled her hand as she waited for the water to warm, enjoying Ana's scent on her fingers. She stepped into the shower and reached for the fancy lavender soap that Sharon probably paid too much to keep in all the bathrooms. "Tomorrow is Monday," she murmured to the water striking her skin. "Monday, Monday." Ana was scheduled to check out tomorrow. She hadn't wanted to bring this up last night nor this morning, but the reality of it now was impossible not to face. She wanted to ask if the flood had changed her plans at all, but that wasn't the important question. Had the past forty-eight hours changed anything?

Riley dried off and went to her side of the cottage. She had asked Sharon yesterday to use the laundry, and she now found all of her clothes cleaned and folded. Riley dressed quickly and went to the main house, hoping to be of some use in the kitchen cleanup at least.

Sharon was in the dining area chatting with some guests who were clearly slow eaters. Riley ate a banana pancake, still sitting on the now-cold grill, and then set to washing the pile of dishes in the sink.

"Morning, sunshine," Sharon said, carrying several plates over to the dishwasher. "Before you say anything, I called over and had my baker send his son with the pastries. So, you can ease up on feeling guilty, but don't stop scrubbing those pans."

"You know me well," Riley said, smiling. "I thought you had to make the pancakes because I forgot."

"No, Sunday is the big brunch. I have pastries, fresh fruit, eggs, sausage and pancakes. I'm first class here." Sharon leaned against the counter, a dishrag thrown over her shoulder. "So, this is just a fling to get Lisa off your mind, right?"

"Ana leaves tomorrow. I'm not letting it go to my head."

"Hmm. We'll see."

"How are things downtown? I'm guessing you've listened to the news last night and probably this morning as well."

"While you were up to better things? Yes, I've been glued to the news. And to the view from the front porch." Sharon started drying one of the serving platters that Riley had finished scrubbing. "We're getting a day of sunshine and then another storm front moves in. They'll have the heavy machinery in tomorrow to clean up the boulders and all of the debris on the north end of town. There are still two streets that you can't get to with a car. I have friends who live over there. They can get out on foot, but otherwise they're stuck."

"Is there anyone in this town that you aren't friends with?"

Sharon smiled. "I can think of a few people who would likely cross to the other side of the street if they saw me coming."

"Sweet little you who never gets into anyone else's business?"

Sharon swatted her with the dishrag. "Speaking of other people's business, I'm going over to help someone today with her flooded basement. It isn't a crisis but she's old and this whole thing has her frazzled. I'm going to bring some of the brunch leftovers as well."

"And you volunteered me to come along?"

"No, but since you mentioned it, you could help me carry a few things."

* * *

The basement stairs were slick with muddy grime, and Riley had to concentrate as she maneuvered past the first corner, carrying soggy box after box into the garage where Sharon sat with the old lady. She lined the boxes up against the garage wall and let Sharon take over from there, patiently going through the contents while the old lady shook her head in dismay. Sharon had sent Riley to borrow a sump pump earlier that afternoon. The machine was making the rounds from neighbor to neighbor, and Riley had promised to pass it on to someone else as soon as the old woman's basement was drained. The basement had a cement floor and unfinished walls, but there were two windows, one of which had shattered in the storm when a log crashed into it. The log was still sticking through the window. Fortunately, there was little furniture in the space, but the number of boxes was staggering.

Thoughts of Ana distracted Riley as she worked. She wondered if Ana would change her plans if she asked her to, but she knew she couldn't ask. Riley had already decided to give Ana her phone number, thinking that there was a good chance she might come back through Denver sometime. But this thought only made her depressed. She was going to be waiting for what? For a call from this beautiful stranger, who knows when, to randomly hook up? They had decided to go separate ways for the day, with Ana expected over at the winery and Riley knowing she'd get roped into helping Sharon's friend for the day. The few hours apart from Ana had brought Riley back to the reality of their situation. Ana lived in Napa and she lived in Denver. Despite everything Riley wanted to believe, Sharon was likely right. Ana was her rebound. Their relationship realistically couldn't be anything more, despite all of the possibilities that swarmed in her mind.

Sharon had to return to the inn to serve Sunday tea. She excused Riley from her job though there were still half again as many boxes to be moved. The old lady had enough to think about with the boxes in the garage and the sump pump needed time to work before they could really get any further.

"You stink," Sharon said as they came out of the house.

"Good thing someone does my laundry."

"You're welcome. But you need more than clean clothes."

They passed through a playground and then crossed the river. Branches were piled up on the park benches, and the swings were entangled with debris. Mud and rocks were strewn across the grass as was a large downed elm tree. They stepped over a log and Riley said, "Hope this wasn't one of Deb's logs. Any word from your park ranger?"

"She isn't my park ranger."

"And?"

"Deb did call my cell while we were over at Edie's, but that doesn't mean anything. We're friends, Riley."

"She wants to be more than friends."

"I know. Anyway, she won't be able to go up to the canyon for a while. They're still moving boulders off one lane of the pass." Sharon looked over her shoulder at the park behind them. "This town is going to be cleaning up for weeks. If we don't get another flood first."

As they neared the main street, volunteers splattered in mud passed them carrying shovels or pushing wheelbarrows. Most appeared to be heading home. The sidewalks were now scraped clean of the muck. Piles of it had been pushed to one end of the downtown plaza, along with at least a ton of branches and rocks. "Maybe this place will be cleared sooner rather than later," Riley commented.

Ana was coming out of the wine shop as they passed her building. She waved to them and then quickly crossed the bridge to meet them. Under her breath, Sharon said, "Someone looks happy to see you."

Ana was nearly clean. Her pants were splattered with mud only at the cuffs. She smiled when she joined them, then gave Riley a once-over. "Did you crawl through a drain pipe?"

"Don't take a deep breath. She smells even worse than she looks," Sharon added.

"I'll take a long shower. With extra soap."

Sharon winked at Riley and then said, "I've got to stop in at Cheddar's to pick up cookies to go with my tea. Drop by the dining area if you want a treat later."

"Sharon, before you go, I need to stay a couple days longer. Any problem with me not checking out tomorrow?"

"With the floods, I've had nothing but cancellations. You're welcome as long as you like." Sharon crossed the street at the next intersection, waving over her shoulder as she went.

As soon as Sharon had gone, Ana stepped closer to Riley. "I want a real date tonight," she began. "I've been thinking about it all afternoon. It helped me get through several hours of painful meetings. I finally had to leave so I wouldn't strangle Joe. Personally, I think he and his wife should throw in the towel. I am, however, being paid by a company that wants him to stay in business. Anyway, I've already got a few ideas for where we could go for dinner."

"A real date, huh?" Riley wanted desperately to ask why Ana had changed her plans and decided to stay longer. She guessed the answer had nothing to do with her, however. "I don't know, appetizers and a bottle of wine in your room worked pretty well before."

"Not tonight. Did you bring any nice clothes?"

"No, this was supposed to be a hiking trip. I had no intention of hooking up with anyone." They had reached the gate for the back path leading up to the cottage. Riley gave the gate a kick and then held it open with one hand and waited for Ana. She had her arms crossed and was staring directly at Riley.

"What'd I say?" Riley asked, though she already knew the answer.

"'Hooking up'?"

Riley shrugged. "What do you want me to call it? Our two-night stand?"

"Nice. That's classy," Ana said, with obvious sarcasm. "Come on, Riley, I want to go on a real date with you."

"Why?"

"Because. We need to talk about things and not just...get distracted."

"'Get distracted'? Is that what classy people call it?" Riley grinned. "Well, I guess saying 'have sex' out loud might be uncouth. It's true, someone might hear." Riley glanced over her shoulder. In a quieter voice, she said, "We could call it screwing. Banging? Definitely not fucking..." She paused and saw Ana shake her head. "Truth is, I'd be fine if you called it any of those. But maybe I'm not high class."

"Maybe not. Good thing I like you anyway." Ana pushed Riley toward her side of the cottage. "Go take a shower. And put on something that doesn't stink. This is *not* just a hookup."

* * *

The restaurant was up on a ridge above the town, nestled among a forest of evergreens. It was built into the side of the mountain with a stone front that looked as if the architect had been trying to camouflage it among all the other boulders. Ana led the way inside as if she'd been here before. The waiter directed them to one of the tables near the kitchen entrance, but Ana quickly interceded with, "I'd really like to sit outside if you have a table on the patio available."

Only one table was available on the patio and it was not yet cleared from the previous diners, so the waiter made a show of the effort it would take to get it ready. Ana shrugged off his attitude and repeated her request. Within minutes, they were seated with a perfect view of Pikes Peak, the washed-out canyon to the north and the swollen river coursing through the town below. The sun was low on the horizon and cast a golden glow on the valley.

"The town looks beautiful from here. Surrounded by the mountains...it looks so peaceful. You never would guess what's happened in the past few days down there."

"Yeah, you can't see the uprooted trees, layers of mud and all of the folks who had their homes, cars and businesses destroyed," Ana added.

"Sounds like you had a hard day at work."

Ana nodded. "I don't think I get paid enough to deal with people like Joe and his wife. I feel bad for them, but maybe they should have decided to carry flood insurance, you know? They did pick a spot on the river. Eventually every river floods."

"I thought you were supposed to be the optimist telling them to pull themselves up by their bootstraps and get back to work."

Ana leaned back in her chair. "Sometimes I think I must be crazy for ever getting involved with wineries. The thought of getting out did cross my mind several times today. Everyone in this business seems a bit crazy."

"They all drink too much?"

"I don't think that makes them crazy, however. I think they are a little bit off before they even get into the wine."

A new waiter came to take their order and then left as quickly as he'd arrived. The tables on the patio were situated far enough apart from each other that the conversations couldn't be overheard well. Riley gazed down at the town, thinking of Edie in her garage full of boxes and of the folks that Sharon had visited the day before whose entire first floor had been destroyed. She glanced over at Ana again. "Why are you staying longer?"

"I talked with my boss this afternoon. He was pissed I missed our phone meeting this morning. Fortunately, he didn't ask for an excuse." She paused and took a sip of water. "He wants me to stay until I have things ironed out with Joe and the accountant that I've been meeting with. On top of everything else, Joe's been in trouble with his bookkeeping. His numbers haven't been adding up the way they should, so we hired an accountant to review everything. After my first meeting with Joe, I was convinced my job was only going to be to smooth things out with the finances and give Joe some tips on realigning his business plan. The flood threw off our schedule and everything else as well."

"Lucky for me, I guess. I was hoping you'd change your plans."

Ana shifted forward in her chair. "Okay, since you brought it up, what are we doing here?"

Riley hesitated. Ana's tone was too serious for her to make a joking response. "I'm not really sure. What do you think we're doing?"

"I don't even know your last name. I don't have your number or email or anything. I know you work as a physical therapist in Denver. That's it. And I really want you to tell me if this is just your idea of a rebound."

"It's Robinson." Riley sighed. "And I don't think this is a rebound."

"Mine's Potrero." She took a sip of water. "How long were you with her?"

"Two years."

Ana tapped her fingernails against the water glass. "So, long enough for this to be a rebound."

Riley shrugged. "Things with Lisa have been off and on for a while now. The first two months were good. But things went downhill as soon as I moved to Denver."

"You moved to Denver to be with her?"

"At the time I claimed it was for a job. In retrospect, I probably should have taken the job in Seattle instead. But Lisa was moving to Denver, so…I got distracted by a girl and made a bad decision."

"You moved after how long?"

"Two months. Do we have to talk about this?"

"Two months?" Ana's eyebrow arched. She took a sip of water and shook her head. "I've made some bad decisions myself, but…"

"I think I realized it was a mistake even at the time. But you have to make those mistakes, right? Anyway, my point is, things weren't great with Lisa and me for a long time. I feel like we'd been in the process of breaking up for a year." Riley stared at Ana. "So, no, this doesn't feel like a rebound. It feels like a really good…fling."

"I'm not sure I like that term any better," Ana replied.

"I live in Denver. You live in Napa." The waiter appeared with a bowl of freshly baked rolls. Riley waited for him to leave.

She kept her eyes on Ana. "I've spent the afternoon trying to think of a way we could make something work, but I can't."

"I fly in and out of Denver once or twice a month," Ana suggested. "Were you even going to ask for my number? Or my last name?"

Do last names matter in a fling? was Riley's immediate thought. She kept this to herself. After a long moment, she asked, "Would something like that work for you? Where you only see someone once or twice a month?"

"I've tried it before."

"And?"

Ana didn't respond. She picked out a roll and then handed the bowl to Riley. "How about tonight we agree to exchange phone numbers and figure out the rest later?"

Riley nodded. She took a roll and set it on the edge of her plate. "And then we call for a long-distance hookup?"

Ana shook her head. "Or because we want to talk, Riley. Anyway, I think I've changed my mind about wanting to have this conversation tonight. You broke up with someone last week. Somehow I keep forgetting about that." She split open the roll and stared at it for a moment, the crusty tan exterior changed to a nutty white. She reached for the butter and then set the roll down and stared at Riley. "And maybe I am crazy. Even if this wasn't your rebound, why should I think we could make this into anything more than a good weekend?"

"Because we both like the possibility," Riley replied. "Even if it's completely unrealistic."

"I want to keep everything easy, just the way it's been these past few days."

Riley lay awake in Ana's bed long after they'd finished making love. Ana's breathing was slow and even. Her arm was draped across Riley's chest. Riley tried to imagine Ana coming to her condo in Denver for the weekend or for an afternoon between flights. In some ways, she thought, it would be nice to have her own freedom, but she knew she'd feel lonely on the days between Ana's Denver trips. Probably too lonely. The thought of eventually moving to Napa crossed her mind but only long enough for her to confirm that it was pure insanity. She'd made that mistake before and knew she wouldn't make it again.

Ana shifted in bed and rolled to her other side, leaving Riley's chest suddenly bare. Riley pulled the covers up to her chin. Maybe this was, in fact, only a rebound. In some ways, it was a perfect rebound. Ana was a beautiful woman who desired her, but having a relationship within the confines of real life was impossible. They fit together well only here, in a cottage in the mountains far from her real life. She decided that they would have to leave it as a fling, but the idea of this made her feel inexplicably lonely. She tried to push it out of her mind, considering every other possibility once more. Maybe a weekend with Ana every two or three weeks would work somehow.

She fought with sleep until she set her hand between her legs and stroked her clit, replaying the scene of Ana's head between her legs and feeling again the flick of Ana's tongue.

Ana nudged Riley awake. "I have a meeting at eight with Joe's accountant."

Riley rolled over and looked up at her. She was dressed in a business suit again and had already put on lipstick and eyeliner. Her dark hair was pulled back with a hairband.

"You look good. Really good."

"This meeting can't wait. Not this morning. I'm not going to be able to explain away this one."

"Damn."

"Meet me for lunch?"

"I need to get out of town and stretch my legs. I'm going hiking after I finish sleeping in."

"Then an early dinner? Why don't you meet me at the winery when you finish your hike."

Riley nodded. She closed her eyes as soon as Ana left but couldn't fall back asleep after all. She got up and dressed in her hiking clothes, then sat on her bed with the trail map spread out and ate a granola bar. Sunshine poured in through the window along with the noise of a street sweeper and some sort of bulldozer that had likely been brought in to remove the boulders and scrape out the mud. She quickly decided on a hike far from the rumbling machines. She scanned the map for a trail far enough from the river to be open and east of town so the roads going to it would be clear. Red Rock Canyon sounded promising.

After a stop at Cheddar's to pick up lunch, she headed out with a book, a bottle of spring water and a sandwich packed in her bag. She drove to the trailhead and spotted one of the park service vans among the half dozen or so cars in the lot. Deb was pacing on the driver's side of the van and talking on her cell phone. Riley parked next to the van. She watched Deb for a moment, then gathered her pack and put on a baseball cap.

Deb held up her hand when she spotted Riley. She ended the phone call and then looked up at Riley. "Taking a well-deserved break from the flood relief work?"

"I am trying to pretend I'm on vacation today."

"Good for you. Have you hiked here before?"

Riley shook her head.

"Try Inspiration Trail. It's one of my favorites." Another park service van pulled into the lot and Deb waved to the driver. "This is our meeting spot. All the trails west of here are closed until the water recedes. We're going to try and see if we can get a crew in to the lower ravine later this week so a couple of us are going to check out the flood damage." She started toward the other van and then looked back at Riley. "By the way, I think I owe you a thank-you."

"For what?"

"Sharon invited me to come over tonight. I have a feeling you might have said something to help things along." Deb turned back toward the van. "Have a good hike, Riley," she called over her shoulder.

Riley shouldered her pack and headed out. The trail, mostly a red gravelly sand, was little more than damp despite the heavy rains. It weaved between towering red rocks for a half mile and then the hike began in earnest as the path steepened. A sheer cliff dropped off on one side of the trail and evergreens were thick on the other side. She reached a stream crossing and stopped to catch her breath. The stream was full, but there was no evidence of any flooding or trail damage. One deer and then several more came out of the clearing on the other side of the stream. They eyed her with suspicion, then one by one sprang over the water and trotted down their own path crisscrossing the steep side of the slope.

She continued on until she found the start of Inspiration Trail and turned to follow this new route. After enjoying a dizzying number of gorgeous vistas overlooking the Front Range, she came to a bench with another remarkable view, this time of the mountains kissing up to the range, and decided to stop. She was in no hurry and the sun and the climb were warming her up. She took out her book and sat down to read, feeling more relaxed than she had in months. Thoughts of Ana and the question of a continuing relationship eventually distracted her again. She had to close the book several times before the characters in the story and the thickening plot finally swayed her mind to pay attention to their plight.

By midafternoon, she'd looped around the canyon twice on different trails and made it back to the parking lot. She had finished all of the food in her pack, including a ration of trail mix, and was out of water. She called work to check in and her receptionist, Laney, chastised her for calling at all. Laney insisted that the relief therapist was doing fine and that she should get back to her vacation. Riley knew they would be fine without her, but it was Monday. She drove back to the inn, downed a bottle of the spring water Sharon had put out for the guests, then cleaned up and went to find Sharon.

"I ran into Deb this morning," Riley said.

Sharon was in the laundry room folding towels. "It's a small town."

"Why are you so hot and cold about her? She told me you invited her over tonight."

"I did. It was a moment of weakness. Or insanity maybe. Now, of course, I'll have to find some way to entertain her, then convince her to leave in time for me to watch my favorite Monday night TV shows."

"You're kidding, right?" Riley wasn't at all certain that she was joking.

Sharon looked up from the towels. "I was lonely last night. So I called her. Maybe you are right. Some nights, maybe, I could use some company."

"She's excited about seeing you."

"I want to be excited about her. I'm just not that excited about anything, Riley. Then I got to thinking about Edie, alone in that garage full of wet boxes of memories, and I decided I wanted company." Sharon shrugged. "Who knows? I might remember why I had a crush on her years ago."

Riley smiled. "She's cute, in that rough park ranger sort of way."

"Yeah, I know we have different types. Although I guess I don't really know what your type is, since I can't imagine how Ana and Lisa are similar."

"They both look good in a skirt?" Riley wondered at this. Sharon had hit on something she hadn't thought of at all. She couldn't think of any traits that linked Ana and Lisa. Nor Blair, for that matter.

"Well, I guess that is a type." Sharon smiled. "And how are things with Ana?"

Riley leaned against the rumbling dryer. "Good. A little too good, actually. I really like her and I think she really likes me. And you are thinking that I'm completely crazy for even thinking about this. Right?"

"Yes. And I do think she likes you quite a bit. She mentioned something this morning that I'm not going to repeat, but it was enough for me to be convinced."

"You're not going to tell me?"

Sharon shook her head. "She'll have to tell you herself. It won't sound as good coming from me."

Riley sighed. The hardest part of this whole situation was that it didn't matter if they liked each other or if Ana was more the type of person she longed for than anyone she'd ever been with—if she had a type at all. "Napa and Denver are more than a thousand miles apart. As much as I rack my brain, I can't make it work out to be anything more than a vacation fling. There's no way I'm ever moving states for a woman again. No one's that cute."

"Maybe she'd move. She travels for work anyway, right?"

"I wouldn't want her to move."

"Just because it didn't work for you and Lisa doesn't mean this time wouldn't be different."

"But it's crazy to even be having this conversation. I only met Ana how many days ago? And I broke up with Lisa a few days before that. No, she just has to be my beautifully sexy rebound."

The dryer buzzed and Sharon looked over at it. "Want to help me fold sheets?"

Riley went over to the winery after she'd finished helping Sharon fill the guest rooms with clean towels. The street sweeper and bulldozers had done a good job on the main street along the river, but most of the lower streets were still clogged with mud. The machines had stopped now, however, and the town was strangely quiet with few volunteers out and about and little traffic.

Riley crossed the footbridge, eyeing the river's water level, which was down a foot or more from the day before. She passed the restaurant with its damaged furniture still stacked along the walkway and then came up to the entrance of the winery. She paused, seeing Ana at the bar with a cluster of three men around her. One of the men was Joe, and Riley thought she could guess which one was the accountant. He had wire-rimmed glasses, a trim gray suit, folders under one arm and a briefcase in his other hand. He might have been the guy she saw Ana and Joe and his wife with the day before the flood. Riley watched as he shook hands with Joe, nodded to the others and then turned to leave. Joe picked up a folder, stared at it for a moment and then turned to head into the kitchen. As he did, the third man turned toward Ana and kissed her. She returned the kiss as his hand caressed her shoulder.

Riley felt her breath catch in her throat. The accountant, or whoever he was, passed her just then, saying, "I'm sorry, the winery is closed today, ma'am."

Riley nodded, unable to manage a response, and continued staring through the glass at Ana and the man, still standing too close to each other. The accountant repeated himself, adding something about the flood, and then shrugged and turned to leave.

Ana and the other man stepped apart as Joe came back into view. Joe handed a bottle of wine to the man, who studied the label, one arm still wrapped around Ana. Then Ana looked out the window and met Riley's gaze. Her hand came up to her lips. They stared at each other for a moment. Riley felt numb. Ana was only a nameless stranger in someone's painting, a beautiful woman casually embraced by a handsome man as he chose a bottle of wine for their evening together. Riley finally turned and walked away.

PART TWO

Sacramento, California
(Two Years Earlier)

The fluorescent lights of the hospital obscured any sense of day or night. Riley took the stairs to jolt herself awake. She'd found it was more effective than coffee at this time of day. She paused at the nurses' desk to check the patient's room number. Two nurses were seated at the desk, busy with records. One of them looked up finally.

"Can I help you?"

"Joe Granzig? Had a stroke five days ago and was cleared for PT by Dr. Jennings?"

The nurse with short curly brown hair and an easy smile nodded. "Room 306. He's had family visiting for a while. Would you mind kicking them out so I'm not the bad guy? I've already tried to convince them to let the guy rest."

"Do you want them to hang out in the waiting area or are visiting hours over?"

"You guess."

"Got it," Riley said. She started to walk away but stopped when the nurse called her back to sign in. Riley wrote her name on the clipboard.

"You work with Sheryl Oberwein, right?"

Riley nodded.

"My mom's good friends with Sheryl. Your name came up a few weeks ago. My mom has a PT practice in Denver."

Riley glanced at the nurse's name badge. "Lisa Derringer? Yeah, I sent Jeanette Derringer a résumé a few weeks ago. Sheryl told me about her practice."

Riley had applied for the job despite her misgivings about moving to Denver. Sheryl had been her supervisor through her clinical rotations, and she'd done an internship with her as well. When Sheryl's associate in the practice took a year off for maternity leave, Riley had the opportunity to fill in for her. Unfortunately, this associate was due back in August, at which time Riley would be out of a job. Sheryl had pushed Riley to apply for the Denver job mostly because she knew the practice owner. By Sheryl's description of the position, there was a good opportunity to do the work Riley wanted to focus on, rehabbing stroke patients, at the Denver practice. And according to Sheryl, Jeanette Derringer would be a good mentor. "Sheryl somehow knows everyone."

"Doesn't everyone know someone else in this business? And everyone thinks they know everyone's secrets as well."

"People love to gossip," Riley returned. The nurse's innuendo about secrets made Riley pause. She wasn't out at work, only because she had no reason to be, but she knew people could guess. "I manage to avoid gossip only because I don't really know anyone. I'm just here to see my patients."

"And then you get the hell out of this place, right? Well, it doesn't stop people from knowing things about you."

Riley paused. "Like what?"

"I know you are from Seattle."

"How did you know that?"

Lisa shrugged. "Like I said, just because you don't gossip doesn't mean someone else isn't gossiping about you. Blame the nurses' grapevine." A man came up to the nursing station and Lisa turned her attention to him.

Riley went to find Room 306, trying to shake off the feeling that the nurse knew more about her than where she was from. Joe

Granzig was exhausted and clearly in no shape to listen to Riley's spiel about the importance of his physical therapy program. She convinced the family to let him rest and made arrangements to come back to see him after he'd had a nap. When she came out of the room, Lisa was still at the nurse's desk, writing. She considered taking the elevator at the other end of the hall since it would get her closer to her next appointment, but instead she found herself walking back over to the nurses' desk. "And I'm guessing you're from Denver?"

"Yes," Lisa answered, without glancing up from her chart. "But that wasn't hard to figure out, Sherlock. My mom's practice is in my hometown, yes."

"Miss home?"

She nodded. "Do you?"

"Sometimes."

"Denver's better than Seattle." Lisa finally looked up from her chart when another nurse came up to the counter, handed over a file and then walked past them to the elevator.

"Why's that?"

"We have less rain."

"I like the rain. And there's no ocean anywhere near Denver," Riley countered. She knew she had seen Lisa before, but she hadn't really noticed her. Now that she had gotten Riley's attention, she was hard to walk away from. Her curly brown hair was pulled back with a bright red headband, and her green eyes kept lighting on Riley. She had a smile that made Riley want to forget about the fact that Joe Granzig's nap had just made her afternoon schedule even busier.

"But Denver's a mile high." She tapped her pen against the counter. "Top that."

Riley smiled at the word choice. She doubted it was accidental. "And why is it important to be a mile higher than everyone else?"

"The sea level's rising." She clicked her pen. "Just saying you'd be better off in Denver."

"I don't think I have a chance if you're going to bring in climate change." Riley wanted to ask her what she was doing that evening. Instead she said, "I'll let you know if your mom wants me to do an interview. Maybe then we can argue about the merits of Denver versus Seattle."

"I already know she wants you to do an interview."

"You're sure?"

Lisa nodded.

Riley moved out of the way as another nurse came up to the desk. She glanced down at the next name on her appointment schedule and tried to refocus. "I've been running behind all day."

"Don't work too late. I'm off at eight."

Riley stopped in her tracks at this. She looked back at Lisa. Her smile confirmed the invitation.

It wasn't exactly a date, but Riley had trouble concentrating on the rest of her patients that afternoon. She went back to her apartment, showered, changed into jeans and a button-down shirt and was back at the third-floor nursing desk five minutes before eight. Lisa was finishing rounds with the lead nurse, so Riley sat down on one of the couches in the waiting area.

Riley had been single for all of a week, but it had felt like an extra long week. She had been with Blair since they'd started PT school together. After graduation, Blair had moved to Austin and Riley had remained in Sacramento. Riley blamed the distance on every problem that had come up since Blair's move, but she'd finally admitted, at least to herself, that she'd lost interest long before Blair had moved. Blair somehow realized this as well.

"Do you dance?"

Riley looked up from the magazine in her hands. She had picked it up to have something to look at but had proceeded to roll it into a tube and was tapping it against her knee rather than reading it. She unrolled the magazine and replaced it on the stack. "Sometimes. Why?"

"I'm meeting up with some friends at one of the clubs downtown tonight. We're getting dinner first." Lisa had changed out of her scrubs and into a pair of tight blue jeans and a white tank top with a horseshoe print on it.

Riley stood up. "Sounds fun. But, as fair warning, I'm a little rusty on the dance floor. I can't even remember when I last walked into a club. You might decide not to go out on another date with me after tonight."

"Who said this was a date?" Lisa asked with a straight face.

"Oh, I'm sorry, I thought that—"

Lisa held up her hand. "Relax, I was just giving you a hard time. Now that I have your attention, I'm planning on teasing you a little. You know, I've tried getting you to talk to me for a year."

"A year? No way."

"After the third time you ignored me, I finally gave up."

"What?" Riley put her hand over the door sensor as Lisa stepped past her into the elevator. Lisa pressed the ground-floor button. "I'm sure I never ignored you. Before today, I didn't know I had a chance with you."

"Or that I existed, right?"

Riley shook her head.

Lisa continued, "I'm not going to admit how many times you have walked right by my desk without even looking my way. You are always in your own little world. Don't worry, though. It wasn't like you were the only one on my list."

"So you have a long list? I just happened to be the one who you caught today?"

"Something like that. Anyway, this isn't a date. Maybe I'm just bringing you along as a favor to my mom."

"Really?"

"Or maybe you just happened to be the one I picked today. You've been looking depressed lately, and I think you need to get out of the hospital anyway." Lisa stepped out of the elevator when the door opened again on the ground floor. She was shorter than Riley, but she had a quick stride. Riley had to jog to catch up to her as she slipped out the sliding glass doors. "Maybe you should pay more attention to people," Lisa continued. "I would have gone out on a date with you a year ago."

Riley caught Lisa's arm as she was about to step off the curb, pulling her back just as a car made a right-hand turn in front of them. The driver had his eyes focused on the oncoming traffic and never glanced in their direction.

Lisa drew in a sharp breath. "That was close."

Riley let go of Lisa's arm. They stood facing each other. After a moment, Riley said, "Maybe I'll pay more attention from now on."

The restaurant served breakfast all day, but it was known as the Burger Joint. The place only closed from three to five a.m., and since it was one of the only alternatives to the hospital cafeteria within a half-mile radius, many of the customers wore scrubs. Lisa quickly introduced her friends, Chris and Marie, who had claimed half of a booth and were sitting close enough to clearly be a couple. Lisa ordered without glancing at the menu as the waitress brought a milkshake to the table. The waitress seemed to know all three of the women but handed Riley a menu. Chris and Marie looked familiar. Riley knew they were nurses, but she didn't try to guess where they worked in the hospital. By the joking banter between the three, Riley quickly guessed that Lisa had either dated one or both of them.

While Chris and Marie were distracted by the chocolate milkshake they'd ordered to share, Riley asked, "So how long have you been at Mercy, Lisa?"

"Two years. It's a good job. I'd stay longer if a few things were different."

"Such as?"

"I want a different city. I'm sick of Sacramento. I need a change."

"Why'd you come here?"

"A girl." She smiled. "But we broke up. And then I met someone else. That didn't work either. The one after her wasn't much better."

One of the other women reached across the table and jabbed Lisa with a straw. "Hey, I heard that. And I can count. That was me you you're talking about, wasn't it? I was second after Jen, right?"

Lisa laughed and turned toward Riley. "I swear I'm not that bad of a girlfriend. Anyway, I've already got a job lined up in Denver. I'm so close to being out of this town. You'll like Denver."

"Sheryl's told me about your mom's practice. It sounds great, but I don't know about moving to Denver."

"Homesick for Seattle?"

Riley paused at Lisa's comment. She hadn't admitted as much to herself, but it was true. She missed home. But that was only part of it. Seattle was the easy choice and she couldn't deny that part of her wanted the simplicity of starting a career in a place that was already home. "I've got a job lined up in Seattle. I know everyone. It's a good practice."

"But I've already made the argument for why Denver is better than Seattle."

"The sea-level thing?"

Lisa grinned. "Why go home now? Seriously, I think you will be surprised at how much you like Denver. You're going to fit in there."

"How do you know? You barely know me," Riley countered.

"Nurses know all," one of the other women said, kissing her partner as she finished a sip of the milkshake.

"It's true. We've got a gossip ring like no other." Lisa reached over to her friends' milkshake and sucked the straw. "Anyway, my mom needs a good associate and you've got the rep. The Seattle job can wait."

Lisa's smile made Riley realize that she was already considering Denver despite all the reasons she'd piled against it a week ago. She'd flown through the city a handful of times but only visited once when she was a kid. Her parents had insisted on sightseeing in freezing temperatures for a day or two before they headed up to Aspen. She could scarcely pull up an image of the city beyond the airport's white peaked tent.

They headed over to the club on foot since no one wanted to drive home later. Downtown was always crawling with cops on the two streets with gay clubs. Chris and Marie walked ahead, arm in arm. Lisa was suddenly quiet, walking close enough for Riley to have caught her hand if she'd felt ready for that. She wanted desperately to reach out for her, but she kept her hands jammed in her jean pockets.

"I'm sorry I ignored you before. I've had a lot on my mind, and I wasn't exactly available until about a week ago."

Lisa eyed Riley but didn't answer. They had reached a busy intersection and caught up with Chris and Marie waiting for the light to change. The club was on the other side of the street and there was a sizeable line of people waiting to get inside. They crossed the street, and then Lisa said, "You know, sometimes I don't like to leave things up to chance or fate or whatever you want to call it. But I got shy with you. And then my mom called me up and asked me if I'd heard anything about you. She wanted to know if Sheryl was biased. I didn't tell her that you were the woman I had a crush on for about a year."

"Thank you for not telling her that."

"Don't let it go to your head." Lisa smiled coyly. "It was a little crush and I had plenty of other distractions."

"Plenty?"

The line moved quickly and they were inside before Lisa answered Riley's question, although Riley doubted she was going to answer anyway. Chris and Marie made a beeline for the bar. They ordered beers and found a table that had been recently abandoned by two guys who had gone to grind on the dance floor. The place played a top forties dance selection with enough bass that Riley could feel it in her belly. She hadn't been out to a club for years, and she felt out of place. The butch women all seemed much cooler than she was with their gelled hair and rolled-up short sleeves showing off a pack of cigarettes, inked arms or machismo-rich muscles. The femme women were equally unattainable with their glances that brushed right past her, their heeled boots, tight jeans and tank tops with necklines low enough to tease cleavage.

Lisa took one sip of her beer and then grabbed Riley's hand. "I don't come here to sit around and drink like these two do," she said, motioning toward Chris and Marie. "Watch my beer, Chris."

Riley was on the dance floor before she could argue against it. Lisa pressed them into the crowded middle section and Riley felt her body moving easily with the motion of the crowd. Lisa's eyes kept darting from Riley to the other dancers. Riley closed her eyes, feeling the beat move her body. Lisa rested her hands on Riley's hips and then inched closer. By the next song, Riley's lips were brushing against Lisa's neck.

They ended up at Lisa's apartment. It was close to the club and Riley's excuse to herself was that she was suddenly too exhausted to walk the fifteen blocks back home and a cab was ridiculously hard to find. Chris and Marie had stayed at the club. Lisa explained that they went there for the beer and the eye candy. They insisted that they never left until last call on a busy Friday night.

"You have a roommate?" Riley asked, picking up a framed photograph of two strangers. A man and woman wearing Mickey Mouse ears smiled back at her.

Lisa nodded. "I share with another nurse. That's her and her brother. He drops in unexpectedly, but otherwise it's a perfect setup. She's almost always working graveyards. And even when she isn't working, she sleeps like a bat. I almost never see her." Lisa kicked off her shoes and went into the kitchen barefoot. "You want a drink?"

"No."

Lisa leaned against the kitchen counter, staring at Riley. "You sure?"

"Mmhmm."

She folded her arms. "I have to admit, I'm feeling suddenly shy."

"Why?"

"You've had a crush before, right? Okay, remember your last crush?" Lisa asked, filling a glass with water.

"Yeah, of course."

"And what if your crush was suddenly, after a really long year of waiting to get that person to even say hello, sitting in your living room?"

"Well, I've never asked a crush to go out for dinner, let alone dancing, on a first date. I usually stick to something low pressure like coffee if I can get up the guts to even say hello." Riley sank down on the couch. "I can go if you'd like. We can try again another time. Maybe a coffee date?"

"No, don't go."

"How about a movie?"

Lisa came out of the kitchen and grabbed the remote. She turned on the DVD player and the TV. "Looks like my roomie was watching old episodes of *West Wing*."

"Perfect. Not sexy at all. We won't even be tempted to hold hands."

Lisa sat down on the couch several inches from Riley. "You think I'm crazy, don't you? I can't believe I'm just going to watch TV with you." She hit the play button and settled back against the pillows. "I'd really like to kiss you."

"Too bad. No kissing tonight." Riley set her hand on Lisa's knee. She smiled when she felt Lisa shift her hand further up to her thigh. By the end of the second episode, Lisa was cuddled up on Riley's chest. Riley fought against sleep until she noticed Lisa's even breathing. She was sound asleep against her and soon quietly snoring. Riley closed her eyes.

* * *

Riley rubbed her face and squinted at her watch. She'd awoken to the sound of the front door opening. The door slammed shut and she recognized the woman from the Mickey Mouse ears picture. She was still in scrubs and without the Mickey ears looked much less happy. She walked past the sofa to turn off the TV. She glanced at Riley and then Lisa, but she didn't say anything. Riley thought she might have scowled at her, but she didn't trust the shadowy light. It was half past eight in the morning. Lisa was snoring. Riley shifted Lisa's head off her lap and onto the couch pillows and went to find the bathroom. She awkwardly introduced herself to Lisa's roommate as the woman came out of the bathroom, getting only a grunt in return. Riley squeezed toothpaste onto her finger and rubbed it over her teeth, then rinsed. She splashed water on her face and smoothed her tousled hair. The last time she remembered waking up in a stranger's apartment was in college.

Lisa was up by the time Riley went back to the couch. She yawned and then covered her head with a pillow as soon as she saw Riley watching her. "I still can't believe I finally asked you out. And brought you home. And then we ended up watching TV."

"I had a good time last night," Riley said. "Dancing was fun." Riley realized that Lisa's coyness yesterday was more likely an awkward shyness. "Up for that coffee date?"

Lisa looked up over the pillow. "Yeah, I'd like that. Let me shower first."

Coffee in hand, they walked over to the farmers' market set up two streets down from Lisa's apartment. Riley guiltily remembered the conversations she'd had with Blair about farmers' markets. Blair had been obsessed with going every Wednesday and Saturday, and it had been a point of contention in the relationship every time Riley picked up an apple or any produce at the grocery store. Riley had come to hate the markets and hadn't been to one since Blair moved to Austin. Now it was her suggestion that they go. She looked over at Lisa and reached for her hand. Lisa smiled and clasped hers. They walked the length of the city block, lined with growers' tables filled to the brim, sipping their coffee and not buying anything. Then they turned around and walked back the other direction. Riley eyed the berries on the last table. Small bright red strawberries filled little green baskets in tidy rows, and behind these were bunches of lettuce, kale and chard.

"Hold on, I want something." She glanced at the greens, thinking of Blair, who had taught her the difference between chard and kale, then she picked out a basket of strawberries. A woman with a blue bandana on her head took her money and emptied the basket of strawberries into a paper bag.

Lisa stood on the sidewalk, waiting. Riley looked at her and winked. Lisa shook her head. "Why are you winking at me?"

"Why not? You've had a crush on me for a year. I figure I might as well catch up."

"Don't. It was a little crush. I shouldn't have told you."

"But you did." Riley opened the bag and popped a strawberry into her mouth. She tossed the stem into a planter box. And then picked out a strawberry for Lisa. "They're delicious."

"With coffee?"

"An acquired taste."

Lisa took a bite. She shook her head and swallowed.

"You might get used to it." Riley knew exactly why she hadn't noticed Lisa before yesterday. She'd been so loyal to Blair and, even more so, to her job that anything else had simply been ignored. And in the process, she'd lost a year of possibilities. "Want to go out tonight?"

"I can't. I'm working swing. Tomorrow?"

"Tomorrow at the same coffee shop?" Riley held up her coffee cup.

"Give me your phone," Lisa said. She entered her number into Riley's phone and handed it back.

"I'm going this way," Riley said at the next intersection.

Lisa glanced toward her apartment. "Thanks for last night." She turned and headed down the street. Halfway down the block, she looked over her shoulder and smiled. Riley felt a warm wave rush through her. She felt as if every nerve that had been asleep for the last year or so was awakening now. She watched Lisa for another moment and then turned to head home.

* * *

The coffee shop by Lisa's apartment had mediocre coffee. The baristas were bleary-eyed and rude at ten on a Sunday morning. Riley ordered two coffees and sat down at one of the outside tables. She recognized Lisa walking down the sidewalk toward her and waved.

"I love spring in this city," Lisa said. "But it's too damn short. The weather report said it is supposed to be close to ninety today and it's only May."

Riley handed her a coffee. "With one pack of real sugar and just a little cream."

Lisa took a sip. "So, sometimes you pay attention, huh? This is perfect, thank you."

"Have you ever seen the rose garden downtown?"

"Over by the Capitol?"

Riley nodded. "I passed the garden on my way here this morning. The roses are ridiculous. But I can't help wanting to stop and smell them. I was just thinking about how I've been in this city for four years now and feel like I don't know anything about it. I didn't even know about the rose garden and it's only ten blocks from my house."

Lisa stood up. "Okay, we've got to take a walk."

"Where to?" Riley picked up her coffee.

"The day I broke up with the girl who I came to Sacramento for, I went on a run." Lisa pointed north and started walking, coffee in hand. "I was trying to decide what I was going to do with my life."

"Slow down," Riley said. "What's your rush? It's Sunday."

"Come on, it's a long walk. Keep up." Lisa smiled back at Riley and walked faster. She slowed down a bit when Riley caught up to her. She continued, "Anyway, at first, I figured I'd go back home but it'd only been a few months since I'd moved and I'd signed a year lease. So, I went on this run, and I wasn't really paying attention to where I was going. I ended up at the river. I followed it for a while and there's a place where the river bends and the city just disappears behind the trees. All you can see is the river, open fields and, way off in the distance, snow-capped mountains. It reminded me so much of home that I decided to stay. I mean, I knew the mountains weren't the Rockies, but seeing them was somehow close enough. I want to show you that spot."

It took less than a half hour to get to the river. They followed the dirt path above the shoreline and then the path slowly dropped closer to the water's edge. Soon enough, every trace of the city did disappear behind the thick line of trees. Riley realized that bird calls and the sound of the water coursing between the rocks had entirely replaced the city sounds in an unsteadying moment. Lisa stopped when they had a perfect view of the mountains.

"Why'd you break up with that girl?"

"The one I left everything I knew to be with?" Lisa laughed cynically. "We just weren't meant to be girlfriends, I guess. I should have known better…Turns out that when she said she didn't really believe in monogamy that meant she slept with whomever the fuck she wanted to whenever the opportunity presented itself. I figured that out two weeks after I'd moved here. But I thought it would get better, you know. We talked about it, and for a while, it was better."

"You thought she'd be happy with just you."

Lisa turned to look at Riley. "Naive, right?"

Riley took Lisa's hand. "It's beautiful here. The city feels miles away."

Lisa kept her gaze trained on the distant mountains. "I know this is crazy, but I think you are going to come to Denver with me."

"Why's that?"

"Fate keeps messing with me. As soon as my mom said your name, I thought, yep, this is full circle. I moved to California for a girl and so a girl is gonna move to Colorado for me."

Riley laughed. "If I take the job in Denver, I'll be moving to Colorado for work. Nice as you seem, we only met yesterday."

Lisa shook her head. "We met a year ago. You asked me if I wanted the last strawberry yogurt. We were in the cafeteria and it was after the grill had closed, so there weren't many options besides the usual—Cup o' Noodle, stale ham and cheese sandwiches or yogurt. We were standing in front of the refrigerated section. I said I liked strawberry so you took the peach. You smiled when you handed me the strawberry and said, 'Enjoy,' then walked away."

"I do like strawberry best."

Lisa took a step closer to Riley and their lips met. They parted for a moment, and then Riley kissed her again. Lisa's lips felt so good against hers that she felt light-headed and greedy.

A bicyclist rang his bell, and they stepped to the side of the path to let him pass. They walked hand in hand back toward the city, each step bringing the city sounds and smells closer. They said goodbye in front of Lisa's apartment. Her roommate was sleeping off her fourth graveyard shift, and Lisa didn't want to risk waking her. Riley wanted to go to the grocery store before the Sunday evening crowd anyway.

"When do we get another date?" Riley asked.

"When's your phone interview with my mom?" Lisa countered.

"Does another date depend on how I do on the interview?"

"No." Lisa hesitated. "But I leave for Denver in two months."

"So, worst case, we hang out for two months and then go our separate ways."

"No, I'm already too into you for that to work. I'm tired of getting my heart wrapped up in a lost cause. Call me after you have the interview."

Riley caught Lisa's hand as she was turning to leave. "Well, in case the interview doesn't go well…," Riley said, stepping closer to Lisa. Riley thought she could spend the afternoon kissing her. Her lips felt strangely empty when they finally parted.

* * *

Jeanette Derringer was nothing like her daughter, at least not over the phone. Riley hung up after the conversation had ended and sank back on her chair. She wasn't sure if the interview had gone well or had been entirely terrible. Jeanette had asked the usual interview questions, ones that Riley had even practiced beforehand, but her responses to all of Riley's answers were so cool that it was difficult to tell if there was even a chance at a second in-person interview. Jeanette's last comment was the standard, "Well, I'll let you know."

Five days had passed since she'd gone to the river with Lisa. Work had kept her distracted during the day, but every night, the feeling of loneliness was all the more acute. Since she'd broken up with Blair and no longer spent an hour with her on the phone every night, she'd suddenly had too much time in the evening. Now, knowing that someone she was interested in was close enough to walk to made the nights all the more long. Riley turned on the TV, flipped through the channels and turned it off a moment later. She was too antsy to sit in the apartment. She grabbed her sweatshirt and changed into running shoes. She'd jogged with Blair but hadn't liked it enough to keep up their workout routine when Blair had left.

The night air was crisp, but she was warm enough after only a few blocks. She ran east toward Lisa's apartment, second-guessing her decision with each passing block. The rose garden was lit by the streetlights, but the roses had lost their daylight luster. She changed her mind about going toward Lisa's place and instead cut across the Capitol building and headed north toward the river. She had run for twenty minutes at a good speed before she decided to head toward Lisa's place after all. She was breathless by the time she reached Lisa's apartment. She stopped and stretched on the stairs leading up to Lisa's door. There was a call box, but she hesitated to press Lisa's button. She hadn't planned out what she would say and wasn't certain Lisa would be happy that she'd dropped by unannounced.

Finally, she turned to leave without pressing the call button after all. She jogged a few paces and then spotted Lisa. She was standing on the street corner watching her. Riley stopped in midstride.

"Did you suddenly get shy or are you stalking me now?"

Riley wiped her forehead with the back of her hand. "I think your mom doesn't like me."

"I just got off the phone with her," Lisa said, holding up her cell phone.

"Did you tell her we went out on a date last week?"

"Maybe."

"Maybe? Okay, did she say anything about my crappy interview?"

"She said she was going to ask you to come out to Colorado to check out the practice in person. She said she didn't want to offer you the job without you having a chance to meet everyone."

"She said that?"

Lisa walked past her and unlocked the front door. "You want to come inside, or are you just going to hang out here looking slightly creepy?"

"I don't know. I've had a crappy week. You might not want to hang out with me tonight."

"One of my exes sent me a text yesterday to say she's thinking of getting engaged—another polyamorous one who never wanted to be tied down to anyone. And I got written up by one of the lead nurses today for something I wrote in one of the charts. I drew a picture of an a-hole on this guy's treatment sheet. The guy cussed me out for half an hour because he didn't like the salt-free diet his doctor prescribed. He's recovering from a heart attack. It isn't the salt that is going to kill him. It's his anger management problem."

"My week was crappy because I wanted to see you or at least call you, but you told me I couldn't."

"That was why your week was so bad?"

"Yeah," Riley admitted. "And they've been out of strawberry yogurt at the cafeteria all week too."

Lisa grabbed Riley's hand and pulled her inside the apartment building's foyer. They kissed by the line of mailboxes, ignoring the teenage boy who walked past them whistling. "You're coming to Denver with me," Lisa said as they parted.

"Where'd the shy girl go?" Riley touched her hand to her lips. Lisa's kiss had managed to make her knees feel weak.

"I'm not shy. But I think I'm done taking it slow with you."

Riley followed up the stairs to her apartment. The door was unlocked, and Lisa hesitated after she'd opened the door.

"You don't usually leave the door unlocked?"

Lisa shook her head. "My roomie's probably home. She always forgets to lock the door when she gets home." She leaned against the doorframe. "Can we go to your place instead?"

"Embarrassed to bring a girl home?"

"It's not that, exactly."

"You know, your roommate and I already met. She came home the night we fell asleep on your sofa. I said hello to her as she was coming out of the bathroom."

Riley pulled the door closed. Lisa didn't argue. "Let's go to my place anyway. I'd love to change out of these sweaty clothes."

Lisa's car was an old Toyota sedan with ripped seats and a cracked windshield. The crack was below the centerline and ran all the way across, giving the glass the same appearance as a bifocal lens. Lisa's radio was tuned to country music. Riley pointed the way through the downtown streets to her apartment building. She wondered if Lisa wasn't out to her roommate. Or maybe the roommate simply didn't like strangers spending the night in their apartment.

Lisa hummed along to the song that was playing. "Do you like country music?"

"Not really. I'll put up with about anything, though."

"'Put up with'?" Lisa huffed. She turned the song down a bit and then squinted at Riley. "Okay, this might not work out after all."

"Because I don't like country music?"

Lisa laughed. "I love country music. Love it. Seriously, this might not work." She grinned as she turned the volume up again.

Riley pointed to an empty parking spot. "My place is on the corner. But I don't know if you even want to bother parking. Maybe you should just drop me off and we'll go our separate ways."

"Maybe you will start to like country."

Lisa pulled into the empty spot and hit the brakes. She leaned across the center console and stared at Riley, then turned off the car. The music died quickly. Riley waited for a long moment and then leaned over and kissed her. They walked up to Riley's apartment hand in hand. Riley had kept the place she'd shared with Blair but had decided against a roommate. Blair had picked the place when she was living there by herself because the rent was cheap. The train tracks were only a hundred yards or so behind the building. When Riley moved in, they talked about moving. But they had both gotten used to the noise of the passing engines and liked to sit out on the back balcony and watch the long freight trains lumber by in the evenings. Riley had thought about moving when Blair left but never got around to doing anything more than looking at rental postings online.

Riley unlocked the door and scanned the place as Lisa walked in behind her. She'd left a few dirty dishes on the coffee table in the living room and there were books strewn about haphazardly. She'd become a compulsive reader since Blair had left and she'd found a secondhand bookstore three blocks from the hospital. "Sorry. It's a bit of a mess. I wasn't planning on having anyone over." She pulled off her sweatshirt and then caught her sweaty scent. "Mind if I rinse off? There's beer in the fridge if you want to help yourself."

Riley showered quickly and changed clothes. She came out to find Lisa cross-legged on the loveseat with a photo album on her lap. She held up the page she'd stopped on and pointed to a photograph in the center. "Want to explain this one?"

Riley could have guessed which photo had caught her attention without seeing the page. "I think it's pretty self-explanatory, don't you?"

"Not one bit," Lisa said, laughing. "Okay, clearly you are on your knees and have your face in someone's crotch. That much I figured out. But what's all over your hair? And is someone spanking you with a spatula?"

"Whipped cream. It was a college graduation party. I don't remember the spatula at all," Riley said, coming over to have a closer look at the photo. Lisa pointed to the object in question and Riley agreed that it did seem to be aimed at her backside. "I didn't actually graduate that year, but it felt like I did after that party." In the picture, she was on her knees, pretending to eat out her girlfriend, who happened to be fully dressed, when someone reached over and squirted whipped cream on her head. It was her girlfriend, Katie, who had graduated. She'd been with her for a year at the time of the party, but they broke up not long afterward. Katie had gone on to graduate school in Michigan, and they'd lost touch.

Lisa looked up at her grinning. "So, someone takes a picture of you, looking like this, and you say to yourself, 'yeah, that one's going in the book.'"

Riley reached over Lisa's shoulder and closed the book. "I like to remember the moment. It was a good night."

"I bet. Was she good in bed?"

Riley nodded.

"You're supposed to tell me she was terrible."

"Why would I do that? She taught me a lot." Riley brushed a curl back from Lisa's face and leaned down to kiss her. Lisa shifted on the seat, making room for Riley to straddle her. "How about you? Have your exes all been terrible in bed?"

"Not all of them." Lisa reached for Riley. "But I don't want to talk about exes."

Riley unbuttoned Lisa's shirt and unsnapped her bra. She brushed a fingertip across Lisa's collarbone and started massaging Lisa's shoulders and neck, watching Lisa's face relax as her hands worked on the muscles.

"I could get used to this," Lisa murmured.

Riley finished with Lisa's shoulders and ran the back of her hand over Lisa's chest. She let her hand rest between Lisa's legs and leaned forward to kiss her. Lisa's eyes were closed, and as Riley unbuckled her belt, a smile briefly crossed her lips. She took off the belt and the pants. Lisa leaned back against the chair pillows and moaned softly when Riley traced a line from her belly button downward with her tongue. Riley paused as the sun set and the room suddenly darkened. Lisa's eyes were still closed and a half smile played on her lips. Riley watched her, for a moment, and then asked, "Will you be pissed if I don't move to Denver?"

Without opening her eyes, Lisa said, "Well, you don't like country music, so whatever." She ran her hand through Riley's hair, then grabbed behind her neck and pulled her close. "I think you should forget about Denver for the moment."

Riley slipped out of her T-shirt and jeans. She ran her hand up the length of Lisa's leg. Lisa clasped Riley's hand before she reached her upper thigh. "Are you telling me to stop?" Riley asked softly.

Lisa shook her head. She caressed Riley's fingers, then placed Riley's hand on her upper thigh. "I was thinking about Denver..."

"I thought we were forgetting about Denver."

Lisa nodded. "I know. But what if you move there and hate it? There's a lot of country music in Colorado."

Riley shrugged. It wasn't about the music and they both knew it.

"Maybe we should just have fun and forget about what comes next."

"Probably," Riley agreed. "But I do have an old cowboy hat and a pair of boots somewhere around here. I used to lease a horse at a barn outside of town. Think I'd fit in if I wore the hat?" Riley teased.

Lisa shifted off the chair and pushed Riley onto her back. The carpet was rough against Riley's bare skin, and she started to sit up but paused when she saw the smile playing at the edge of Lisa's lips. Lisa's look made her willing to yield, at least for the moment.

"I'd like to see you in a cowboy hat. Nothing else, just the hat." Lisa climbed on top of her. She pressed her hand on Riley's chest, pinning her down. The hair between her legs brushed against Riley's skin as she shifted position, her free hand stroking from Riley's breast down to her hip. She moved lower and slid her tongue between Riley's legs.

Every muscle in Riley's body quivered at Lisa's touch. She was used to initiating sex with Blair and nearly always taking the lead. Blair seemed to be more comfortable on the pillows than on top and neither of them had tried to reverse the roles they'd fallen into early on. But this wasn't Blair, she reminded herself as Lisa's hands and tongue moved deftly over her body. She reached for Lisa, wanting to feel more of her, but Lisa grinned and pinned her down again.

"Don't worry, I'll let you have a turn. But right now I want you on your back."

* * *

The phone rang, jostling Riley from a sound sleep. She climbed out of bed and found the phone, answering it on the last ring. It was Jeanette. As soon as Riley heard the woman's voice, she looked over at Lisa, stretched across her bed buck naked. Lisa had spent the weekend at Riley's house. It was Monday morning and the clock claimed it was already half past seven.

"I want you to come out to Denver," Jeanette was saying.

"I'd like that," Riley said. She rubbed the sleep out of her eyes and cleared her throat.

"I'm sure you have a full schedule, but I'm hoping that Sheryl can spare you for a day or two at the end of the week?"

"As in this Thursday or Friday? Yeah, I think I can make that work."

Lisa rolled over and rubbed her face. She squinted at Riley and mouthed, "Is that my mom?"

Riley clapped her hand over the phone and said, "Yeah, do you want to say hi?" She grinned at Lisa and then answered Jeanette's next question. When the details were settled, she hung up the phone and tossed it onto the bed. "Looks like I'm going to check out Denver."

"What if you move out there and hate it?"

"Then I hate it."

"But you'll blame me."

Riley picked up the dildo that was lying in the middle of the bed. She went to the sink to rinse it off and then put it back in her underwear drawer. The sheets needed to be changed, but she wasn't going to have time get laundry done anytime soon. "I don't even have the job yet. And, for the record, it is really weird to be looking at you, naked in my bed, while I'm setting up an in-person interview with your mom. Can we agree not to tell her about anything that's happened between us until after she decides whether or not she wants to offer me the job?"

"Fine. But if she asks if you're good with your hands, I'm going to tell her the truth."

"Which is?" Riley climbed on top of Lisa. She smelled of sex and the scent made her want her all over again.

"Your massages make the top of my list," Lisa replied.

"How long is that list?"

"Not saying. And I'm pretty sure I'd never say anything about sex to my mom, but I'd love to see her expression if I did." Lisa grinned. "It might sway her opinion of you."

"One way or the other."

Riley was late for her first patient. She rarely had to come up with an excuse for the nine o'clock appointment and doubted that the patient really believed the line about traffic delays. By lunchtime, she'd caught up and had enough time to meet with Sheryl to discuss their end of the week schedule. Jeanette had, however, already called Sheryl to let her know and the schedule had been tweaked accordingly. She was doubled up on Tuesday

and Wednesday to fit everyone in, but Sheryl was excited enough about the Denver job to inspire Riley as well.

By the time she left the hospital, it was dusk. Riley walked home, planning out dinner and thinking about Denver. She admitted that the move would be less about the job and more about the girl. And she barely knew Lisa. The job would have to be worth the move, not the sex. Every hour that had passed without Lisa made her realize this fact all the more. She considered the standing offer at the practice in Seattle. It was only ten minutes from her folks' place and she had friends in the neighborhood. Her mom would say she was crazy for not taking the job, and she'd probably be right.

Riley unlocked the door to her apartment and dropped her wallet and keys on the front table. She went to the kitchen and opened the fridge, then the freezer. She took out a bag of grapes and sat down at her computer. She pulled up the website for Jeanette's practice. Jeanette's face smiled back at her. The resemblance to her daughter was easily noted. They had the same curls and the same smile. Jeanette's face had more wrinkles. After scrolling through the website for a few minutes, she clicked over to her email. She knew she wasn't going to take the Seattle job. It was the easy decision, too easy. Her cell rang and she recognized Lisa's number.

"What'd you forget?"

"How did you know I was calling to say I forgot something?" Lisa asked.

"It's too soon to call and say you want to come over without it seeming like you're going to be clingy."

"In that case, I'll admit it. I can't make it even one night without you," Lisa laughed. "And maybe I left my keys."

Riley stood up and walked around the apartment, scanning for a set of keys. "Wait, how'd you get home?"

"I walked. It's a long walk, by the way. You live in the boonies. Fortunately, my roomie was home so I wasn't locked out. Didn't you notice my car was still parked outside your place?"

"Nope. Maybe it got towed." Riley picked up the keys. They were on the nightstand.

"Don't joke. I've had a few too many parking tickets, and I think I'm about one away from a tow. I hate street sweepers. I swear it's just a crock to make money on traffic tickets. The streets are still dirty."

"I found them. I'll be over in a half hour."

Lisa was out on the sidewalk when Riley walked up to her building. Riley tossed the keys to Lisa. "I wouldn't have minded if you'd just asked me to come over tonight."

"I swear I didn't leave them on purpose."

"A likely story," Riley said, clasping Lisa's hand. She kissed Lisa on the cheek. "Do you want to invite me up anyway?"

Lisa shook her head. "Let's go out."

"Roommate home?"

"Maybe. It's just awkward. Do you like Thai food? It's the closest place and the food's cheap and not bad either."

"Sold." Riley wanted to ask if she was out to the roommate but held her tongue. If Lisa wanted to tell her why they weren't going up to her place, she would have already, Riley decided. They walked one block south, and Lisa pointed out the restaurant sign.

"It's possible that they know me by name."

Riley walked home after they'd finished dinner. Lisa had wanted to drive her, but Riley said she wanted the walk. She guessed by Lisa's reaction to this that it was clear to her that Riley wanted some space. The more she considered the interview with Jeanette Derringer, the more she realized that she needed to make a decision on moving to Denver because of the job, not because of someone she'd just met. The more time she spent with Lisa, though, the harder it was to consider a job in Seattle. She'd laughed more in the weekend they'd spent together than she could remember in the past year. They'd planned more trips for the year than either would have time to take in the next ten years. She felt as if she'd woken up in a room flooded with light and blamed Lisa entirely. Moving to Seattle would be like reaching for the light switch. She didn't want to go back.

There were several bars between Lisa's house and hers, but on a Monday night there was little noise coming from any of them. The liquor stores were busy enough, though, and she made her way past two separate fights before being followed. The guy picked up her trail outside the entrance of one liquor store and kept not more than ten feet behind her, asking for change all the while, until he finally gave up when they reached the next liquor store.

From there, she kept to the main streets with stoplights. The side streets held too many shadows. Even between the stoplights, streetlights made halos on the ground and she kept her pace quick through the dark places. The sky was cloudy and the moon was hidden away. When she finally reached the Capitol grounds, she was too tense to take the shortcut through the rose garden. She made it home and snapped the lock into place, every nerve on edge. A train rumbled past and she realized she'd left the balcony door open. She closed it, then turned on every light in the place and walked around with an empty beer bottle in her hand, scanning even the closet and under the bed with a paranoid, raised-hair feeling that she couldn't shake.

Her phone rang and she felt a shiver race up her spine. It was Blair. She answered the phone and then went to the fridge to get a fresh beer, turning off the unneeded lights as she went.

"Is it too late?" Blair asked.

Riley relaxed as soon as she heard Blair's voice. "No, I'm awake looking for a boogeyman."

"Why?"

It was a reasonable question. Riley had lived in a city for most of her life and was rarely afraid of being out alone. But something felt off about the night. "I left the balcony door open when I went out tonight. Stupid, huh? Anyway, I'm looking in the closets and under the bed. No one's here but me." She paused, realizing that she'd told Blair enough for her to guess that she'd been out on a date. She rarely left the house after work otherwise. "What's up?"

Blair was silent for a long moment. "I was wondering how you were doing. That's all. So you were out tonight? On a Monday?"

"Yeah." Her forced upbeat tone was poor concealment. Riley sat down on the loveseat and popped off the beer cap. "It's good to hear your voice. What are you up to?"

"Nothing really. I just finished reading the book you loaned me a year ago. I wanted to call to tell you it was really good and that I kind of hated it."

"Which one?"

"*Bittersweet*. It was really fucking sad. I didn't really get the sweet part of the bitter. But I couldn't stop reading it."

"I loaned you that book a year ago and you decide to read it now? Haven't I loaned you like a dozen books by now? I think I even warned you about that one."

"You did. That's why I picked it. You told me it didn't have a happy ending." Blair sniffed and then drew a breath in sharply, trying to hide the fact that she was crying. After a while, she said, "So are you going to tell me what you were out doing tonight?"

"I wasn't going to, no."

"Okay, I'll start. Who is the person that you were out with tonight?" She paused and then said, "I know you, Riley. You don't do anything after work on a Monday night unless there is a good reason. How do you know her?"

"Can we not do this?"

"I just want to know."

"What do you want to know?"

"Is she the reason we broke up?"

"No."

"Yeah. Whatever. I'm in Texas. How am I supposed to know what's really been going on with your dating life? All I know is, you don't go out with someone you just met on a Monday night. That isn't you. You aren't spontaneous."

Riley set the beer down. She had no taste for it now. She stood up and paced, then sat down again. Blair was crying and the sound of it was poorly muffled, likely by Blair's hand covering the end of the phone. When she heard Blair sigh, she said, "I met her last week. You know I wouldn't have lied to you. We've talked about the reasons why we broke up. It had nothing to do with this person."

"Actually, you talked about the reasons why you wanted to break up."

"I told you. It's hard being so far apart, and you know I don't want to move to Texas…"

"I really don't want to hear this again."

Riley thought of tossing the phone out the back door. If she hurled it, there was a chance that she'd hit the tracks. "I want to keep you as my friend. Do you think that I'm crazy for even asking you to do that?"

The line was silent for at least a minute. Finally Blair said, "I think you are crazy to ask, but you know I'm not going to let you out of my life. Not completely." Blair cleared her throat.

Riley heard a door open and guessed Blair had gone out on her back balcony. She had an apartment in downtown Austin with a great back porch with an overhang and room for a patio set. She heard one of the patio chairs scrape against the concrete. She pictured Blair sitting down on the balcony with the sounds of the city all around her.

"How's work?"

"Good. I'm going to be laid off at the end of July but otherwise, I love it. How's your job?"

"Just great. Fuck, Riley, you've been out having a good time with some new girl and I'm calling you up as if there's still some chance. What the hell is wrong with me?"

"Nothing. You know that. You are amazing, and funny, and beautiful and—"

"Don't give me a pep talk right now. Seriously." Blair cussed, the muffled words scarcely as loud as the accompanying snap of a lighter. "The person I'm still in love with has moved on to the next girl and wants to be *friends*. Don't try and make me feel better. I'm pissed that you're going to have sex with someone else. I just want to sit here and be pissed."

"And you do pissed off so well too. I wish I could be there to see it."

"Then get on a plane."

Riley listened to Blair's breathing, slow and even. She thought of all the nights that had slipped away with that sound lulling her to sleep. "By the way, you scared away all the boogeymen. I'm sitting in this lonely apartment that I left unlocked on the wrong side of the tracks on this weird night without a moon, but I'm not scared anymore."

"You're welcome." Blair took a deep breath and exhaled slowly. "You could afford a nicer place."

Riley knew she had lit up a cigarette. Blair had quit smoking while they were together and gone on a health kick. This had inspired the farmers' market trips and the jogging. "This place feels like home now. And it has good memories."

"Memories, huh?"

"I'll send you a book with a better ending."

"Don't. I don't think I'm going to read anything for a while. And a happy ending would only make me more depressed. I gotta go, Riley."

With that the call ended. Riley stared at the phone for a moment. She got up finally and went out to her balcony. A cat howled and then a dog barked as if in answer. She searched for the moon but still couldn't make out even a shadowy light through the thick clouds.

* * *

The Denver flight was scheduled to leave at six in the evening. Riley had left work early to pack and barely made it to the airport before the scheduled boarding time. She only relaxed when she read the departure sign and realized the flight had been delayed a half hour. She fished out her cell phone from the backpack she'd taken as her only luggage. There was a missed call from Lisa. She pressed the call button and then hung up before the first ring.

Riley had told Lisa that she thought they should wait to hang out again until after the interview. Lisa seemed understanding but was not happy about this. In part, Riley knew it was because of how she'd left things on Monday night. Riley knew she should have explained why she wanted some space but she'd left instead. Lisa obviously knew something was wrong but apparently wasn't going to ask. On the other side of it, Riley didn't want to bring up her uncertainties about their moving to Colorado together. It seemed too obvious. If she liked the Denver job well enough to justify the move, none of her worries would matter anyway.

Blair hadn't called since Monday night either. Riley had been too busy at work to really think about it much, except in the evenings when she sat out on her balcony to watch the trains pass. She had stopped in at Whole Foods one night to buy a pre-made dinner but ended up with kale, tofu, garlic and red bell peppers. She chopped everything up and tossed it all together in the pan with oil. She added soy sauce when the kale had turned to a brighter green, then took the pan outside and sat down on the balcony with a pair of chopsticks. Blair had cooked this recipe up nearly once a week when they'd lived together, and it had taken Riley a very long time to be convinced kale was even edible. Blair had always sprinkled sesame seeds on top of the dish, but Riley had forgotten to buy these. Without the sesame seeds, it hadn't tasted nearly as good as she remembered.

When she finally got to Denver, Riley took a cab to the hotel. It was near midnight, and the cab driver kept rubbing his head as if to stay awake. The half-hour delay had turned into a two-hour delay, and Riley had finished the book she'd brought for the trip. Riley turned on her phone and saw another missed call from Lisa. Blair had called as well. Neither had left messages.

The hotel bed was hard and the pillows overstuffed, but Riley fell asleep almost instantly. She awoke when an alarm she hadn't set went off at five a.m. By seven, she'd had two cups of bitter hotel coffee and had watched the morning news on two different stations. She called a cab and was at Jeanette's clinic a full half hour early. She chatted with the receptionist and met the rest of the staff as they arrived.

Jeanette arrived last. She glanced at Riley and then pointed to the one closed door that she had yet to see anyone go through. "You're Riley? Good, I like promptness. Let's go to my office."

Jeanette unlocked the office door and then switched on her computer. She hung her jacket on the coat hook but shook her head when Riley started to sit down. "We aren't staying in here. Don't get comfortable. I just want to double-check my schedule and figure out who we are seeing this morning."

Riley rocked from her heels to the balls of her toes and then, realizing what she was doing, froze in place. She eyed the office space, noticing a prominent framed picture of Jeanette and a much younger, though still recognizable, Lisa, on the wall behind Jeanette's chair. There was one plant on Jeanette's desk, a Christmas Cactus, that strained out of the confines of the pot in which it was planted and half covered Jeanette's keyboard, brushing the back of Jeanette's hand as her fingers struck the keys.

Jeanette glanced up at her. "So...I'm going to tell you some things that you probably already know. Stop me if I'm becoming a bore. I realize that your work with Sheryl focuses primarily on hospitalized patients. You understand that you will have very little opportunity to work in the hospital here, correct?" Jeanette paused only briefly and did not look up from the computer screen before continuing. "Here we work almost exclusively with patients who have been recently discharged or are in need of long-term PT programs."

"I'm ready to get out of the hospital. And I want the long-term clients."

Jeanette nodded. "And I understand you want to spend more time with patients in stroke recovery. Of course, we also see sports rehab patients and you would have some responsibilities overseeing these programs. We see most of the stroke patients in their homes, but between me and Elaine, who is the only other full-time therapist I have right now, we keep a full appointment schedule seeing just the post-op sports rehab patients in the clinic." Jeanette checked the time on her wristwatch and then said, "And we are starting out five minutes late for our first patient. I don't like to keep them waiting. Shall we?"

Riley shadowed Jeanette throughout the morning. Little of Lisa's bubbly personality was evident in Jeanette. Although she chatted with her patients in a friendly way and the patients seemed to like her quite a bit, when Elaine, the other therapist, asked her a question Jeanette was quite short with her. Realizing that Riley had taken note of the harshness of her tone, she later admitted that everyone had been overworked since the last therapist had left, and were likely not being as patient with each other because of it.

By the time they were ready for a lunch break, Riley was still unsure if Jeanette was going to offer her the job or send her packing.

"I usually take about five minutes to eat in the clinic, but I blocked off enough time to go out for a bit," Jeanette said. "There's a place that the staff likes a few blocks away."

It was near the end of May, but the wind was icy. Riley wished she had thought to bring her coat as well. The morning had seemed warm enough, but now the sun had moved behind the clouds and the temperature had dropped quickly. Jeanette asked Riley's opinion on the cases that they had seen that morning, and Riley realized that her interview was just beginning. After a grueling forty-five-minute session, with Riley barely able to eat half the sandwich she'd ordered between Jeanette's questions, Jeanette finally leaned back in her chair and said, "There is one last thing we need to discuss, even though I can't really ask you directly about it."

Riley felt her neck muscles tighten. She took a sip of water and shifted back in her chair, deciding how direct she wanted to be with her. Finally, she said, "Jeanette, I want this job. And I think I'm a great fit for your practice. Lisa introduced herself to me weeks after I'd sent you my résumé. I'd already made the decision to apply for this job before I knew her."

"She told me as much. But you know her now. And since she's my daughter, I want to know how you are going to handle issues that come up down the line. I don't know your history, obviously, but I know my daughter's. I can't remember the names of the women she's dated in the past year because there've been that many."

"It won't affect my decision to stay at your practice. I'm very good at separating my work from my personal life."

Jeanette was clearly still hesitant. Her arms were folded across her chest, and she continued to stare at Riley.

Riley added, "I understand that you can't help but weigh all of this in your decision to offer me the job. If you need more time, I can wait. I do have an offer at a practice in Seattle, but I want this job more."

"Sheryl told me that you put work above everything else. As a practice owner, that's what I need right now. We've gone through some changes since our last associate left. She took two of our staff with her and the rest have been overworked since. I need someone to step in whom I don't have to babysit." The waiter came to refill their glasses and Jeanette was silent until he'd left. She reached for her iced tea and took a sip, then glanced at her watch. "When can you start?"

* * *

"How many times have you changed a flat?" Lisa asked.

"More than once." The sun was directly overhead, and Riley could already feel beads of sweat dripping down her back. "Pop your trunk so I can get the spare."

Lisa climbed back into the driver's seat and the trunk popped open. Riley pulled out their camping gear and set the packs on the side of the dirt road. They hadn't seen another car since they left the trailhead, and neither of them could get a cell phone signal. The backcountry trailhead was a little over twenty miles up a winding rocky dirt road. It was too early in the season to have tourist traffic and they'd picked this place specifically because of the reputation it had for being a hidden gem. She found the spare and the jack and set to work.

They'd just spent three days backpacking. With loaded packs, it took a full day to get to the waterfall. They spent the next day swimming in the icy pond underneath the fifteen-foot falls, swatting away mosquitoes and eating cold soup and oatmeal because the propane burner wouldn't light and they had somehow forgotten matches. They had peed in holes they dug, spent every night naked from the moment they slipped into the tent and away from the mosquitoes, hiked along the river, discussed religion, politics and, finally, all the books they had both read. Lisa had a book habit that was possibly worse than Riley's.

Once she had the jack in place and supporting the flat, she searched the trunk for the wrench. Lisa was sitting on top of their packs, watching her. "What's wrong?"

"I can't find your wrench."

"I don't keep any tools in the car."

"Well, yeah, but this is for the tire. Usually there's a wrench with the jack, but I can't find it."

Lisa came over to the trunk and peered inside. "I don't remember seeing anything like that but, you know, I always just call for road service when I get a flat."

"You've never changed a tire on this car?"

"I've never changed a tire, period."

Riley stopped herself from swearing. She pulled out picnic blankets, twine, empty plastic water bottles, three screwdrivers of various sizes and one hammer, that had all ended up in Lisa's trunk despite her being convinced she had no tools. Each item that she removed elicited some comment from Lisa. There was no wrench. Riley closed the trunk finally and looked at Lisa. "We can't get the tire off without a wrench."

They both stared at the now useless spare tire. "Well, someone will drive by eventually, right?" Lisa asked hopefully. "Sounds like everyone else except me has a wrench. How much food do we have?"

"We have one canteen of water left. It won't last long. We need to walk into town."

"I think we should wait and see who comes up the road." Lisa sat back down on her pack.

"It's Monday. The weather report said rain on Wednesday. I don't think anyone else is coming." Riley had taken the day off but was due back at work in the morning and they still had a four-hour drive back to Sacramento.

Lisa looked up at her but didn't move. "This ridgeline is actually a pretty spot. We have a good view in both directions.

I didn't notice all of the trees before. Look at those manzanitas taking over in the gap between the ponderosas."

"I don't really want to look at trees right now."

"I'm just saying that it's pretty. It's really different here than it was just ten miles back where we camped."

"Okay, I'll give it one hour," Riley said. "If no one comes in an hour, I'm walking into town."

"You mean, we're walking into town. No way in hell am I going to stay here if you leave." Lisa patted Riley's pack. "Come sit with me. There's no mosquitoes."

Riley looked up and down the road. Waiting was useless. She knew no one was coming and the last thing she wanted to do was sit on the side of a dirt road in the middle of nowhere.

"You're one of those types that get pissed but don't say anything, aren't you?"

Riley shook her head. "I'm not mad. I'm frustrated."

"That's just a different word for the same feeling," Lisa countered. She patted the pack again. "You agreed to one hour. Sit down and relax."

Riley realized that she was mad but didn't admit as much aloud. She turned her pack over so the squishy part was up and sat down. "Okay, I'll try and relax."

"We can talk about something."

"We've spent the past three days talking."

"Wow, you are really mad, aren't you?" Lisa said, whistling through her teeth. "I'm sorry I'm not the type of dyke to keep a wrench in my car. But I don't think you'd like me as well if I were that type." She grinned at Riley, and Riley felt the tension ease.

"I'm not mad about the wrench."

"Then why are you mad?" Lisa waited for Riley to answer, then took a deep breath and exhaled, spreading her hands outward with open palms. When Riley looked at her skeptically, she said, "Yoga. I don't go to class three times a week just to get a nice butt."

"You sure about that?"

"Don't joke. I'm finding my center so I can be ready when you finally open up to me."

"I already know where your center is. And I think I've already opened up to you. And vice versa," Riley said, grinning back at her. "I'm not mad."

Lisa stopped her deep breathing and playfully punched Riley's shoulder. "All right, just tell me."

Riley nudged a rock with the toe of her shoe. It rolled down the slope for several feet before settling to a stop. "It's been a month and I haven't been to your place since the first night. I'm not sure if there's a reason why you don't want me at your apartment or not, but why is it a good idea to move in together when we get to Denver if you don't want me in your space here? Sometimes, I feel like we hardly know each other." Riley felt the ball forming in her throat. She'd tried once before to have this conversation with Lisa, but the ball had stopped her. Riley continued, "I've been hoping you would tell me a reason why you never want me at your apartment without me having to ask."

"How am I supposed to know something is bothering you if you don't tell me?" Lisa looked away. "Sometimes you have to ask."

"Well, I'm asking now."

"And if we didn't get this flat tire, would you have gotten around to it? Hell, Riley, we've spent three amazing days together. I was beginning to think I knew you better than anyone I've ever dated. And now you tell me that you feel like you hardly know me?"

Riley picked up another rock and turned it over in her hands a few times. "Why haven't you wanted me to come over to your place?"

"It's nothing really." Lisa sighed. "My roommate doesn't like company."

Riley tossed the rock on the ground and dusted her hands off on her pants. "But it's your place too."

Lisa shrugged. Riley guessed there was another reason, something that Lisa wasn't admitting.

"Is your roommate not comfortable with you having women over?"

"That's one way to put it." Lisa eyed Riley. After a long pause, she continued, "She's the one who convinced me to leave Colorado."

Riley felt all of the pieces of the puzzle click into place. "So, she doesn't like you to have anyone else over because she's still jealous of you being with others?"

"The whole thing is complicated." Lisa's gaze was fixed on the distant tree line where they'd spent the past three days.

"Are you guys really finished?" Riley felt sick to her stomach. How could she have let herself get this close to moving in with Lisa and not see that she was still involved with someone else? Lisa didn't answer, so Riley continued, "'Complicated' as in maybe we are still together, maybe not?"

"It's not like that."

"'And don't worry, Riley, she's no lay compared to you.' That's what you were going to say, right?" Riley shook her head. "Shit. You know what I thought? I thought that maybe you were embarrassed. I thought maybe you weren't out to your roommate and…"

"She's nothing compared to you," Lisa said, interrupting her. "She is still my friend but we don't sleep together." Lisa reached for Riley's hand. "Maybe I should have told you she was my ex. I can see how you'd think it was weird that we always go to your place. But it's just easier. I don't want to deal with having you and Jen together in the same room. We're moving to Colorado in a few weeks and it won't be an issue then."

"Yeah," Riley said. "There will be all sorts of new issues."

"You don't want to live together, do you?"

"I'm not sure. I'm used to trusting people."

Lisa shook her head. "I didn't lie about anything, Riley. And don't tell me that wasn't what you just implied."

"Well, you certainly omitted a few details."

Lisa stood up, pushing her pack over as she did. She walked to the car, opened the door and sat down in the driver's seat. She looked back at Riley and shook her head. "Maybe you are right. Why the hell should we move in together? We can both move to Denver and live in separate places. That way you won't have to worry about trusting me."

Riley realized she was cornered. She had wanted to suggest living in different places as soon as she decided on taking the job, but Lisa had been so excited about the prospect of sharing a place that she'd given up the idea. Now that Lisa was offering it, could she accept it without Lisa being pissed?

"I can understand that you didn't want to talk about your ex. And I didn't mean to imply that I don't trust you. But we've only been seeing each other for a month. How well can we know each other?"

"I guess I was a complete idiot then, thinking I knew you so well, huh?"

Lisa got out of the car and slammed the door. She paced down the road and back up again, finally stopping in front of Riley.

"I don't care if I make Jen jealous by having a million girls over. It isn't about that at all. Jen has depression issues. She's on meds for it, but no combination of pills ever really seems to fix her. She's been really down since I told her that I was moving back home. She even threatened to take a full bottle of Vicodin along with whatever else they give her to sleep."

"And if she thought the move was because of a new girlfriend, it would make everything that much worse," Riley added.

"If you knew her, you wouldn't blame me," Lisa defended.

After a moment, Riley said, "I don't blame you."

"We're moving to Denver, Riley. We need to be able to talk to each other about stuff like this."

Riley nodded.

A cloud of dust billowed on the road below them and a moment later they could hear a car's rumbling engine. Lisa looked at Riley and arched her eyebrow. "I knew someone would come."

"Is that an 'I told you so'?"

As the car neared, the driver immediately slowed down and waved.

Lisa glanced over at Riley. "I still want to finish this conversation. Later."

Despite being very eager to help, the man and woman in their late fifties had a wrench that fit only American-sized lug nuts. They left, promising to call roadside assistance for them as soon as they had a cell phone signal.

"I don't think we should wait," Lisa said, as soon as the Ford rumbled away. "What if they call for assistance, but no one can get up here for another four hours? We'd have no way of knowing. Or what if they forget to call?"

Riley was already packing their things back into the car. She grabbed the canteen, now only half full, and her wallet. "I want to stretch my legs anyway."

The ten miles back to town were almost entirely downhill. It was near four when they reached a paved road and a truck immediately came into view. "It's a Toyota," Lisa said, waving at the driver. "I don't think I've ever been so happy to see another beat-up Toyota."

The truck was in nearly as bad a shape as Lisa's car, but the driver not only had a set of wrenches but time on his hands. He drove them back up the dirt road, helped switch the tire and then gave them directions to the nearest tire shop. They were driving back down the dirt road, following the truck close enough to catch all of his dust, within the hour.

Unfortunately, the tire shop was closed, and the town was small enough to only have one such store. Lisa and Riley had already agreed that her spare tire was in no shape to drive back to Sacramento, not at highway speeds anyway. They got a room at the one motel in town and Riley called Sheryl to explain their dilemma. If all went well, the earliest she could make it to the hospital was noon.

Lisa had showered and collapsed on the bed. When she got off the phone with Sheryl, Riley stripped and showered as well. She came out of the shower and Lisa looked over at her.

"You look good in a towel."

Riley had the towel wrapped around her waist. She had no clean clothes to change into and didn't really want to get dressed anyway. She sat down on the bed and reached for Lisa's hand. "Want to finish that conversation?"

"I'm not sure. I'm exhausted." Lisa closed her eyes. "And I think I'm still mad."

Riley leaned over and kissed her. Lisa made no attempt to reciprocate. "Well, I'm not mad anymore. Thank you for telling me what was going on with you and your roommate. I'm sorry I didn't ask sooner."

PART THREE

Wagers

Riley found the gate for her flight from Denver to Seattle sandwiched between a flight to Cleveland and one to Sacramento. She was a half hour early and there was a good chance that the snowstorm was going to delay the flight. With the weatherman's prediction for heavy snowfall through Christmas Eve, she figured she'd be lucky if she got home before her family finished off Mom's Christmas cookies and Dad's homemade beer. Riley pulled out the paperback she'd brought and sat down with a window view of the swirling snow. A de-icing machine worked on one of the planes, and the figures moving about on the ground below looked entirely miserable.

Two hours passed and Riley got up to stretch. The gate attendant had already announced that the Seattle flight would be delayed a minimum of three hours. The Cleveland flight had been canceled. The folks waiting for the Sacramento flight milled about the gate, sending anxious or angry glances at their gate attendant. Riley decided he must be new at the job. Every twenty minutes or so he announced that the Sacramento flight would be loading within the hour, and then ten to fifteen minutes later, he'd come back on the loudspeaker to explain that there was another delay.

Riley had missed breakfast trying to get to the airport in time, worried about traffic with the snow, and her stomach rumbled now. A woman sitting next to her had a bagel and coffee. Her hands cupped the coffee as if she were as cold as the tarmac workers outside. Riley eyed the bagel and finally decided she wanted food more than she wanted to read any more of her mystery novel.

When the gate attendant for her flight announced yet another new flight time, now a full four hours late, Riley shouldered her backpack. She walked the length of the terminal until she spotted a café with bagels and empty seats. The coffee was better than expected. She opened her book to the dog-eared page and settled back into the scene. Every few minutes she took a bite of her cinnamon bagel, which was slightly stale and more chewy than she'd hoped, and then washed it down with the coffee.

"Is this seat taken?"

Riley glanced up from the book, and her breath caught in her throat. "No," she managed, motioning to the empty spot next to her. "I guess it makes sense that I would run into you in an airport. But…"

"But? You were hoping I was some stranger who just happened to be politely asking for the last open seat in the place." Ana set her coffee and scone on the table, but she hesitated to sit down. "Do you want me to leave you alone?"

Riley scanned the café. The place had filled, and there were no empty tables. "No. Please sit down. I'm sorry."

"Don't be. I'm the one who owes an apology." Ana sat down and stared at Riley. "Where are you going?"

"Maybe nowhere if this snow keeps up." Riley looked out the window. "Home for the holidays. What about you?"

"Same. Lodi, here I come." Ana sipped her coffee.

"This is weird," Riley said. "I mean, it makes sense that you're here, but it is still weird."

"I think you mean awkward." Ana smiled. "You didn't return any of my calls."

"Or the texts or the emails. Go ahead, you can say it. 'What the fuck, Riley?'" Riley paused. She had never thought she'd have to face a conversation with Ana after what had happened. "Do you know why? The only thing I could think to say, was, 'What the fuck, Ana?' and I didn't want to leave that on your voice mail or your email or your damn text. Why? Because in the back of my head, I heard my mom's voice telling me not to swear on the phone. Seriously. My mom. And I couldn't think of anything to say that didn't start or end with a swear word."

Ana took a deep breath. She glanced at the table next to theirs. Three men in business suits were arguing about tech stock prices. Riley had been trying to tune out their conversation for the past thirty minutes.

"Yeah, what the fuck?" Ana repeated. "'What the fuck, Riley?'" She shook her head slowly. "I'm sorry, Riley. That's all I wanted to say. I'm sorry."

"Okay." Riley sighed. The apology didn't feel like anything now. It was too late, she wanted to say. If Ana had come out of the winery, right after the kiss, and grabbed Riley then, her words would have meant a lot more.

"I wanted to apologize and even more I wanted to explain what had happened. I know I left too many messages on your answering machine, and I texted you after those voice mails, knowing you would probably think I was a crazy stalker. But I didn't really care. I was mad that you wouldn't let me explain."

"It was a fling, Ana. You don't really need to explain anything. Clearly you were already in a relationship with someone else, and I don't really care why you wanted to have a fling with me. But it was just a fling." Riley looked at her, but Ana didn't respond. She set the book down, not bothering to dog-ear the page, and took her empty coffee cup over to the trash can. She stared at the trash can and at the people pacing in the terminal. Nobody's flight was going to leave anytime soon. She walked back to the table and stood by the chair, not wanting to sit down and yet wanting to sit down so badly she felt ill with the thought of leaving. Maybe it could have been more than a fling. Maybe she couldn't walk away now.

"It's December 23rd."

"And?" Ana rubbed her eyes.

"I'm going to go reschedule my flight to tomorrow. My mom wants me home for Christmas, but if I get out of here today or tomorrow, I'll still make it in time to sing the cheesy Christmas carols she loves."

"Okay. Well…"

"Change your flight too. Fly out tomorrow."

"Why?"

"Because you're sorry and so am I." Riley struggled to think of any reason that Ana should stay. She didn't have a logical one. "And we need to talk. Change your flight and spend the next twenty-four hours with me."

Ana stared at Riley. Her expression was enough for Riley to guess that the answer was no. Finally, she shook her head confirming it.

"Yeah, I guess you're right. What difference would it make?" Riley slipped her paperback into her backpack. "I missed you so damn much. Way too much for a fling."

"I wish you'd called."

"Why? I wouldn't have listened to an apology. I was too mad. That first night was hard. But then I realized how stupid I'd been even thinking…" Riley shook her head. "And then I was just jealous of the guy you'd kissed. For about a month after, every time I tried to go to sleep, I would wonder where you were, what you were doing and I'd hope you were falling asleep alone. Finally, I got you out of my brain, and so of course, that's when you show up again." Riley forced a smile. "I guess all I can say now is I'm sorry you aren't going my way."

Riley went to the gate. She waited in line to speak with the attendant, who was more than happy to change her flight to the following day. He admitted that he was about to announce that the flight was being canceled. She turned to leave and nearly collided with Ana.

"I just changed my flight," Ana said.

"You did?"

"I'm not sure if I made the right decision," Ana said.

"We could be making a mistake," Riley agreed. She pointed to the ground transportation sign. They took the shuttle to long-term parking, found Riley's car and got in quickly. The engine warmed up and Riley turned the heat on high. Ana hadn't said a word since they'd left the gate. A thousand questions sprang up in Riley's mind, but she held them back and focused on driving. Gusts of wind turned the snow sideways, and the roads had changed from wide blacktops to narrow slushy strips between sheets of ice.

When they finally made it back to her condo, Riley found a parking place right out front. She led the way inside, turning the thermostat up as soon as she'd taken off her coat. "It'll warm up in a minute."

Ana kept her coat on but took off her shoes. She set her luggage in the front hallway and followed Riley into the living room. Riley switched on the gas fireplace, and the room felt warmer almost immediately. Ana sat down on the sofa cross-legged.

"You live alone?"

Riley nodded.

"Your ex moved out after the Alaska trip?"

"Sort of. When we first moved out from California, I wanted my own place, at least at first. She was supposed to be living with her mom, but all of her stuff ended up in my spare room because she spent every night here. I asked her to leave when we broke up, but most of her stuff hasn't moved."

Riley stood next to the fireplace, watching the flames wave between the fake logs. "I decided I didn't really care about her stuff being here anyway. It was easier to ignore a few boxes and a pile of clothes than call her up and get in another argument about it. This place is closer to her work, so she still comes by sometimes."

"When I broke up with Tom, I threatened to take all of his stuff to the Goodwill if he didn't get it out himself. It's still there. His argument is that I'm never home anyway, which is mostly true. But whenever I do come home, I can't stand to look at all of his crap all over the place."

Riley stiffened at this. She thought of the man she'd last seen Ana with and tried to push away the image of their embrace. "Do you want tea? I don't really like the taste, but I like to hold a warm mug."

"I'd like that."

Riley went to the kitchen and set the kettle on the stove. She got out two mugs and dropped in the tea bags. The living room and the kitchen were in one open space divided by a counter bar. Ana was watching her.

"It's strange to see you here," Riley said. "For some time after that trip, I thought it would be easier if I'd just imagined you and the entire thing. Now it's hard to deny that you exist."

"You left so fast."

Riley opened her mouth to ask the question that had been on the tip of her tongue for months, but she stopped herself short. Instead, she said, "Suddenly, I had no reason to stay."

Ana pulled the blue throw blanket off the back of the sofa and wrapped it over her shoulders. She stared at the fire. The kettle whistled, and Riley poured the water into the mugs. The tea bags popped to the surface. Riley carried the mugs and a little jar of sugar over to the sofa. She set a mug in front of Ana, along with the sugar, and sat down on the other end of the sofa. The steaming mug warmed her more than the fire.

Ana picked up her mug and held it inches from her chin. She breathed in the steam and closed her eyes. "When are you going to ask?"

"I don't really want to ask. I've asked all of the questions too many times in my head. And I've heard all of the answers. For a while, my brain was busy answering for you. I didn't like any of your answers, by the way."

Ana snorted. "Why are you such a pain in the ass?"

Riley sipped the bitter tea. She never added sugar or cream. She stared at Ana's profile. She was, in fact, beautiful, exactly as Riley had remembered. Her wavy brown hair dropped to just below her shoulders and a wisp of it fell forward whenever Ana dipped her chin to sip the tea. "What happened next?"

"No, that isn't the right question. What you need to ask is, what happened before the kiss? Not in the moment before the kiss, but in the years that led up to it. A kiss is nothing without all of the moments that lead up to it."

"Poetic, but I don't really want to know about all of those moments," Riley replied.

"I know you don't. You just want to sit there and feel like you made the right decision by leaving."

"Ouch."

Ana arched her eyebrow. "I could hit much harder than that. I might still."

"Why did you decide to come home with me?"

"Why'd you ask me to come?" Ana countered.

"Because I fell for you in one weekend. One weekend. It should have been a rebound." Riley set the mug down on the coffee table. She rubbed her forehead. "I'd been with Lisa for two years and never felt what I felt with you. In some ways, being with Blair, the girl I was with before Lisa, came close. And I still love both of them, in different ways. They drive me crazy, but you know, I don't want them out of my life entirely. But that weekend with you was different."

"What was it about that weekend?"

"I thought I had met someone who, if our living situations had been different, I could be with for longer than a year or two. I knew even then that it was a stretch, but you made me think it was possible. I don't know why." She stopped and looked at Ana. "I guess I was your distraction for the weekend. But why did you play it up so much? Why not just be honest and tell me you wanted to fuck around on your boyfriend?"

Ana shook her head. She was silent for several minutes, sipping her tea intermittently and not looking at Riley. Finally she said, "You wanted to know what happened next? I went looking for you. Where did you go? You didn't go back to Sharon's house. You weren't in the cottage."

"I went to a café. Remember the guy who made me cookies?"

"I remember the cookies."

"He was standing out on the street when I crossed the road. I nearly walked right into a car. I was so pissed I wasn't really paying attention to anything. He pointed to me like I was in trouble for something. Then he pointed to the café. I guess I must have looked like I needed an intervention. I followed him inside and soon had spilled the whole story. We weren't alone. There were four or five other random people who were there waiting for a guitar player who never showed up, and so they listened to my story and gave their own bits of advice. They got my story instead of the song they were hoping for. The really strange thing was, I had a good evening. I laughed about it. I laughed about how you'd played me, and all these strangers laughed along with me. I left the café feeling as if I didn't give a damn whom you slept with, but I didn't want to see you ever again. That was how the story ended."

"But did you start at the beginning?"

Riley was puzzled by her question. "As in, when we met?"

Ana shook her head. "You know that wasn't the beginning. When we met in Sharon's kitchen, you already had baggage. And isn't there always more to a story than girl meets girl?" She set her mug on the table next to Riley's and took off the blue blanket. She shifted her place so she was closer to Riley and held out a hand.

Riley clasped her hand. She felt a tremor race from her belly to her chest. Ana's hand was soft and warm. They stared at each other. "I'm still not sure why you are here."

"I wanted a chance to tell you my end of the story. For weeks, I was angry. I didn't waste any time thinking about how it would be nice to hold you again. I just wanted you to call so I could yell at the top of my lungs. I was too damn mad to even think that I might have fallen for you." She shook her head. "But I did fall for you. Otherwise, I wouldn't have cared that you left before I could explain."

"You can yell now."

Ana smiled. "No, I just feel sad now."

"Why?"

"I think you are right. I don't see how it could work for us without one of us taking a very big risk or the relationship fizzling out in some sad, long-distance way. I don't really want that. Maybe it needs to be our one fabulous fling."

Riley reached out and wrapped her arms around Ana. Ana moved closer to her, resting her head on Riley's shoulder. It felt so good to be holding her that Riley didn't care anymore about what had happened before. She wanted to say, "Let's pretend this is the beginning," but even as she said the words in her head, she knew it couldn't be true for them. Ana was right. They didn't meet in the beginning. They both had history.

"I went back to Catori in early November for work and stayed with Sharon. She said you were doing okay. She even gave me your address here so I could stop by on the way to the airport, but I never did." Ana exhaled. "Tom's my boss. We'd been together going on five years. In fact, we were engaged. But we never set a date."

"So you figured you didn't really need to mention him then? Since there was no set date?"

Ana pulled out of the embrace and squared her jaw at Riley. "I'm nowhere near done unless you want me to be."

Riley felt the distance between them double with her words. "I'm sorry."

"You." Ana pointed her finger at Riley. "Have no idea how sorry I was." The nails were manicured and a ridiculous dark red, but her hands were beautiful all the same. "Just listen, okay? Give me the benefit of doubt for the next five minutes. Tom wanted to help. He flew in, thinking he'd surprise me. He surprised me all right. Joe and his wife were glad he came. They were old friends. He was the one who finally convinced Joe not to throw in the towel after the flood."

"I don't want him to be the good guy in this story."

"There is no good guy. Just a series of shitty things that all happened to ruin something I had convinced myself might be amazing. I know better now." Ana brushed her hand across Riley's cheek. "We had been on the rocks off and on for several months leading up to that trip. We both knew we were close to done. Tom and I had talked about it right before I flew out to Colorado, in fact, but we had agreed to wait until after that trip to finish the conversation. Tom thought he'd try and sweep me off my feet once and for all. Instead, I pulled the carpet out from under him."

Ana reached for her tea. She took a sip and kept her hands wrapped around the mug as she continued. "We broke up that night. Remember that restaurant up on the hill that we went to? It's one of Tom's favorites. He insisted we go there, even though I was too pissed to even talk to him. We got the same terrible waiter. I have no idea what he thought of me. When we first walked in, he said, 'Back again? You stay busy.' Tom heard and asked what the waiter meant as soon as we got our menus. So I told him. But I started at the beginning."

"Which was?"

"My first girlfriend. She started the story."

"What was her name?" Riley asked, feeling on steady ground now that she knew Ana had in fact broken up with the man she'd been so jealous of for months.

"Marcelle. We were high school sweethearts. I mean, we never told anyone, you know. I thought we were going to grow old together. She had other plans. She has five kids now and a husband named Bruno. Whenever I go back to Lodi, I try to stop in and bring presents for her kiddos. They call me auntie. I think that secret will go with Marcelle to her grave. She calls me once in a while to complain about Bruno, and she always asks if I've found a woman."

"Was she the only one?"

"The only girl?" Ana nodded, answering before Riley could respond. "Until you. But the story isn't just about Marcelle and you, with Tom in between. There are five others that deserve mention."

"Do they really all deserve mention?"

"Yes." Ana set the mug down. "After Marcelle, there was Craig." She held up her index finger. "Craig was my college crush who ended up being a total asshole, but it took me two years to figure that out. I met Randy when I had a tire changed at Sears." She held up a second finger. "He still works at Sears in the tire department. You should see his forearms."

"No thanks."

Ana grinned. She was clearly enjoying this. "Seth was a friend with benefits that I met in my MBA program." Three fingers. "I thought everyone needed to have one of those, but I realized one night in a bar that Seth was holding me back. That was the night I met Terrell." Four fingers, raised higher. "He played basketball and the stock market. And women, as it turned out. Terrell knew how to spend money, but he somehow made more than he wasted. He was handsome. Too handsome, in that catch-your-breath sort of way."

Ana reached up to her neck and touched a pendant that hung from a gold chain there. Diamonds encircled a bright ruby teardrop. "From Terrell, with love. But he loved a few too many women at the same time. I couldn't deal. So I moved to Napa chasing the dream of my own fortunes and met Ernie. His real name is Ernesto, but he hates to be called that. Ernie got me into places that I needed to be and helped me make the connections." She held up all five fingers.

"What happened with Ernie? You know, you're missing a diamond."

"I know. One fell out right after I got it. I retraced my steps but I never found it. Terrell said he wanted to replace it. But like most things with him, he never really planned on following through and I knew it. Anyway, I think it's pretty even missing a diamond, and no one notices unless they are close enough to kiss me." Ana sighed. "Tom was the reason I'm not with Ernie."

"You fell in love with Tom and broke Ernie's heart, didn't you?"

"And he's the one I thought about after you left. After I'd sent Tom back to his hotel room alone, left you three voice mails and a very long, probably pathetic text, which I hope you deleted before reading, I called Ernie. Funny, huh? It'd been five years since I had even thought about how things had gone between us, but I called him that night. He still lives in Napa.

He's the head chef at a four-star restaurant. When I called, he asked if it was because I wanted to get a table reservation. They book four or five months in advance unless you know someone. He's helped me before when I had to woo clients. I told him I just wanted to hear his voice and that I wanted to say I was sorry. Sorry for everything. And that I wanted to see him sometime to say hi. He said his wife wouldn't want him to be having that sort of conversation and he hung up. I felt terrible. I knew I'd broken his heart and at the time that it happened, he'd been no big deal to me."

"I didn't read your text or listen to the voice mails. I didn't want to hear any excuse. Why didn't you think about the other girl? Marcelle? Why Ernie instead?"

"Yeah, I don't know. I think I needed to say sorry to someone." She glanced at the fire with a faraway look in her eyes. "But that's what I mean. They're all part of the story but not the whole story, of course. All of the things that had happened between Tom and me...you know, I had just gotten off the phone with him when I walked into Sharon's kitchen that morning we met. He had really pissed me off, but I was determined to let it go. You helped."

"You didn't look like you hated his kiss."

"And, finally, this is how you are going to ask about that kiss. Tried to slip it in, huh? A bit underhanded, maybe."

Riley shrugged. "I felt like I'd been slapped across the face. I'm not trying to slip anything past you."

Ana stared at her for a long moment. "I'm sorry. I bet you hated me at that moment. He took me by surprise."

"You kissed him back."

Ana sighed. "Yeah, I kissed him back. I'd planned on talking to him about everything but...Not right then. Not in the winery. Not in front of Joe. And then I saw you standing there. I saw the look on your face, I knew what you'd seen, and I knew you weren't going to hear any explanation. I'm sorry."

"Me too."

Ana caressed Riley's arm and then rested her hand on Riley's neck. "But we don't have a chance, do we? And it really has nothing to do with what happened."

"I don't really believe in chance or luck. I think I saw you kiss him for a reason, and I think we were both at the airport today for a reason as well. But this might be how our fling was supposed to end."

Ana leaned close, and Riley moved into the kiss automatically. Ana's lips were warm and full, pressing exactly the right amount to make Riley need more. They kept kissing until Ana shifted on the sofa and pulled Riley down on top of her. The room had warmed now and their clothes came off easily. Riley looked down at Ana once they were both naked. Ana's tan skin was a beautiful contrast to the dark brown sofa. Ana shivered and Riley pulled the blue blanket over them. She lay back down slowly, feeling every point of contact that their naked skin made. She wasn't ready to make love to Ana, but she had no desire to stop caressing all of her parts, the smooth parts, the parts with short trimmed hair and the well-muscled parts. She was familiarizing herself with Ana's body all over again. It could take the rest of the day for all she cared.

Ana was curled up against Riley's backside with one arm draped over her. Riley remembered suggesting that they go upstairs to the bedroom but didn't recall exactly how they got there. She hoped Ana had fallen asleep as quickly as she had. Riley shifted Ana's arm and climbed out of bed. She squinted at the clock. Five a.m. She went to pee. When she got back, Ana was propped up on her elbow and she'd turned on the nightstand light. Ana pulled the covers down and Riley slipped back into the warmth. Riley settled onto her pillow and closed her eyes.

"Don't try and go back to sleep," Ana said. "You can keep your eyes closed, but we need to talk."

"When's your flight?"

"Three o'clock," Ana answered. "You said you wanted twenty-four hours."

"Then we'll have plenty of time to talk in two hours. Let's just sleep until seven."

"No sleeping," Ana repeated, tickling Riley's ear and neck until Riley was sitting upright in bed trying to keep her hands away.

Riley was completely awake now. Ana grinned back at her. She was still naked. Riley had to consciously stop her hand from reaching out to touch Ana's nipples. "I don't think I've ever spent this much time naked with someone I wanted to have sex with and not done anything more than kiss."

"You were pretty clear that you didn't want to go there last night," Ana said. She reached for Riley's hand and guided it to her breast.

"My body and my mind disagreed."

"And this morning?"

Riley shook her head. She could feel Ana's nipples responding to her touch. "This isn't fair."

Ana found Riley's other hand and moved it to her other breast. "Some things aren't fair."

Riley encircled the nipples with her fingertips and then moved to straddle Ana. Ana kissed her and moaned softly when Riley pulled away. Riley shifted down to brush her tongue over Ana's nipples, then took her time, moving up and down the length of Ana's body with soft kisses, her lips barely brushing over the places she knew Ana wanted to be touched. Ana let her play this game for some time before reaching down to slip her hand between her legs. Riley felt a surge between her own legs as she watched Ana. She pulled Ana's hand away and sat upright, still straddling her, then moved Ana's fingers to her own swollen clit.

"You're wet," Ana murmured.

Riley nodded. She let Ana play until she could feel the start of an orgasm, then shifted away from Ana's hand. Riley reached down to find Ana's warm center, moving her fingers inside, and Ana pressed her hips upward at Riley's touch. Riley matched Ana's rocking, watching her all the while. Her eyes were closed and her head was pressed back against the pillows, chin tilted up. Riley could hardly believe Ana was in her bed, could hardly believe they were again pushing each other to the edge, and even as she doubted that she should have brought Ana here, she wanted her all the more. Ana pressed down on Riley's hand as she climaxed, then reached for Riley and pressed her finger against Riley's clit. Riley didn't try to quiet the sounds that came with the rush.

A moment later, she rolled off Ana and lay on her back with her eyes closed, thinking that she might easily slip back asleep if Ana would let her. *What happens after this doesn't matter*, she thought. She had needed the release of an orgasm and guessed Ana did as well. Maybe that was all they would get.

Ana's hand was under her nose. "Smell that?"

"Pussy?"

"I love it."

"You're weird," Riley said half-heartedly.

"No, I'm weird for falling for someone I barely knew in one weekend. And I'm weird for wanting to find a way to have you in my life after today."

Riley was silent.

"You're going to leave me hanging with that one, aren't you?"

Ana climbed on top of Riley and crossed her arms. Her chin rested on her fists and she stared at Riley. "Do you remember the last day we were together? That Sunday morning?"

Riley nodded. "I remember waking up late. I didn't pick up Sharon's pastries like I was supposed to. Some girl had me distracted."

"That morning I whispered, 'I love making love to you,' in your ear. You were sleeping, but I saw you smile. I have a realtor friend in Napa. I called her that afternoon and asked her how much she thought I could get if I rented out my condo. I told her I was thinking of renting a place in Denver for a while. She said she had a buyer who was interested in my neighborhood and she thought I could get a pretty good price if I wanted to sell. That gave me cold feet, so I told her I'd think about it and hung up. I knew I wasn't really ready to sell my place. I probably wasn't ready to rent a place in Denver, either, but I did consider it. Doesn't really matter what city all my stuff stays in anyway. I'm always traveling through to somewhere else."

"Denver? You really thought about moving? You know you're crazy, right?"

"In retrospect, yes, it was a crazy idea."

Riley shook her head. "You said I was crazy moving states for a girl I knew for two months. You were thinking about it after one weekend?"

"Well, I'd been thinking about moving closer to an airport for some time. As it is, I commute from Napa to the San Francisco airport or to Sacramento once or twice a week, and nearly all of my flights are eastbound. I thought I could route everything through Denver or move there and save the commute. Besides, I thought I was ready for a change."

"And now?"

"I don't know. I didn't really know then either. I was just thinking about possibilities." She touched her fingertip to Riley's lips. "How long are you in Seattle?"

"'Til New Year's Day. But I don't go back to work until after the weekend."

Ana started to speak and then stopped. She rolled off Riley after a moment and sighed. Riley waited for her to say something, but the only sound was the heater. It ticked, then knocked, then rumbled when the heat switched back on.

Riley found Ana's hand and clasped it in hers. "I wonder what you'll say about this part of the story when you meet your next lover. What will be my one-line description?"

"You have to spend a little more time in my life before you get included in that list."

"Will you spend New Year's with me?" Riley asked. "I can change my flight, leave earlier. My parents will understand. I'll meet you anywhere."

"Your parents were going to be your New Year's date?"

"Well, me and a hundred other people or so. Every year they throw a party on New Year's and invite everyone they know. Everyone. They never really know who will show up, but it's usually a big crowd. I won't be missed much."

"Ever been to Napa?"

"I drove through once on a spare tire. Don't ask. Didn't stop, though." Riley paused, remembering the backpacking trip she'd taken with Lisa to the waterfall. Their tire fiasco had ended at a tire store that happened to be out of Lisa's particular tire and they'd ended up driving the entire way home on the spare, taking care not to go any faster than forty-five miles an hour. They'd talked about going back to Napa sometime when they had time to stop, though. "I'd love to go again and actually get out of the car."

Ana smiled. "Good. If you want to go back to sleep, now I'll let you. But I'm starving, and I am going downstairs to see if I can find anything in your kitchen."

"I can make you something."

"No, all I want is toast. I saw the bread out on the counter last night." Ana climbed out of bed. She pulled her shirt and pants on, without underwear, and turned off the nightstand light.

Riley pulled the blankets up to her chin and closed her eyes.

They ate brunch at the café five blocks from Riley's townhouse and then went for a walk around the park. The grass, long since turned yellow from frost, was now blanketed in several inches of snow. The trees were bare except for their dusting of snow crystals, and when the sun finally poked through the clouds, the branches seemed to glow.

The icy patches on the sidewalks made the going slow, and they returned to Riley's house just before noon. Ana made tea and opened the *Denver Post* she'd bought. Riley went upstairs to shower and change. She turned on her computer to print out boarding passes, double-checked her flight time and Ana's as well, then started down the stairs. She paused when she heard Ana talking with someone. She figured she was on the phone until she heard Lisa's voice.

"Where's Riley?" Lisa asked, her voice full of suspicion.

"She's upstairs. I'm Ana."

"How do you know Riley?"

Riley waited on the staircase. She was partly curious to hear how the conversation would play out and partly sick that Ana and Lisa were talking together at all.

"It's a long story. Are you Lisa?"

Riley couldn't hear a reply. Finally, she made her way down the stairs. She saw a look of relief on Ana's face as she entered the kitchen. Lisa's expression was hard to read. She had on her mint-green scrubs and the red wool cap Riley had given her last Christmas. Her jacket was hung over one arm; she had the house key in one hand and her red mittens in the other.

"Lunch break?" Riley asked.

"Yeah," Lisa said. "I saw your car out front and figured you'd missed the flight. I heard most of them were grounded."

Lisa's casual words didn't mask her nervous tenor. Ana had left the newspaper spread out on the kitchen table. She held her empty teacup as if she had been interrupted en route to refill it. She looked over at Riley and smiled calmly. With the two women suddenly in the same space, their differences were starkly apparent to Riley. Ana could have passed for a model. Lisa was just…Lisa, a little rough on the edges from a consistent lack of sleep and no effort to make herself look any better than she had to, but still pretty just as she was. Riley realized in that moment how comfortable she felt with Lisa. Maybe it was only time and shared space that made her feel that way. Or maybe Ana was in a different class than Riley altogether and she would never be able to really relax with her.

Turning to Lisa, Ana said, "The weather was terrible. Riley offered to let me spend the night and we changed our flights."

Lisa's gaze darted from Ana to Riley and then down to her mittens. "You know, I think I'm going to get lunch at Sesame instead. I feel like soup anyway."

"The Sesame Café? We just ate there. I had their corn chowder. It was delicious. The tomato soup sounded good too." Ana acted as if there was nothing awkward at all about the two of them discussing lunch options.

Lisa turned toward Riley. Her brown curls, untamed by the hat, poked out in every direction. "You're still going to Seattle, right?"

Riley nodded.

"I'll see you then in a few weeks, I guess." Lisa turned to leave. The sound of the front door opening and closing behind her came only a moment later. She hadn't stopped to put on her coat or mittens.

Riley leaned against the wall. She had the impulse to go after Lisa and apologize, but she looked at Ana instead. "Sorry about that. It was probably more than a little awkward."

"No, it's fine. Whatever. You told me she stops in occasionally."

"Yeah, but…"

"Lisa's pretty."

Riley recognized Ana's baited statement. "She is pretty," she said, watching Ana closely. "But you two are in a different class."

"Is it really over between you and her?" Ana went over to the table and folded up the newspaper. Without looking up at Riley, she said, "And for the record, you have a terrible poker face. I hope you didn't want her to know that we were sleeping together. She had that figured out the moment you came into the kitchen."

"At least you won't have to guess what I'm thinking. Or worry that I'm hiding something from you."

Ana shook her head. "This time it's about you, not me."

"We're friends, yes. But Lisa and I aren't lovers anymore. I haven't had sex with her since we broke up in September."

"There's more to a relationship than sex. Are you or aren't you having sex is only part of the equation."

"Being friends with an ex is always complicated. But it is possible to be just friends."

"I think you are more than a friend to her. Just now you didn't act like she was only a friend."

"Well, no, she isn't just my friend. Obviously we have history. Even after everything that's happened between us, when I see her blindsided like she was, I can't help but feel for her. To her knowledge, I haven't dated anyone since we broke up. And then she comes in and sees you here."

"If things work out between us, would you be able to tell her to stop coming over here?"

Ana still hadn't looked up at her. Riley considered the request. It wasn't unreasonable. She had wanted to ask Lisa to do much the same thing with Jen but hadn't for fear of sounding jealous or, worse, controlling. From Ana, it didn't sound like either of those things. Instead, she only seemed fearful of being hurt.

"If that needs to happen before we can go forward, I'll let her know right now," Riley said. She walked over to the table. Ana was staring out the window. The sky had clouded over, and it had begun snowing again. Snow crystals swirled like dust particles, disappearing before they landed. Riley reached for Ana's hand. Ana turned and kissed her. She felt the charge race through her body.

* * *

Riley called Blair on Christmas morning, as had been their tradition for years. Blair was in Sacramento with her family. The noise of a coffee grinder and Blair's parents' banter was enough to get her to take the phone call outside where it was quieter.

"My job sucks. I'm thinking about moving back here," Blair said. "Did you know that it is sixty degrees and sunny here? Even the weather is trying to convince me to move back to California."

"I thought winters were nice in Austin."

"Yeah, it's fine in the winter. But for six months out of the year it is too hot and humid to even step outside. Anyway, the weather isn't the reason. It's the job."

The practice in Austin was high volume and Riley knew she was making good money at it, but they'd talked several times before and it was clear that the place had her stretched too thin. "Your family would be happy if you moved home."

"You know, they still ask about you. My mom wanted to know if I was still keeping in touch with you. She's ready to have me married. She wants grandchildren, and you were the only one I dated long enough for her to think of when the subject came up."

"You're thinking of having kids? Like soon?"

Blair laughed. "You sound freaked out by the idea."

"I'm just surprised."

"Don't worry. I'll give you plenty of time to get used to it before I get pregnant. And you know, I don't exactly have anyone lined up to help me with the whole process yet."

"No cute girls in Austin?"

"I've been dating. But, you know, nothing serious. I think I need to get out of Texas," Blair replied.

"I saw Austin listed on some 'top gay cities' thing a while back. Maybe you just need to find a different job."

"Maybe. What about you? How are things with your on-again, off-again girlfriend?"

"We've been off since September."

"Your decision?"

"Well, that depends on how much it is anyone's decision to break up with a person when she's been cheating on you. You know that nurse she was roommates with in Sacramento? She moved to Denver. I wasn't sure if anything was going on, but I suspected. When I found out for sure, I told her we were done. But does that make it my decision?"

"Yeah, I don't know. Wait, how did the same nurse she was sleeping with in Sacramento end up in Denver? The one who you were pretending was only her friend even after you realized they had a one-bedroom apartment?"

"Thanks, Blair. You have a knack for making me feel even worse then I already do. Yes, that one. Jen moved out to Denver for a job. They basically picked things up where they'd left off. I figured it out and called her out on the whole thing. Then it happened again. Took me a few times to learn the lesson, I guess."

"You know, it isn't all bad living alone. I go out dancing with friends from work, run with a club on Tuesdays and spend Thursday nights singing karaoke like a badass. Sometimes I think I'd be happier if there was someone waiting up for me. But then she would probably give me a hard time about kissing girls at the karaoke bar. I don't know. Maybe relationships are overrated."

"They probably are." Riley wasn't ready to mention Ana. She and Blair had made a pact that they would tell each other about new relationships, but she didn't consider Ana to be a "relationship" yet. She wasn't ready to consider it as that, anyway. "It's good to hear your voice. Maybe we should try and talk more than once a year. Merry Christmas, Blair."

"You too, Riley. Hey, Riley." Blair paused. "I quit smoking. Again. I knew how much it pissed you off that I'd started back up at it, so I wanted to let you know. It's been a year today."

"Good for you, Blair. That's awesome." Riley hung up after Blair's line clicked. She felt guilty not telling her about Ana, but she knew it was too soon. Blair would latch onto the idea of her having a new girlfriend and would make a big deal of it, and Ana wasn't a girlfriend, not yet.

Riley had missed Ana's call earlier, but she wasn't ready to call her back yet. She headed downstairs and her phone rang. It was Lisa. She answered, sitting down in the middle of her parents' staircase. "Hey, there. Merry Christmas."

Lisa echoed the same words. "How's Seattle? How's the fam?"

"Good. My brother already came and went. He was sober, which is good, but I don't know how long it will last. My mom's in the kitchen making pies. My dad's cracking walnuts. What about you?"

"Mom bought a pie. We're ordering Chinese food. Jen's working tonight, so she's sleeping now, of course."

"Party on," Riley joked.

"Exactly." The line was silent for a long moment before Lisa added, "Okay, so who the hell was that woman?"

"You know, I am allowed to see other people. We finished things how many months ago?" Riley added, "Though that doesn't really make a difference in your world, I know."

"Is she even queer?"

"She seems to know her way around."

"Jeez, Riley, you could have more tact. I don't want to hear how she is in bed."

"My point was, I don't give a damn what box she's checked. And you could keep your nose out of this," Riley countered.

"I'm just watching out for you. I know you are going to get your heart wrapped up in this."

"And then what? Are you worried that maybe she will cheat on me with her old roommate? Yeah, she's been into guys so that would suck, but in the end, I don't think it really matters who someone is with when they cheat. They're just not with you."

Lisa was silent.

"You know, you are right, in some ways. I barely know her. And, yeah, I could have let myself fall for her too fast. My heart was wrapped up in her the first time we kissed." Riley sighed. "Why are we even talking about this?"

"I just know it won't work out. She looks like she drops a small fortune every time she buys shoes. Or goes to get her hair cut. And you know she isn't painting her own nails. I bet you didn't notice the label on her purse."

"Lisa, I'm not going to notice anyone's purse."

"It's legit. No cheap knockoff looks that good. And she wears makeup. Not just lipstick and eyeliner, but the kind of thing that takes a half hour to do every morning."

"So? She looks good without makeup too."

"Look, Riley, just don't get in over your head, okay? She isn't going to stay around long. If she's into you at all, it's only because she decided dykes were trendy this week. Women like her end up married to rich old men who like to splurge. She might be into you for a while, but it isn't going to last."

"Words of advice from my cheating ex. Thank you."

"I really am only looking out for you. And you can go ahead and say it isn't any of my business. But I still love you and I'm going to stick my nose in when I need to so you don't get hurt."

"I'm not sure why we are even having this conversation. *You* are going to watch out for me so I don't get hurt? Look, Lisa, I have to go."

"Are you ever going to let what happened go? I want to be friends with you at some point."

"My dad's asking me if I want some of his home-brewed beer. I don't think this day is going to end with anyone sober."

"All right, fine. Just think about what I said, okay? I know you're going into this blinded by the fact that she's all done up and gorgeous."

"For the record, she said you were pretty. And she was a bit jealous that you were still coming over to my place."

"She wants you to tell me to stay away, doesn't she?"

"Yeah."

Lisa sighed. "Okay, whatever. Have a merry Christmas, Riley. I'll be here when this woman breaks your heart. Call me anytime."

Riley sent Ana a text. She had decided not to call when the late afternoon passed into the evening and she ended up watching a movie with her folks. It was nearly eleven when she climbed into bed. Her parents had kept her room essentially the same as it had been when she'd left for college. Now, all these years later, it was disorienting to be lying in the same bed after so many other things had changed. Her cell phone rang and Riley first reached for the old cordless phone. Eventually, she found her cell and saw Ana's number flash on the screen.

She climbed back in bed and answered the call. "Hey."

"Is this a bad time?" Ana asked. "I only realized how late it was after I'd started calling you."

"I'm in bed, but I'm not asleep yet. Are you okay? You sound tense."

"I'm sitting in my car, trying to breathe."

"Uh-oh. What happened?"

"My little sister, Sabrina, got pregnant, and my mom has totally lost it. She's been screaming at her, calling her a whore and every other bad word she can think of, all because my sister doesn't want to marry the guy. So Sabrina, who of course is hormonal, has spent most of the day crying. My other sister, Isabel, is married and has four kids, so she's excited that my little sister is gonna have one. This is only making my mom more pissed. I'm trying to stay out of the whole thing. I came out here after Sabrina admitted the baby-daddy was sent to jail last month. That's when the shit really hit the fan. I'm wondering how much longer it will take before they notice I'm out in the car."

"You could help your little sister out and tell everyone that you like pussy."

Ana laughed. "You have no idea how much I want to say that, just to see their reaction. I think I could only do it if you were standing in the room with me, though."

Riley listened to Ana detail the day's events from her nieces' and nephews' presents to the obligatory Catholic mass, the big afternoon dinner and, finally, the evening's fight. Ana's world sounded so distant from the one in which she lived that Lisa's comments kept springing to mind. She almost asked Ana what type of purse she had and if things like designer labels mattered to her. What did they have in common, Riley wondered, and did commonality matter?

Ana's sister finally put an end to their call. Sabrina had come out to the car and Ana said, "Oh, Sabrina, sweetie, you know she'll be excited about the baby by tomorrow morning. Let her sober up." Then, "Riley, I'm sorry. I've gotta go. Can you call me when you have a chance tomorrow?"

The line went silent. Riley stared at the phone until the screen darkened. She set her cell phone on the nightstand alongside her old cordless one and closed her eyes. Lisa's face came to mind first. She concentrated on Ana and a moment later pictured her instead. Then a moment later, it was Blair she saw. Blair sitting on their old back porch in Sacramento with a beer in one hand and a cigarette in the other.

That cigarette was the last one she'd smoked while they were together. She'd lit it up after their first real fight. The fight was about organic produce. Riley had always bought the cheap conventional stuff and Blair wanted them to buy only organic. Riley's defense argument rested on one thing. "But you smoke, so why does it even matter?" So Blair had given it up and they'd bought organic after that. Riley still couldn't articulate what cigarettes had to do with the value of organic produce, but Blair had accepted it as the cost of compromise.

* * *

Riley waited outside the Sacramento airport wearing a long sleeve shirt and jeans. Her coat, gloves and hat were all packed away. The pilot had said that the expected high for the day was seventy, and it felt every bit that warm. She had forgotten to ask Ana what type of car she drove and so she had to watch every car that slowed down near her spot. Finally a black BMW pulled up to the curb and Ana hopped out of the car and waved. Riley gingerly placed her suitcase in the trunk when Ana popped it open and then sank into the leather seat. She glanced over at Ana, who was wearing gold hoop earrings and a matching necklace that flashed in the light streaming through the sunroof. She grinned. Lisa was probably right, after all. Ana was in an altogether different league than anyone she'd dated before, and if things like this mattered, it was unlikely they would last.

"Why are you smiling like that?"

"It's just good to see you," Riley said.

"You are a terrible liar. But I like that about you. If I can tell when you are lying, I'll have the upper hand if we ever play poker."

"You play poker?"

"And I'm good at it." She zipped between two cars going the speed limit, then stepped on the gas and sped until the road merged onto the freeway. Clearly, she had driven this route many times before. The wind picked up, and Ana closed the sunroof. She eyed Riley. "It's a long drive. You might as well tell me now why you were grinning. I'll have gotten it out of you by the time we reach my place, one way or the other."

"I was thinking about something Lisa said about you."

"That's a good way to start off our long weekend," Ana said with sarcasm. "Okay, let's hear it. What does your ex have to say about me?"

Riley stared out the window, wondering why she had even started down this path. Fields of tilled earth crisscrossed with narrow waterways slipped past her view. "She doesn't think…"

Riley hesitated, then started again, "She thinks you're playing around and will drop me when someone more in your league comes along. I was grinning because of course you drive a shiny BMW. My Honda is ten years old, and I bought it used. I keep it in really good condition, but, you know, I drive a sensible sedan." Riley grinned. "Not a luxury driving machine."

Ana's jaw was set, and Riley realized from her expression that she'd hit a nerve. "My ex bought me this car." She cut around a truck and then pressed her foot harder on the gas pedal. "His family owns the winery, and they have their hand in a bunch of other business ventures as well. Money isn't the same to them as it is to you or me."

"It's easy to get used to being around people who like to spend money, isn't it?"

Ana's glare was enough to make Riley want to swallow her words.

"You don't know me well enough, Riley," she started. "Not enough to say things like that. If this conversation hadn't started from something your girlfriend said, I'd be giving you a bigger piece of my mind right now."

"Ex."

"Ex-girlfriend," Ana agreed. "Though clearly she is still someone you listen to, unfortunately."

"She knows I don't want her dropping by my place anymore."

"Easy to blame that one on me, wasn't it?"

Riley pulled at the seat belt, the shoulder strap of which was cutting too close to her neck. Riley thought of all the ways she could have explained her issues with luxury lifestyles, but she knew her tone would sound judgmental, and it was too late anyhow. The last thing she wanted to do was to bring up the subject of money. "Can we get out somewhere? I want to start over."

"This is Woodland."

"And?"

"There's nothing in Woodland." Ana shook her head and pulled off at the next exit. She pulled into a McDonald's parking lot and turned off the car. Riley got out and went around to her side of the car. She leaned against the door, staring through the window until Ana finally lowered the glass. "So you drive a BMW."

"Yep. What else have you got lined up against me?"

"I guess you have fancy purses with designer labels. I wouldn't have noticed. And I have no idea where you'd go to buy a purse like that"—she pointed to the purse in question—"because I've never even heard of that brand. You wear expensive clothes that don't hide the fact that you are sexy as hell. Meanwhile, I'm worrying about whether you've noticed that my jaw's hanging open when I look at you. Only takes one look from you and I'm stopped in my tracks." Riley paused. "It's not hard at all to see why I'd want to be with you. Thing is, I'm not sure why you want to be with *me*. I know I'm going about this all wrong, but I need to know if you're only playing a game."

"My purse came from a designer in Italy. I went to Florence last summer with Tom, about a month before I met you. The trip was terrible. We were both in bad moods, and then we got food poisoning. But I love the purse." Ana's hands still gripped the steering wheel. "What would you do if I said yes? Maybe I am just playing a game."

"I'd say let's have a good New Year's then." Riley waited for two teenage boys to walk past. They stared at her, then at Ana's car before heading into McDonald's. "And then I'd get back on the plane on Sunday after having a sex-filled long weekend and I'd miss the crap out of you. But I'd go back to Denver and my boring life knowing some things aren't meant to last."

"And if I said no?" Ana looked at Riley. "What if I want this fling to finally turn into something real?"

"I don't know if I'd believe you."

"Of course you wouldn't. And I thought I had issues," Ana said, shaking her head. "Thank you for being honest anyway. Get in the car."

"Not yet."

Ana sighed. "What else?"

"What's your answer? Are you playing at this?"

"No. My answer is no. And fuck you for even asking."

Riley wanted to believe Ana. But nothing about their relationship felt real and Lisa's words haunted her. She closed her eyes and tried to think of a way to start back at the beginning. "It's good to see you."

"Now I don't know if I believe you."

"I know it's only been a week since the whole thing at the airport, but you've been in my head every moment. I keep trying to get you out and I can't."

"Sorry."

"No, you're not. I can tell. You're hoping I'm hooked." Riley leaned through the window and pressed her lips to Ana's. Ana smiled, then grabbed the front of Riley's shirt and pulled her closer. They kissed again, Ana's lips parting to allow her to press her tongue against Riley's.

Ana pulled away finally. "Why are you such a pain in the ass?"

Riley shrugged. "Baggage, I guess. What else?"

"Well, that kiss was how I was hoping we would start out," she said. "Okay, get in. I'm going through the drive-through for fries and a Coke."

The drive to Napa took a little over an hour. Ana's condo was one in a long row, all salmon-colored with tile roofs and stucco exteriors. Her block faced the highway, but the patio backyards all butted up to a hill lined with grapevines. The sun was setting when they pulled into the garage. It was immaculate and clear evidence that she didn't much spend time at home.

Ana led the way from the garage down a narrow hallway past a tiny laundry room and into the kitchen. She dropped her keys in a basket on the counter and then filled two glasses with water. She handed one to Riley and then continued through a small dining area, past the family room with one oversized sofa with a matching, excessively large footrest and a flat-screen television that took up most of one wall and up the staircase to the bedrooms.

"Tom still has some of his stuff in the spare room," she said, motioning to the first door they passed, "but I stopped giving him a hard time about it. Like you, I decided I didn't really care about stuff. Nearly everything in this house was bought on his credit card, anyway, so it's all basically his."

"Including the TV downstairs?"

"Yeah, he loves that screen. In fact, that's his excuse when he comes over unexpectedly. There's always a game playing." Ana entered the master bedroom, and she pointed to a sitting area. "You can leave your suitcase there. I remember that you don't mind living out of a suitcase, but there's room in the closet if you want to hang anything up."

Riley dropped her suitcase in the corner. "Is it likely he'll show up unexpectedly over the next few days?"

Ana shook her head. "He knows you're here."

"How'd that conversation go?"

Ana shrugged. "Better than I expected, actually."

"Let me guess. He didn't mind that you were seeing someone else because I'm not a guy."

Ana tilted her head. "Yeah, something like that. Then he said something completely inappropriate and I made him apologize. He actually looked genuinely sorry. Tom isn't a bad guy, really. I wouldn't have been with him for that long if he was."

"What ended things?" Riley asked. "I mean, I know it wasn't us getting together. If you wanted to, you could have lied about all of that."

"Do you really want to talk about Tom?"

"No, not really." Riley sighed. She settled her hands on Ana's hips. "How about you tell me he was a dick and you knew you could do better. Then we met."

Ana laughed. "Because you wouldn't believe me. And you'd give me some line that made it seem as if you had believed me, but I'd know better." She paused. "We kept fighting. About anything and about everything. Most of the time, neither of us wanted to be having the fight, but then we couldn't seem to agree on the terms of a truce. I knew we just didn't love each other enough. He knew it too." Ana didn't speak for a long moment, then she leaned forward and kissed Riley. "Good enough?"

Riley nodded. In some ways, it was better than her ending with Lisa. If Lisa hadn't wanted to keep Jen in her life, they might have reconciled. But all that was in the past. She didn't want to go back to her life with Lisa, even if things didn't work with Ana. The past week in Seattle had made that all the more clear. Even if Ana hadn't asked, she wanted Lisa out of her life. "So…what are we doing for New Year's Eve?"

"I thought you'd never ask. There's something I've wanted to go to for ages. I think you'll like it. I found out about it three or four years ago, but it wasn't an option for me then."

"Why's that?"

"I had the wrong type of date before."

"Is this a fancy sort of thing, or am I okay in jeans?"

"No jeans. But I took care of that." Ana opened her closet door and pulled out something on a hanger covered in plastic. "I may have rifled through your closet to find your size. And you don't have anything like this, but I think you'll look good in it. It's on loan from the black-tie shop downtown. I know the owner." Ana handed the hanger to Riley and sorted through her closet until she found something else. She held up a red silk dress with a low neckline and an even lower drop in the back. "I'm wearing this."

"Okay, really fancy. What is this thing we're going to?" Riley said, pulling the plastic off the hanger. She felt the fabric underneath. It was a tailored black suit with a thin black necktie and white dress shirt. High quality.

"A members-only ball."

"A ball?" She grinned. "Seriously?"

Ana nodded.

Riley had never been to a ball and had no desire to go now. The look of excitement on Ana's face, however, was enough to convince her to go along with it. "How'd you find out about this members-only thing?"

"In the wine business, you get to know everyone. I met the woman who organizes the New Year's gala a few years back. She knows Tom, but then, everyone in this town knows him.

Anyway, it's women only, so I never could go. They rent out a ballroom in one of the wineries. The venue switches from year to year."

Riley hung the suit back in the closet and reached for Ana. Ana's kiss filled her lips. She had Ana's blouse off a moment later. Ana pulled her toward the bed, moving the comforter and sheets back as she sank onto the mattress. Riley took off her shirt and jeans while Ana watched. Riley moved on top of her, finding Ana's waiting lips once more.

Ana nudged Riley awake at eight o'clock. "Wake up. I already showered. It's your turn."

Riley rubbed her eyes and climbed out of bed. Ana was already in the red dress. "You look amazing," Riley said, her hand tracing the drop at the back of the dress. The fabric only just covered Ana's lower back, leaving the rest exposed. "Maybe we should stay here. I don't know how long I'm going to want you to keep that on."

"I've been wanting to have a date for this for years." Ana shook her head. "And I want to see you in that suit. Go shower."

The suit fit perfectly. Riley stood in front of Ana's mirror and looked at herself. Ana came up from behind her and adjusted the tie. She rarely had a reason to get dressed up and had never been to anything formal enough to need a suit. Compared to her usual attire of either scrubs or jeans, it was a strange costume, but she had to admit, it felt good.

"Not bad for a rental," Ana said, kissing her neck. "It looks like it was made for you, in fact. I'll have to thank Susie with a case of wine. She was doubtful she had anything that would fit a woman's build, but I figured with your broad shoulders you could pull it off." She stepped in front of Riley. With her heels on, she was suddenly at eye level. "You have no idea what you are in for tonight."

Riley went over to her backpack and fished out a small black box. She handed it to Ana. "You left this at my place."

Ana opened it up and then glanced at Riley. "You replaced the missing diamond." She took the gold chain out and held it up to the light. The ruby pendant slid down the chain, spiraling and catching the light as it spun. Ana held it up to her neck and then touched the spot where the new diamond had been set. Five diamonds circled the ruby now that the missing one had been replaced. She handed the ends of the chain to Riley to fasten. "Thank you," she said, turning to face Riley. "You didn't have to get the diamond replaced."

"It didn't look right with the empty space."

Ana glanced in the mirror and then touched the pendant. "I didn't even realize I'd left it. Clearly I was distracted."

"My mom was really excited when I told her I wanted to go to a jewelry shop. She has this idea that one day I'm going to start liking shiny things. The fact that I am seeing someone who likes this sort of thing might be close enough."

Riley didn't want to offer any more details to Ana and hoped she wouldn't ask. The fact that her mother knew the jeweler by name and had his number on speed dial on her home phone was not something she was ready to tell Ana yet. Too many questions would follow.

"You told your mom about me?"

"As it turned out, my parents were really disappointed I was going to miss their New Year's Eve party. They needed to hear a good excuse."

* * *

Ana drove to the winery hosting this year's event, which looked more like a castle than a winery. The front was made from blocks of stone, and turrets cropped up on all four corners. Torches lit the circular drive in front of massive wood doors. It was set far from the main road up a long narrow drive and a huge iron gate blocked access. A guard stood at the gate. He checked Ana's name on the list before pressing the code to open the gate. They parked in the nearly full lot and followed the path to the front entrance. A guard opened the front door and without asking pointed to the spiral staircase at the far end of the foyer. They passed a marble fountain and walls with full-length gilded mirrors before climbing the stairs. Ana led the way down a corridor dotted with naked Grecian statues in various seductive poses. She knocked on the door at the top of a narrow flight of stairs leading down to what seemed to be a back entrance.

A woman in a suit answered the knock. She glanced briefly at Riley and then smiled as she recognized Ana. The ballroom opened up behind her. A live band was playing and the dance floor was filled. There were a number of women in drag, and aside from the formality of it all, Riley felt at once strangely comfortable. Riley caught Ana's hand and brought it to her lips.

Ana pointed out socialites that she recognized as they moved from the entrance to the bar. Riley couldn't keep track of their names nor the descriptions Ana gave of their fortunes. Some were locals in the wine business, but most seemed to be up from San Francisco or thereabouts with fortunes in everything from oil to IT. Riley wondered how Ana could possibly have met so many of them.

"Ana, good to see you here." A gray-haired woman in a long black dress stopped them in front of the bar. She extended her hand to Riley. "I don't believe we've met."

Riley shook her hand as Ana made the introduction. Riley noticed that Ana hadn't mentioned the woman's last name. She'd only said "Madam Bea." Bea had a square diamond that was distractingly large on one of her fingers.

Bea studied Riley for a long moment before saying, "I hear you are a physical therapist in Denver."

Riley nodded and glanced at Ana. She hadn't guessed that this woman was someone Ana knew well and wondered what else Madam Bea knew about her.

Bea seemed to notice Riley had been thrown off balance by her comment. She smiled and continued, "Ana is quite smitten and now I can see why. I'll leave you two to get your drinks and expect to find you on the dance floor soon."

They reached the bar and ordered their drinks. After the bartender turned away, Riley asked, "So how exactly do you know so many of the women here? And Bea? She's a close friend?"

"I don't know if I'd call her a close friend or not. But she is someone I like to keep close. You know the saying about enemies and friends? Well, I'm not sure which side of the fence I'd put Bea on. She's Tom's aunt and part owner in the family winery. She's the financial brains of the family and runs the ship, even if Tom's dad thinks he does. She also has invested in practically every tech company that has made it big in the past twenty years. And if you screw up on something she's asked you to do, you are out of the company by the next morning."

Riley watched Bea converse with another couple, then make her way through the crowd until she reached a woman sitting alone at a table across the way. "And is she out? Or is it a family secret?"

"From what I gather, she's one of the founding members of this club and they've been doing this for nearly thirty years. Aside from New Year's, they have an annual spring ball as well. But she's not out. Tom thought I was crazy when I asked him if she was a lesbian after the first time I met her."

"This is a little weird. I feel like I've been thrown back into a different era," Riley said as the music changed to a waltz. "And, for the first time in my life, I'm actually glad my mom made me take ballroom dance lessons."

Ana's face lit up at this. She set down her drink and grabbed Riley's hand. They were on the dance floor before Riley had time to argue. She hadn't learned the footwork for lead, but Ana smoothed over her mistakes without a misstep and by the third song, Riley had a better handle on it. The band changed from playing classical to a swing piece, and Ana quickly outdanced Riley. Riley felt a tap on her shoulder and stepped aside as another woman, in a suit that was clearly not a rental, took over.

Ana spun about the room with her new lead. Riley leaned against one of the tables near the dance floor, watching them. A woman in dark green gown approached her table. She motioned to the dance floor, pointing out Ana and the lead who was guiding her around the room. "They dance well together, don't they?" Her accent was French. "I don't know Ana personally, although we share the same circle of friends. I never once suspected I'd run into her here. I'm Patrice." She extended her hand.

"I'm Riley." She shook Patrice's hand. Patrice let her hand linger on Riley's for a moment. "Nice to meet you," Riley added.

The woman nodded. "You're from Denver?"

Riley felt unsettled once more. "Word on the street."

Patrice laughed. "There's two hundred guests tonight. Each one of them has been first vouched for by one of the members, then vetted, aliases checked, et cetera."

"And then they publish the list?"

Patrice laughed again. "Absolutely not. They are going to play another swing song. You've lost your dance partner."

"I don't mind," Riley said. "It's nice to have a break."

"So I shouldn't ask you to dance then?"

Riley smiled, trying to hide her surprise. Patrice had steel blue eyes and sharply beautiful features. Riley stood and took her hand, letting Patrice lead them onto the dance floor. She was as tall as Riley but lithe against her arm. They danced the swing, with Patrice leading, and then Riley took over when a waltz followed. Riley had tried to keep track of Ana's place on the dance floor but soon lost track of her. She felt Patrice hesitate when the music changed to a samba.

"I don't want to be the cause of any drama tonight. Your date is alone at the bar. At the moment, she's waiting for you. But I wouldn't trust that to last too long."

"I enjoyed dancing with you," Riley said.

Patrice smiled. "Likewise."

Riley let Patrice go, enjoying another look at Patrice when she turned to leave. Riley wouldn't have minded another dance with her, but when she looked again at the bar and spotted Ana, she felt her breath catch. She made her way over to her, finding Ana chatting with the bartender between his drink orders.

Ana seemed distracted when Riley approached. She handed Riley a wineglass. Riley sipped it and smiled. "I remember this."

"Peach sauvignon. Jonathan makes his own version, but it is essentially the same as what you tasted before."

"Jonathan?"

Ana motioned to the bartender. He looked over at Ana and smiled. "We dated once. For about five minutes. He's the reason I met Ernesto, the chef."

"He wasn't part of the original story. I remember the numbers. Before Ernesto was Terrell. The guy who played basketball and the stock market."

"Not bad. You were paying attention." Ana motioned toward Jonathan's back. "Well, there were others between the numbered ones. Some of my lovers didn't quite earn a number. Jonathan and I, we never made it to a third date."

Riley set the glass down. It was a half hour until midnight and the band had gone on a short break. Jazz music played in the intermission. She saw Patrice at the other end of the bar, ordering a drink from Jonathan. Riley reached toward Ana, her hand brushing along Ana's jawline. She turned Ana's face toward hers and kissed her lips.

"You're feeling jealous, aren't you?"

"No," Riley lied.

"I know a jealous kiss when I feel it." Ana caught Riley's necktie. She pulled Riley's face close to hers. "And I like it. Give me another."

Riley guided Ana into another kiss, this time pressing harder against her lips. She was jealous of the look Ana had given the bartender and uneasy about the sea of eyes that seemed to all be watching Ana and silently judging her escort.

"We're not leaving before midnight so don't get any ideas," Ana said when they'd parted. "Who were you dancing with? She looks familiar."

"Patrice. She's French."

"And exquisite in that French way, isn't she?" Ana watched Jonathan hand Patrice her drink. The other bartender, a woman in her mid-twenties, squeezed behind Jonathan and slapped his butt as she did. Jonathan winked at her. "You liked dancing with Patrice, didn't you?"

"Who's jealous now?" Riley took the wineglass back and took a long sip. "She asked me to dance. I wasn't going to say no while you were otherwise engaged."

"Maybe. But you were talking with her for a while."

"'Cause you were off dancing with twinkletoes."

Ana took the wineglass out of Riley's hand. "That was Cris. She's a fabulous dancer, isn't she?"

"Oh, I don't know about that. I've seen better," Riley replied with a sniff.

Ana playfully slapped Riley's shoulder. "You're the one who called her twinkletoes."

Riley kissed Ana again. The alcohol was going to her head and she liked the buzz. "Maybe I was jealous. A little." She traced the line of Ana's dress as it draped over her shoulder and dropped down her back. "It's just this dress."

"Just the dress…?"

"I keep thinking how easy it would be to slip it off your shoulders." Riley paused. She spotted twinkletoes coming up to the bar. The woman eyed Riley and Ana. She waited for a bartender, now pointedly looking the other direction. "Somehow, I know I'm not the only one who was thinking about your dress as you spun around the dance floor."

"While you were dancing with Patrice, you kept stealing glances over at me. I caught you several times."

"Maybe."

Ana finished her drink as the band reappeared. "I don't want to dance with anyone else for the rest of the night. Only you."

Riley drove Ana's car back to her condo. She'd stopped drinking several hours earlier, at midnight, but Ana hadn't and was still tipsy. She fell asleep, still in her dress, while Riley was changing out of her suit. She'd kicked off her high heels and collapsed across the middle of the bed. Riley helped her out of the dress, barely stirring her from sleep and covered her with the blankets. Riley was still too keyed up from their evening to drift right to sleep. They had danced until her feet hurt, and Ana had loved every minute of it, shaking her head when Riley asked if they could sit the next song out and dragging her back on the dance floor after each short break.

Ana rolled over and the comforter shifted off her back. Riley sat down carefully on the bed, pulled the comforter up and stared at her. Her profile was becoming familiar, and yet Riley still couldn't believe that the face on the pillows didn't belong to some beautiful stranger. She wanted to wake her, to watch her eyes open and to tell her how lovely she had looked as she slept. But more than this, she wanted to memorize the image of her sleeping, slackened muscles erasing any lines on her forehead or around her eyes and a half smile playing at the edges of her lips.

Ana's chest rose and fell with each even breath, but Riley knew she might wake at any moment, catch her staring and reach for her. She suddenly realized that the privilege of sitting beside her, watching her as she slept and waiting for her to wake was more than she was entitled to if this was still just a fling. She couldn't go back to Denver under that pretext now. Her heart was in too deep.

She went downstairs and got a glass of water. She found her cell phone and checked her messages. Lisa had called and left a voice mail. Riley didn't bother to listen to it. Blair had left a one-line text wishing her a Happy New Year. Riley turned off her phone and went back to Ana's bed. She spooned against her, enjoying her warmth, and fell asleep with her hand on Ana's belly.

* * *

The sun streamed in through Ana's bedroom window. Riley woke first and went downstairs to find something to eat. She scouted the pantry, which had little more than two twelve-packs of Coca-Cola, chips and enough cans of soup to enable someone to survive a month housebound. Ana apparently wasn't attached to any particular brand. She had at least ten different varieties of soups, all vegetarian, and all stacked in even rows with the labels clearly visible. There was an open box of Life, but the cereal in it was stale. The contents of the refrigerator were sparse as well.

Riley finally opted for the stale cereal, which was marginally more tolerable once soaked in milk.

"Sunny and in the sixties today," Ana said, coming in to the kitchen. She was in a pair of cargo pants and a long sleeve T-shirt. "Want to go for a hike?"

Riley nodded. "You look different. I like your hair like that."

"Ponytail and no makeup. I'm on vacation." She rested her hands on Riley's shoulders and leaned down to kiss her cheek. She kept her hands in place and massaged lightly. "I have no idea how old that cereal is. I don't even remember buying it."

"I was hungry enough not to care."

Riley finished the last bite, and looked over her shoulder at Ana, who had stopped the massage and was now staring out the window. The question that had been nagging her all morning resurfaced.

How likely was this to work out?

The hike that Ana had picked was one she'd been on before and she'd promised a nice spot for a picnic by a little lake halfway up the trail. The trailhead was just outside of town. A wide gravel road trimmed on either side with grass led them upward, narrowed to pass through a dense forest of oak and then narrowed further to a rocky deer path that wound up to a ridge. Once they were on the wider ridge trail, Ana slowed her pace. She reached for Riley's hand and gave it a squeeze, then let go. The view of Napa Valley opened up below, with rolling hills unfolding in layers that stretched as far as the horizon, all dressed in varying shades of green. The sky was a cloudless soft blue.

"In Denver, you get used to brown winters. The snow rarely sticks for longer than a day or two. But there are months and months of bare branches and dead grass. When I go home to Seattle, my eyes feel like they are on vacation. It's like there's no end to the green. But the sky is gray, and it rains, of course. It never looks quite like this. I could get used to this."

"We're almost to the lake," Ana said. "Depending on the season and the rains, sometimes it looks more like a frog pond. But I like it even then."

The lake was little more than a large pond, in fact, but it was framed with oaks and set in a box canyon. A picnic bench whittled with initials and hearts had been placed at one end of the lake. Ana sat down atop the table, propping her feet, clad in expensive-looking, shiny leather hiking boots, on the bench. Riley took out her phone and snapped a picture. She shook her head when she saw the image frozen on the screen.

"What is it?"

"You look like a model posing for some trendy boot company."

"A model?" Ana laughed. Her tone turned serious when she added, "It bothers you, a little, doesn't it? I'm not trying, you know. Not today."

"Does what bother me?" Riley stalled. She didn't want to articulate what she felt. Ana wasn't simply good-looking. She was stunning. Riley hadn't worried that Ana was too attractive to be with her when it had seemed like only a fling. Now, however, she felt her insecurities about her appearance mounting. It wasn't a matter of comparing her body to Ana's. They were too different. Riley's lanky build gave her a boyish look, she knew, but she'd never particularly wanted to look more feminine. She doubted, on the other hand, that Ana could make herself look unfeminine if she tried. Ana didn't need to hide behind makeup or fancy clothes. In some ways, in fact, they took away from her beauty. Her graceful curves and delicate lines, at once appealing and mystifying in their perfection, were all Riley wanted to see.

Riley had dated pretty women, but she had to admit she had always felt more comfortable dating ones who were just average good-looking women, not model-pretty ones. Blair and Lisa were both beautiful, but in different ways.

It really wasn't about the women she'd dated before, anyway. As handsome as she felt when she was wearing jeans and a collared men's dress shirt, she knew she wasn't in the same ballpark as Ana. No doubt someone could find lots to psychoanalyze about this—but she didn't want to hear what they might have to say. And she certainly wasn't comfortable enough with Ana to admit her feelings.

"When I'm working, I have to dress the part, Riley. And maybe I like dressing up. But you know, it doesn't matter how I dress. Or if I'm wearing makeup. I still like women."

"I'm not suggesting you don't."

"Then what are you suggesting? I think you have some image in your mind about what a woman who likes women is supposed to look like, and I'm guessing you don't think I look the part. So, because I look like I should be modeling boots, I'm probably only playing a game with you, right?"

Riley shrugged. Ana was partly right. "Maybe."

"Damn. I basically had this same conversation with Tom. He told me I was making a mistake. That I was 'too attractive to be with a woman.'"

Riley slipped her phone in her pocket and sat down on the table too. The wood was damp from the moist air. She traced the lines of a heart that someone had etched into the plank closest to Ana. "It's possible that it is going to take me a while to get used to being with someone who looks like you do."

"Who looks like they are modeling boots?" Ana shook her head. "I like you, Riley. Get over it." She touched the same heart that Riley had traced. "Have you always had trust issues, or is it something about me?"

"Why do you think I don't trust you?"

"I don't think you believe that I really like you. I don't think you'll believe me when I admit exactly how much I like you." Ana brushed her hand against Riley's cheek. She pulled her hand back. "I'm not playing around."

"Not this time?"

Ana turned her gaze toward the lake. Her voice sounded distant when she finally answered. "I wasn't playing last time either. Is that why you don't trust me?"

Riley didn't answer. Was her experience with Lisa adding to her own doubts about a relationship with Ana? Or was she still waiting for something to resurface with Tom?

"I've always been wary of people saying they like me, I think. How do you really know? Do you like me only until someone better comes along? Yeah, what happened has played into some of my fears, maybe, but I think I was probably insecure before all of that. I'd blame my ex, but she isn't here to defend herself."

"I have this crazy idea that by the end of this weekend you will accept that I like you. A lot."

"And what if I feel the same? Then we come back around to wondering how we are supposed to make this work…There are so many other issues beyond the fact that I think you might be out of my league."

Ana sighed. "Long distance, for a while. I have a layover in Denver sometime in the last week of January. And I'm not too attractive for you, Riley. You're beautiful. I told you that last September and I meant it."

Riley leaned over and kissed Ana. "At the moment, I'm not going to argue."

* * *

The following day, Ana had planned a drive to the coast. They woke up early but didn't get out of bed until noon and only then because of Ana's growling stomach. They took a long drive but didn't end up at the coast. Instead they drove inland, then circled back, and soon Ana was pointing out the winery that Tom's family owned. "It's one of the smallest wineries in Napa. In fact, most of their grapes are grown in the central valley. But they have a nice tasting room in a redwood cellar, and of course, the restaurant brings in a choice crowd."

"Can we stop?" Riley asked. She wanted to see the winery mostly as background. She wanted more than a mental picture of the world Ana knew.

Ana seemed hesitant but turned the car off the main road and headed toward a beige stucco building with a red tile roof. She pulled into the parking lot. "Maybe this will be fun." She paused. "I haven't taken anyone on a tour before that wasn't all about the business."

"You don't have to give me a tour. I just want to look around your world."

"My world?" Ana shook her head. "I wouldn't call it that. Anyway, I think you'll like it. We'll go to the tasting cellar first, then we can wander around the garden. Nothing will be in bloom, but they have the best collection of gaudy sculptures that I've ever seen. It's impressive, really."

The stucco building housed a restaurant and a banquet hall. It wasn't clear where the wine was processed, but Riley guessed most of this happened off-site. The real estate in Napa was premium and most of every bit of space was dressed in grape vines or gilded for tourism. They passed the stucco building and walked through a courtyard which had a large statue in the center of a horse bending his head to an angel. It was just as gaudy as Ana had warned it would be.

Riley half expected to see Tom strolling about and looking exactly as she remembered him from the scene in the flooded mountain winery so many months ago. Instead, as they entered the tasting cellar, they ran into Madam Bea. Bea greeted Ana with a cool smile and made no hint at ever having met Riley. Ana even introduced Riley again, this time saying only that she was a friend visiting from Denver. Bea shook her hand with practiced civility. Riley noticed that the three people working the tasting room all paid close attention to where Madam Bea was at all times and what she was saying. It was clear Bea had her mask on in front of them.

Riley didn't like any of the wines they served but pointed to the most tolerable one when Bea inquired which one she liked. They were sent out with a bottle of this one, and Bea refused to let them pay. Riley tipped the server and they headed back outside, with Riley finally feeling at ease once they were back in the daylight. The feeling didn't last long. Tom was standing outside the cellar, talking with an older man. Riley glanced over at Ana to see her reaction. She was as cool as Bea had been earlier when he raised his hand in greeting, shook hands with the older man and headed toward them.

"Tom, good to see you," Ana said. "Riley, this is Tom," she continued, introducing them with poise.

Tom shook Riley's hand, smiling like a salesman all the while, his expression obviously forced. His hands were cool, but sweaty.

"So, Riley...I've heard a lot about you. I didn't think I would get a chance to meet you. It's a pleasure."

Riley nodded. "Mine as well." She had little idea what Ana had told Tom. She glanced at Ana for a hint, but Ana's gaze was focused on Tom. She was on her own. "You know, I haven't heard all that much about you, come to think of it. I basically only know you like expensive cars and big TV screens."

He laughed loud enough to attract the attention of a couple heading in to the tasting cellar. Tom raised a hand when they looked back at him. "In fact, I was over at Ana's yesterday watching the game. You two must have been out. How do you like the screen?"

"It's a little big. But I'd bet football tackles look pretty good in high def on a screen that size. You can probably see the ACLs tear."

"We'll have to watch a game sometime and you can tell me what you think."

"Yeah, that wouldn't be awkward," Ana said quietly.

Tom's forced smile disappeared at Ana's words. He eyed her for a moment and then turned back to Riley. "Are you a Broncos fan?"

"No. Seahawks."

"Really? I bet that goes over well in Denver." Tom chuckled. "Do you have dinner plans?" He motioned to the entrance to the restaurant to the left of the tasting cellar. "I think Ernie can be convinced to squeeze in two attractive women. I can have a word with him if you'd like. You really haven't had a fine meal until you've tasted a four-star chef's creations. Ernie is something else."

Riley noticed Ana's flinch. It was subtle but nonetheless present. When she didn't answer Tom right off, Riley said, "Thank you, but we already have plans for tonight, I think."

Tom looked at Ana and said, "Of course. It's last minute and a holiday weekend anyway. Ernie would probably strangle me for even asking." He pointed at the bottle of wine in Riley's hand. "Enjoy. That pinot is one of my favorites."

Once Tom had left, Ana let out a long sigh. "I don't know if I'm still up for the garden. Maybe we should get out of here before we run into anyone else."

"Who else are you worried about?"

Ana shook her head.

Riley pointed to the angel and horse statue. "If this is any indication, I don't think I should miss the garden."

Ana didn't smile. Her face was as unrevealing as Madam Bea's had been earlier. She led the way through the courtyard and past two small stone buildings, opened a wrought-iron gate and stepped down onto a strip of grass lining a wall of green bushes. The bushes were at least seven feet tall and too thick to see through. They followed the grass path, which weaved between the bushes and opened up every twenty feet or so to display another statue. Before long, it became clear that the garden had been laid out in a maze-like pattern. Even with dormant roses and pots holding only green foliage, it was a beautiful spot.

After a few minutes, Ana's pace slowed. Riley reached for her hand. They paused in front of a koi pond with a large leaping frog statue towering over the water. Orange and white fish circled in the shallow water. Riley dipped her hand in the pond. One of the fish came up to the surface, as if testing her fingers for food, then darted away as quickly as it had appeared. Riley sat down on the stone blocks framing the pond. Ana had her arms crossed and was staring at the bushes as if she could see right through to the other side of the maze.

"I told him you were coming. We talked on the phone after Christmas. I felt I should tell him so he didn't drop by the house unexpectedly. He was supposed to be in LA this week. I guess his plans changed."

"Running into him this time was way easier than last. I had this idea that he was much better looking. Now he just seems rich and well-dressed."

Ana came over to the koi pond and stared at the water. "I think he wanted to meet you. He still thinks we are just going through a rough patch, no matter how many times I tell him it's over. He was sizing you up. He is so damn competitive that he won't accept that I decided when we were done."

"It's nice to feel like I'm not the only one with baggage."

Ana smiled, but her eyes were still focused on the fish. "We do have dinner plans tonight. I called Ernie yesterday, and he arranged a table for us."

"What are the chances that we'll run into Tom?"

"Slim. Unless he finds out we're on the reservation list." Ana shrugged. "I can't believe he came to my house yesterday, and yet, I can. He just can't accept that it's time to quit. Now I'm really glad we went on that hike." She rested her hand on Riley's. "I swear things are over with Tom and me, even if he isn't acting that way."

Riley laughed. "Damn, haven't I heard that line before."

"Don't compare me, Riley."

Riley stood up, inches from Ana's lips. "I couldn't. But I have heard that line."

"Fine. I'll watch my step in that territory." Ana clasped Riley's hand. "Come on, we haven't even gotten to the best statues yet. They've got a replica of Michelangelo's David next to a pair of mating squirrels that are quite unforgettable."

The only time Ernie was able to work them into the reservation list was at the last seating. They finally were seated at a table at a quarter to nine. Riley was light-headed from the wine they'd consumed while waiting and let Ana order. A loaf of freshly baked sourdough arrived first and Riley ate two slices. Ana had been quiet since their walk in the garden. Riley hadn't been able to shake the newly refreshed doubts she had about Ana having really ended things with Tom. After the food arrived, Riley felt less tongue-tied.

"This place is nice. Not at all like the dark tasting cellar with metal chairs."

"I tried to convince them to get rid of those chairs a long time ago."

Ana had finished her pasta dish and leaned back in her chair. She sipped her wine. "Don't tell Ernie, but my favorite thing here is the bread. They make it every morning and I love the smell of it baking. I've gotten Ernie to give me a loaf on more than one occasion."

Riley finished the last bite on her plate as a man wearing a chef's apron came up to their table. He nodded at Ana and held out his hand to Riley. "Thank you so much for coming this evening. I hope you enjoyed your meal."

Riley knew without asking that he was Ernie. Ana smiled comfortably at him and showed none of the tension that had been evident when Tom had appeared.

"The halibut was delicious. So was everything, in fact. Especially the bread."

"Everyone always mentions the bread. That's one of my grandmother's recipes." Ernie smiled. "But the halibut is all mine." He turned to Ana. "A pleasure seeing you, as always. And don't worry about calling at the last minute. You know I can almost always work in another table. For you, anyway."

Much as Riley was happy things hadn't worked out for him and Ana, she did feel a bit sorry for Ernie when she saw the tender look he gave Ana before heading back to the kitchen. He even stole a glance back at their table as he pushed through the double doors.

* * *

Sunday morning arrived too soon. Riley awoke early and made breakfast for them both. She'd gone to the grocery store the night before and bought ingredients for omelets and rolls. Ana came down to the kitchen as Riley was pulling the rolls out of the oven.

"It smells amazing in here," Ana said, wrapping her arms around Riley.

"So, as I was cooking, I realized the stiff competition I'm up against. No comparing my food to your master chef ex, all right?"

"Riley, I burn toast. That's the competition you are up against."

Riley set the omelets on the table and put the rolls on a plate. She'd searched for a bread basket but finally came to the conclusion that Ana didn't own one. She had little besides a set of four plates, bowls, utensils, three coffee mugs and two wineglasses.

Ana took a bite of the omelet and nodded approvingly. She ate several more bites and then reached for a roll. "I looked up the details for my Atlanta trip. I had a four-hour layover in Denver, but I'm going to reschedule the second leg so we have the evening together. I'll arrive at noon in Denver and fly out to Atlanta at six a.m. the next morning. I don't need to be in Atlanta until that afternoon anyway. I'll text you the dates and times and everything."

"Okay, sounds good."

Ana looked up from her plate. She set her fork down and reached for the coffee. "Wow, that was really unconvincing. You do still want to meet up in three weeks, don't you?"

Riley stopped eating. "I do. But I'd rather have a date next Thursday and maybe Saturday night too."

Ana sipped the coffee. "You make better coffee than I do."

"I like you."

"But you're not sure you are up for this? For long distance?"

"I don't have much choice, do I?"

By the time they had finished breakfast, the airport shuttle driver was waiting outside. Riley kissed Ana goodbye at the front doorstep. The driver looked impatient and kept the engine running.

PART FOUR

Denver, Colorado
(A Year Earlier)

"It's almost nine," Lisa said without getting up from her spot on the sofa. The canned laughter of the sitcom she was watching followed her words.

"Yeah, I had a couple home visits this evening." Riley kicked off her shoes. She went into the kitchen and opened the fridge. A nearly empty milk jug was on the top shelf. Chinese takeout leftovers from two weeks ago were on the middle shelf. One egg remained in the carton. Riley found what was left of the block of cheddar and grabbed a handful of spinach. Lisa never ate vegetables so she never ran out of those. She stared at the back of Lisa's head as she made an omelet. "I'm sorry I'm home late. Are you upset about something?"

Lisa's head shook.

The fact that she hadn't answered was a clear signal that something definitely was wrong. "You can talk to your mom about my schedule. She's the one who has me booked twelve hours straight." Riley flipped her omelet onto a plate and fished a fork out of the dishwasher. She never had time to put the dishes away and was hard-pressed to say if the dishes in the washer were clean or dirty. She rinsed the fork off and dried it on her shirt.

Lisa made room for her on the couch but didn't look away from the TV screen. The sitcom was nearly over. Riley stared at the fireplace next to the television. It was a gas log fireplace and easy enough to turn on, but getting up and flipping the switch seemed like too much hassle. The television would take away any of the relaxing atmosphere the thin blue flame could possibly create anyway. She hated having the television in the same room as the fireplace, but Lisa wanted it enough that they had compromised. Riley kept a dark brown shawl that her mother had sent her and that she never would wear as a throw to cover the screen whenever it was off.

"Christmas is in less than a month. Are you planning on keeping up this schedule through the holidays?"

"I'm planning on going home to Seattle for a few days, but I don't think that's what you are asking about. Why are you suddenly upset about my schedule? It's been this way for a year."

"I don't understand why you have to do the home visits anyway. You know you could make more money and have better hours if you worked at the hospital. My mom would understand."

"Would she?" Riley shook her head. "I doubt it. Besides, I like long-term clients."

"But you work harder and make less money."

"I don't mind." Riley finished the omelet and set the plate on the coffee table. "I like the follow-up. If I worked at the hospital, I'd see them for maybe two or three times and then they'd get a little better and get booted home. And I'd be on to the next patient."

"You'd have more time at home," Lisa countered.

"So I could watch another hour of bad sitcoms?"

Lisa turned off the TV and stood up abruptly. "Do you even like spending time with me, Riley?"

Riley realized her mistake too late. The bathroom door slammed shut. Lisa had the habit of going pee before she wanted to have any serious conversation. Riley went over to the fireplace and flipped on the gas. She listened for the familiar hiss of gas and then the three clicks that preceded the first weak blue flame. With a snap, the entire thing blazed in an orgy of red and orange-white licking flames. Riley sat back down, waiting for Lisa. She emerged a few minutes later, but she walked right past Riley without a word.

Riley considered following her upstairs but stared at the fire instead. In the time that they'd been together, she had learned the price of delaying this conversation. But she was too tired tonight to play the game. After a while, she went to get the pile of mail from the kitchen table and sorted through it. She found a credit card bill nearing the past due date and went to get her checkbook and pen.

Lisa met her on the stairs. "Are you coming to bed?"

"Not yet. I'm paying bills." Riley walked past Lisa's spot on the middle landing and went to the office that had become Lisa's de facto room. It had a twin-size bed that was never slept in and a desk with a computer and printer setup, the place where papers were dumped that needed filing but instead landed in more or less one big pile. Lisa had filled the closet with her clothes and shoes. Lisa had more pairs of shoes that were never worn than Riley thought normal, but she had yet to ask her about this.

More importantly, Lisa wasn't supposed to have moved her things into the room at all. They had agreed to retain some autonomy by living in different houses and seeing each other on set days or planned dates. Lisa had even suggested this. But not long after moving to Denver, her things began piling up in Riley's room and later the guest room. She was at Riley's house every night.

Riley found her checkbook and headed back downstairs. Lisa was sitting cross-legged in front of the fire. She had torn out several pages from a Lands End catalog and crumpled them into a pile. She held one of the pages to the flames until it singed and caught fire. When the flame reached her fingers, she dunked the paper remnant into her glass of water and waited while it sizzled.

"What do you have against Lands End?" Riley joked. "They make pretty decent coats."

"We haven't had dinner together in two weeks."

"Yeah, we've been busy." Riley attached the stamp to the envelope and filled out the check as Lisa lit another page on fire. "Let's set up a time for a date night."

"People with kids have date nights. We shouldn't have to schedule it."

"You've been working swing on the weekends and I work late. What difference does it make if we plan a date or do it spontaneously?"

"Jen's in town."

Riley felt her breath catch in her throat. "Well, that's spontaneous, I guess. Why is she in Denver?"

"I'm telling you now so you don't get mad later. I want you to know I'm being honest with you." Lisa rolled up the last few pages into one ball and tossed it into the fire. It caught within seconds and burned brightly for a minute or two. "We're having dinner tomorrow night. She flies back to Sacramento on Sunday."

"Why is she here?" Riley repeated.

"She's interviewing at the hospital."

"Why is she interviewing in Denver? Oh, yeah, because the ex she still has feelings for lives here."

"It isn't like that. I mean, she…Yeah, well, probably I have something to do with her considering it. We're still friends."

"Probably? You already told me that you think she still has feelings for you. We went through this last year when you took a trip to California and came back saying she wanted you to move back to Sacramento…So, how long has this been planned?"

"I would have told you sooner, but I swear you are never home. And what am I supposed to do? Mention it as you're walking out the door? Or some night after we finish having sex? 'By the way, my ex, you know, the one you hate, is coming to town. How do you feel about that?'"

"I don't hate her, Lisa. I hardly know her. You're the one who told me that you want to keep her in your life but you're not sure how since she's still interested in you. How am I supposed to feel about that?"

"I'm not trying to hide anything. That's why I told you all of that."

"Yeah, but you didn't tell me the trip to California was to see Jen. I didn't find out about that until afterward. And you've obviously had this dinner date planned for a while. You could have found a way to tell me sooner." Riley stood up and went to the kitchen. She paced back to the living room. "What if I said that I don't want you to have dinner with her? Would it matter?"

"Riley, don't go there. This is just dinner. I'm not going back to her hotel room."

"Right." Riley paced back to the kitchen. She braced her hands against the counter, staring at Lisa. It was true that she hadn't been home enough. It was also true that the result—Lisa starting things up with Jen—infuriated her. "I think you should go home tonight."

"I am home."

"You know what I mean."

"You want me to go to my mom's place?"

"Yeah. Where you are supposed to live." Riley closed her eyes. She was exhausted. "I need some space to think."

"Space to think? That's what people say when they want to break up but don't have the guts to do it."

"I'm not saying that."

Lisa shook her head. "If you want to break up with me, tell me. I'm not going to do it for you. I don't want to break up with you, Riley."

"You're the one who is bringing Jen back into the equation. I thought things were fine with us."

"Yeah, we're fine," Lisa said. Sarcasm edged her voice when she added, "We hardly see each other so how can there be any problems?"

Riley felt the pressure of tears forming in her eyes. She rubbed her face and clenched her jaw, determined not to cry. She knew it was just that she was too tired. That made it hard to hold back tears. "Look, I don't want to break up tonight. I don't want to do anything tonight. I only want to be alone for the night."

"Not 'tonight'? But after you've been alone and had some time to think, then you'll call me and we can schedule a break-up night?"

"I'm not saying that."

"Fine. Whatever. I told you the truth about Jen. I've answered every question you ever asked me. We're only friends. Why do you think I told you that she was coming here if I wanted to start things up with her again?" Lisa kicked the fireplace grate. Her ball of ashes rolled closer to the logs with the rush of air. "I told you that I wanted to have dinner with her. It isn't like I needed to ask your permission." Lisa flicked the gas switch and the flames ceased a moment later. She grabbed the coat that she'd left on the loveseat and hesitated a moment. "I'm going out to dinner with her. I'll call you after." She went out the door without looking back at Riley.

Riley had bought Lisa's coat from Lands End and now the catalogs came monthly. For whatever reason, Lisa had decided to give away all of her warm coats when she moved to California. A cold snap in late September came when Lisa was broke and Riley had ordered the coat without giving it much thought. Lisa was always too broke to buy anything decent anyway. But Lisa had been pissed when the coat came and she saw the price tag. She'd thought Riley had spent too much money and wanted to return it. Money hadn't really come up as an issue before the coat, and Riley hadn't told her anything about her own finances. She nearly did then, but Lisa ended up apologizing and wearing the coat after all.

Riley stared at the fireplace, suddenly cold. She was homesick and the only person she wanted to talk to, other than her mom, was Blair. It was too late to call Blair, and she didn't have the energy to tell her mom the entire story, even if she knew what that was. Her mom would ask.

Riley only knew one thing for sure—Lisa was lying. She was more than just friends with Jen. She had seen Jen's name come up more than a few times on Lisa's phone in the past year.

The California trip last spring had been the tipping point. At first she'd accepted the story that Lisa had given her, but slowly she'd begun to question everything Lisa said. Lisa had claimed that she'd gone to California to visit her old friends Chris and Marie. She'd said that they had "happened" to run into Jen. She'd known Lisa kept in touch with Jen, but after that trip her name came up more and more. Lisa's excuse was always that she was worried about Jen's depression and needed to check in on her regularly.

Though Riley had elected to believe her, beeping notifications about missed calls, text messages and online posts popped up regularly on Lisa's cell phone with Jen's name flashing beneath them. She'd never read the messages; until now, she had convinced herself that they didn't matter. Now she desperately wanted to scan through them.

The following evening, Riley awoke to the phone ringing. It was past midnight. She stumbled over to the dresser, found her cell phone and answered the line. She didn't need to look at the caller's number to know who would be calling.

"I'm at my mom's," Lisa said. "I can't sleep so I'm calling you. I had dinner with Jen tonight. And I wanted to let you know that I'm sleeping in my own bed. Or trying to sleep, anyway. We hugged. That was it. Are you still mad?"

Riley didn't answer. She crawled back under the covers and balanced the phone on the pillow.

"Okay, I can tell you are still mad. My mom said you blew up at Laney today. Possibly misdirected anger?"

Laney was the receptionist. She had scheduled two of Riley's clients at the same time and then called a different client to try and reschedule. Riley had to call all three to explain the problem. Then she yelled at Laney. It wasn't the first time she'd made a mistake. In fact, it was a nearly weekly occurrence. But it was the first time Riley had ever raised her voice at anyone she worked with and so unprofessional that she'd wanted to melt into her office chair afterward. Laney had left early with a headache, and Riley never had a chance to apologize. She'd gone to the gym after work and terrorized a treadmill for an hour, then done too many sets at the weight bench. "Possibly."

"I think Jen is going to get this job. She has good references and she thinks the interview went well. They asked her if she could start in two weeks if they ended up hiring her."

"So, are you two planning on getting a place together? Roomies with benefits?" Riley wondered if she and Lisa would, in fact, break up over the phone. She was wide awake now and almost said, "Okay, good luck, Lisa," but she felt nauseous and couldn't bring herself to say the words aloud.

"No." Lisa paused. She took a deep breath and exhaled. Lisa's old yoga habit of deep breathing always made Riley tense. "I'm calling to ask if I can move in with you. I want to make it official. I want you to know where I am every night. I want you to know that I'm in love with you and don't want to sleep in anyone else's bed. And I don't want to feel like I'm just keeping my stuff at your place. I want it to be our place. I want to pay half the bills."

"You know I don't need you to do that." Riley rolled onto her back. She stared at the ceiling. The streetlight shone through her window and made strange long shadows. She had left the drapes open tonight. Lisa was usually the one who closed them. "The thing is, Jen will be a part of your life. You'll be working together."

"It's a big hospital. I may run into her, yes, but that's it. This isn't about Jen. It's about you and me. I don't want you to be able to kick me out of your life so easy. I was pissed when I left your place. Then I cried the whole way home. I kept expecting you to call and apologize for nearly breaking up with me. Over an ex showing up again in my life. That's it." Lisa paused. When Riley didn't answer, she said, "Then I realized you are so damn scared that I will hurt you that you'd rather hurt me first. So, then I felt sorry for you. In some weird way, it made so much sense. Of course you would kick me out first."

The words hit Riley like a fist in the stomach. She felt tears well in her eyes. "I'm sorry about what I said. I really am."

"Ask me."

"To move in?" Riley took the phone off her ear and stared at the black screen. She tapped the phone and Lisa's picture glowed. In the image, Lisa was wearing a black sports bra and jean cutoffs. Her feet were submerged from the calf down in a silvery black pool of water. Behind her, the waterfall that formed the pool cascaded down a gray granite slab. Riley had climbed out on a felled tree, the trunk and branches half submerged in the water, to get the shot. The screen went dark and Lisa's image disappeared. Riley stretched across the bed, her arm covering the depression in the mattress where Lisa always slept. The bed was too big without Lisa lying next to her. She closed her eyes and put the phone against her ear again. "Would you like to move in with me?"

"Yeah, I would." Lisa took a deep breath and exhaled slowly. "Damn it, Riley, why didn't you ask me this last year?"

"I'm sorry," Riley murmured.

"Me too. Now I'm going to get back in the car and drive home."

Lisa hung up before Riley could say anything else. If she'd asked her to move in with her right when they'd moved to Denver, would all of this with Jen not have come up? Was that what Lisa was suggesting? Riley set the phone on the nightstand and stared at the ceiling.

* * *

When the last client finally left, Riley changed in the office, shut off the lights and set the alarm. Everyone else had left over an hour ago to get ready for the annual holiday party. Riley passed the Italian restaurant that made her favorite calzones. The place looked warm and inviting, and she longed to go inside, but she was expected at Jeanette's house in twenty minutes. Gary, the manager, waved to her as she paused by the front window. He only had two customers seated; most of their business was delivery in the winter months. It was snowing, but the pavement was still warm enough to melt the flakes when they hit. She waved to Gary and trudged to her car.

Counting the clinic's staff, a few referring doctors, nurses Jeanette knew from the hospital and other therapists in the

Denver area, Jeanette had invited more than eighty people to the event. Riley had to park a block away. She made her way through a crowd of strangers in Jeanette's front room and then spotted Laney, the clinic receptionist, who was waving at her enthusiastically. Riley nodded and went over to say hello. Laney had a frothy white drink in her hand and pressed close to Riley to say, "You have to try Jeanette's eggnog."

Riley forced a smile. "Better than last year?"

Laney took a big sip to confirm this and patted Riley's arm as if they were close friends. Riley tried not to stiffen with the touch. Things had continued to be strained between them since she'd yelled at her. Riley had been trying to make amends for her unprofessional outburst, but she had been upset enough about the recurring errors to tell Jeanette that she thought Laney ought to be fired for all of the mistakes that she'd made. Jeanette was strangely loyal to her staff, though, especially the dysfunctional ones among them. She'd promised to speak to Laney about the need to serve their clients better, but Riley doubted she would.

Jeanette had hired a caterer for the occasion. A server wandered past now with a tray of appetizers. Riley shook her head as he walked up to her. Laney reached for one and started to chat with him, giving Riley the excuse she needed to slip away. She noticed two nurses that she recognized from the hospital and stopped to speak with them, thinking Jeanette would be pleased if she happened to walk by, but she made a quick excuse to move on when the conversation turned to work topics.

She headed to the family room. Jeanette had high ceilings and the tree she'd gotten towered at probably twelve feet. She spotted Lisa standing opposite the tree. Jen was next to her. Riley paused. She stepped to the side when a couple tried to squeeze between her and the sofa.

A different server came up to her with a tray of drinks. "Eggnog? With or without rum?"

Riley shook her head and let the server move on. Jen leaned close and whispered something into Lisa's ear. Riley felt her stomach tighten. Lisa laughed in response and then pointed at the tree. Despite all of the assurances that Lisa had given her, seeing them interact still made her question if either could keep the friendship platonic.

"Riley?"

Riley turned and recognized one of Jeanette's friends. She remembered her from the Christmas party the previous year. They'd had a long conversation, but she couldn't quite remember the woman's name. She did remember that the woman had been a nurse for years and then had come to work with Jeanette but had finally retired. She also remembered very clearly that she'd been mourning the loss of her lover and had gotten quite drunk while they'd chatted. She'd also been generous with stories from Lisa's past.

"You've forgotten my name, haven't you, sweetie? I know that searching look." She chuckled and extended her hand. "I'm Sharon."

"Sharon, right. Thank you. I'm terrible with names. I remember our conversation very well, however."

They had begun talking last year, by chance, mostly because Lisa had worked late and didn't show at the party until nearly ten o'clock. Sharon had started the conversation over a cheese platter. She'd gone on for quite a long while about different cheeses and Riley had tried to find an escape. But then after several glasses of wine, the conversation turned to love and philosophy and Riley was hooked. Sharon talked mostly about her partner, who had died the year prior, but her views about love and the pursuit of it had fascinated Riley.

Sharon raised an eyebrow and then tilted her head toward Lisa and Jen. There were at least a dozen others between Riley and where Lisa stood, but she knew what Sharon was motioning toward. "Jeanette tells me that you are still together."

"I don't want to know how much Jeanette tells her friends about her daughter's dating life."

"She only mentioned it because I asked if you were still in the picture," Sharon admitted. "I thought you would have moved on, to tell you the truth, and I wondered if Jeanette had managed to keep you in Denver. So, how are things going with you and Lisa?"

"Fine. I've been busy with work and so has she, but we are doing okay overall." Riley paused. She sensed something underlying Sharon's question. "Why do you ask?"

"Oh, I'm old and nosy, I guess." Sharon glanced again at Lisa. She shook her head then and said, "I should know better than to get into other people's business, but I'm going to ask anyway. How do you feel about Lisa's ex moving back here?"

"Since Lisa has mentioned that Jen still has feelings for her, I don't like it, of course. But I'm trying to trust Lisa." Riley glanced over at Lisa again. She was standing close enough to Jen to kiss her. "You think I shouldn't?"

"I wouldn't."

Riley knew what Sharon was implying, but she needed more than someone's doubt to sway her from believing Lisa. "Why not?"

"Maybe I trust intuition more than a lover's promise. And maybe I've heard something that I wish I could tell you. I know it's none of my business." Sharon sighed. "You were so sweet last year letting me go on about my Cherie. I don't think I let you talk with anyone else that night. After I left, I started to feel awful for dumping all of that on you. Especially at a party. It must have been the wine. Or the combination of that and too much of Jeanette's eggnog. I'm not usually like that. But it was also the first Christmas after I'd lost her…" Sharon held up her glass of water. "No eggnog tonight."

Lisa walked up to them. "Hey, Riley. You're finally here. Working late again?" Lisa gave her a peck on the cheek before Riley could respond. "You know Sharon?"

Sharon smiled. "I met Riley at your mother's last Christmas party. I was just thanking her for giving an old lady a shoulder and an ear last year. I needed it." Sharon clasped Lisa's hand. "Did you know, Riley, I've known Lisa since she was a little girl with pigtails?" She laughed. "Now I feel really old." She pointed to a server carrying a tray of pastries. "Time for dessert, ladies. I'm following those baklava."

Lisa slipped her arm between Riley's. "Tried the shrimp yet?"

"No." Riley glanced over at the tree. Jen had disappeared. She pulled her arm free. "I think I'd like a drink."

Lisa seemed to notice the cool response. "You okay?"

"No."

"What is it?"

Riley stopped the next server who walked by with a tray of filled wineglasses. She took a glass of red.

"You don't like wine," Lisa said flatly.

"I don't feel like eggnog, and I doubt your mom bought beer for this event." Riley took a sip, then set the glass on the nearest counter. It was bitter and she had no stomach for it. She didn't want Lisa to be right about anything at the moment, but the wine was too much.

"Something's wrong. I can tell. You are easy to read."

"You told me once that you would never want an open relationship. I thought it was a funny thing to say, at the time, because we were sitting on the back porch of my old place in Sacramento looking for shooting stars. There was supposed to be a bunch of shooting stars that night, I don't remember why, but the moon was too full to see much of anything besides the moon. I wondered why you suddenly were thinking about open relationships, but when I asked, you said you didn't have a reason."

Lisa stared at Riley. After a long moment, she said, "Why were you thinking about that now?"

"I guess I was wondering if you'd changed your mind."

Lisa shook her head. "Maybe I should ask if *you* want an open relationship. Something you want to tell me, Riley?" Lisa smiled.

Jeanette walked up to them. She nodded at Lisa and then turned to Riley and said, "Everything okay at the clinic tonight?"

"Yeah, fine." For all of Jeanette's gruff exterior, Riley had learned quickly that she was quite sensitive and very capable of deciphering Riley's mood as well as nearly everyone else's. Overall, Riley had to admit that she managed the clinic well, despite her propensity to keep employees that made too many mistakes. Her relationship with her daughter was a different matter altogether. Jeanette did seem to love Lisa, but they clearly didn't get along well enough to exchange more than a few words. This had made Riley's position between them uncomfortable on more than one occasion.

Elaine, the other therapist from the clinic, came up to the group. She had a small plate of crispy fried shrimp and dipping sauce. "Have you all tried the shrimp?"

"My stomach's a bit off tonight," Riley managed when Elaine pushed the plate toward her. "I think I might need some air." She headed for the back patio.

"It is a little stuffy, isn't it? Lisa, do you mind opening a few windows? Just a crack. It's snowing out there, and I don't want to freeze anyone."

Jeanette's patio had a panoramic view of the city, but its lights were blurred by low-hanging clouds. When she stepped outside, Riley nearly bumped into Sharon. "I'm sorry. I just need some air."

"I can imagine."

"I don't want to invade your quiet time here, however."

"Don't worry about it. I used to smoke and on nights like this, I miss it. I just wanted to step outside for a moment and watch the snow fall, you know? Anyway, I'm trying not to reminisce about anything this year. This is my year for moving forward."

Riley shivered. "Sharon, what did you hear?"

"What did I hear? Well," Sharon gazed past her. The house lights struck the snowflakes and made them shimmer as they fell. "Jeanette said something...I doubt she would want me to tell you, however."

Riley waited. She needed to know why Sharon had spoken up in the first place. "Please."

"You know, Jeanette has never liked any of Lisa's girlfriends except you. This Jen is one of her least favorites. She gave me an earful about her after everything that happened in California. I also know she told Lisa that Jen wasn't invited to this party."

"Well, Lisa and Jen are still friends."

"Sweetie, Jeanette called me last week. She said that Lisa and Jen had spent the night here. She was upset that Lisa was back together with Jen and beside herself knowing that you had no clue about any of it. They are definitely more than friends."

Riley realized she'd been holding her breath. She took a step away from Sharon and glanced back at the living room window. She couldn't pick out Lisa among the crowd. "Wait, when was this?"

"Last week."

Lisa appeared at the back door. Her green blouse and black slacks were thin polyester, and she shivered as the wind blew a gust of snow. "Riley, find me when you come inside, okay?"

Riley nodded. Lisa closed the door but watched her for a moment longer before finally turning and walking back toward the family room.

Sharon reached into the pocket of her jacket. "This is my number. I run a bed-and-breakfast in Catori. Remember?"

"Yeah, I do." Riley answered her automatically. She could hardly believe what Sharon had told her. "You invited me out there last year."

"This year I mean it. Come stay for a few nights and clear your head—my treat. I really appreciated you listening to my story last year. I didn't know how much I needed to talk about it until afterward."

Riley took the card. She stared at the picture of a little Victorian house set up on a hill and framed by towering mountains. She had no intention of taking Sharon up on her offer, but she jammed the card in her pocket anyway. "I don't know what I'm going to say to Lisa."

"Let her do the talking. Maybe you two can get through this. If she's honest when you ask her about it…"

"Maybe. But I doubt she'll tell me the truth. And I believe Jeanette's story more than any excuse Lisa is going to come up with."

"And you can't be in a relationship with someone you don't trust." Sharon shook her head. "In my younger years, I would have taken you out to a bar to flirt with some cuties. Sometimes nothing feels better than playing someone else at their own game."

"I don't even feel up for a drink."

"Then go home. Because the last thing you're going to want to see is Lisa and that other woman together."

"You're right. I've gotta get out of here." Riley hugged Sharon. "Thank you for telling me. I feel like shit, but at least I know." She reluctantly headed back inside. The family room felt more crowded than before and the hallway, made narrow by clusters of strangers, was stifling. She cut a path to the front dining area and found her coat. She was finishing with the buttons when she saw Lisa. Jen was with her at the bottom of the staircase.

Riley ducked out the front door as a couple was coming inside, shaking off snow as they did. The sidewalks were covered with powder and crunched as she walked. She turned her car on and blasted the heat, then grabbed her ice scraper and set to work clearing off the windows. Lisa appeared on the passenger side of the car. She glanced at Riley, then climbed into the front seat without a word.

Riley finished scraping. She wanted to yell at Lisa to get out of the car but said nothing as she climbed in the driver's seat. Lisa had turned off the radio, and the only sound was the roar of the heater. Riley dialed the heat down and buckled her seat belt. She pulled out into the street and drove to the freeway.

"Tell me."

"What?" Riley asked.

"What's wrong? You are so pissed that you can't even look at me."

"Take a guess."

Lisa shook her head. "I don't know, Riley. What? You don't want me talking to Jen?"

"You can talk to whoever the hell you want to. You can sleep with them too, for all I care." Riley punched the steering wheel and the horn honked in response. She was parked at a stoplight and the red lights glared back at her. No other cars were anywhere in sight. "Jeanette told her friend, Sharon, about you and Jen…So, that friend of hers, basically a stranger to me, decides to be the one decent person and tells me to get my head out of the sand."

"What the hell did my mom tell her?" Lisa cussed under her breath. "There's nothing to say about me and Jen. There's nothing going on."

"Yeah. Your mom likes to make shit up, right? But you know why I'm really mad? I knew something was going to happen with you and Jen. It was only a matter of when. So, now I'm stuck wondering…Was this a one-time thing or were you fucking around in California too?"

"What exactly did my mom say? Damn it, you won't believe me anyway."

"I won't believe you because I can tell when you are lying. Get out of my damn car."

"Here? Seriously?"

The light had turned green and Riley floored the gas pedal. The car sped through the intersection onto the freeway onramp. "How long have you been sleeping with her? Three weeks ago you promised me that nothing was going to happen. Fine. It did. Just tell me. When did Jen start at the hospital anyway? Last week? How has your week been? Been having a good time?"

"I'm not sleeping with her," Lisa said, nearly yelling. "But you obviously aren't going to listen to anything I say. Riley, would you slow down? The roads are terrible."

Riley slowed down despite her inclination to gun it. They drove in silence until they reached their street. The roads were icy, and the tires slid through the first stop sign. Riley pulled half onto the curb and parked. She closed her eyes. "Tell me what your mom knows."

Lisa was silent for a long while. When Riley turned off the car's heater and started to get out, she said, "Jen slept at my mom's place. One night. My mom was livid. Jen and my mom have never gotten along, so everything was awkward. Jen left as soon as my mom started yelling."

"Thank you, Jeanette."

Lisa shook her head. "I told her nothing happened. But she didn't believe me."

"I can't see why she wouldn't," Riley said. "I mean to me it makes so much sense that you two would just bunk together for the night and stay in your PJs the entire time. I'm sure there was no touching. Fuck, Lisa. When was this?"

"We didn't have sex, Riley."

"You know what?" Riley climbed out of the car. "I don't care."

"I didn't tell you because I knew you wouldn't believe me. Jen didn't have time to find an apartment before they wanted her to start working so she got a hotel room, but the place was terrible and she wasn't sleeping well. On Tuesday she asked if she could stay at my mom's place. She just needed a room for a night or two."

"And then she could sleep in your old room, which is fine because you're not sleeping there anymore, right? But instead of coming home last Tuesday, you decided to stay at your mom's. It was snowing that night, remember? You told me you had dinner with your mom and you'd had a few drinks. You didn't want to drive once the snowstorm hit. Convenient, right?" Riley unlocked the front door and turned to Lisa. "Except, even when you called me, I had this funny feeling that something was off about your story. I remembered later that Jeanette had concert tickets for that night. The next day I almost asked her if she'd liked the concert but I didn't. Know why? I wanted to believe you." She went inside and took off her coat. "Where's your car?"

"I left it at the hospital."

"Of course you did. Why drive when Jen can give you a ride to the party?" Riley didn't wait for Lisa's answer. "I don't believe that nothing happened. That nothing is happening between you two…And I'm so damn tired of this crap."

"You aren't listening to my side of things," Lisa started. "You've already made up your mind because some old friend of my mom's had nothing better to do than spread rumors."

"And you know, if at the very beginning you had said that you wanted to keep Jen in your life, maybe I would have been okay with this. But now I'm questioning everything, because you told me more than once that there was nothing going on—

that nothing would ever happen—because you were done. Why lie?"

"I wasn't lying, Riley. Jen and I are friends. That's it."

Riley shook her head. She hung her coat and took off her shoes. She headed for the stairs, brushing off Lisa's hand as she reached for her. "I don't care how you've made this weird threesome thing all work out in your brain, but as soon as you start lying, I'm done. I'm not going to play along anymore. You can sleep on the sofa or in the spare room. Just don't come into my room."

Lisa sank down on the first stair. Riley heard her crying but didn't turn around. She had no words to comfort her. Riley took off her clothes and showered in the dark. She didn't want to see her reflection in the mirror. She climbed in bed naked, pulling the comforter up to her chin, and buried her head in her pillow. She fought back the tears that pressed at the corner of her eyes.

A few minutes later, she felt Lisa slip into bed. She was naked as well and pressed herself against Riley's backside. "I'm sorry, Riley."

Riley didn't answer.

"You're right. My mom was at a concert, and I had dinner with Jen. But then it started snowing and I didn't want to drive. Jen and I slept in the same bed, but like I told you earlier, nothing happened. We didn't have sex." Lisa ran her hand down Riley's arm. "You have to believe me. I'm so sorry."

Riley didn't move when Lisa kissed her neck. She gave no response to Lisa's hands as they moved up and down her back. She let Lisa roll her onto her back and kept her eyes closed as Lisa climbed on top of her. She felt Lisa's lips lightly kissing her chest, her belly and all the way down to her thighs. Lisa moved Riley's legs apart and shifted in between them. Her tongue flicked lightly over Riley's clit and her hands slipped under Riley's butt cheeks. When she pulled Riley into her waiting mouth, Riley didn't move away. She let Lisa's tongue work up and down and felt the climax coming as a craving that had taken over. She'd lost control. The rush filled her and washed over her in the moment that Lisa's tongue pushed hard on her swollen clit.

Lisa lay on top of her for a while afterward, then rolled off without a word. Riley stared at the ceiling, thinking again of the night Lisa hadn't come home. She'd been trying to spend more time at home in the evenings when she knew Lisa was off. When Lisa called with the excuse about having dinner and drinks with her mom, Riley had wanted to believe her. But Jeanette's concert plans had nagged at her. A few days later she'd finally asked Lisa if her mom hadn't gone to the concert because of the snow. The look of confusion and panic that had crossed Lisa's face as she stammered out an excuse about her mom leaving the concert early had left a hard knot in Riley's stomach. Jen had started work at the hospital that week. Part of her knew that somehow she was the reason Lisa was stammering. But she couldn't accuse her of anything. She'd only had her suspicions to go on then.

* * *

Riley went to the gym early the next morning. She left Lisa sleeping. The place was crowded for a Saturday morning. Her favorite trainer was setting up to teach the morning weight class and waved when Riley walked past. As had been her habit four times a week for the past year, she went directly to the treadmill and ran for twenty minutes to warm up for the class. Her phone beeped several times; she knew it was Lisa, sending a message. Instead of thinking of Lisa or of the image of Jen and Lisa standing together by the Christmas tree, she thought of Sharon. When the class finished and she'd showered, she went out to her car and called Sharon.

"Morning, sunshine!"

"Sharon? This is Riley." Riley wondered if she always answered the phone with that line or if she was expecting someone else to call. "We talked at Jeanette's Christmas party last night."

"Oh, I know who you are, sweetie."

Riley wondered at the surreal friendliness in her voice. "You know, I'm not sure why I'm calling. I guess I wanted to thank you for telling me what you knew."

"Don't worry about it. You want to take a drive up to the mountains this morning? It's beautiful. I spent last night in Jeanette's guest room and drove home with the sunrise. It's a gorgeous time of year."

"That's right. Jeanette does have a guest room, doesn't she?" Riley felt the last bit of doubt that she had been holding on to slip away. Even if Jen had wanted to get out of a bad hotel situation, there was no reason, other than the obvious, that she would need to sleep in Lisa's old room when Jeanette had a nicer guest bedroom available.

Sharon repeated her question. "So, you want to take a drive to the mountains this morning? Snow's sparkling in the sun."

"I do. But I've got clients to see. I'm doing a few home visits today…Anyway, there's no point in running away from this, is there?"

"I suppose not, sweetie. Just know the offer stands. Any time you need it, just call."

Riley hung up the line and did not answer the next call coming from Lisa. She drove to work, stopping on the way at a coffee shop to pick up breakfast. The baristas were friendly with the regulars and knew Riley's order before she said it. She grabbed an extra coffee for Laney, who was supposed to be at work already unlocking the doors, though Riley guessed she'd be running five minutes late as usual.

Riley saw her first two appointments in the clinic and then gathered up her things to head out for her home visits. Her schedule was light, so she planned to grab lunch somewhere along the way. Elaine was working in the clinic that morning and seemed a bit hung over from the party. Riley waved to her as she left the office, and Elaine only nodded in response.

Lisa walked into the front lobby as Riley was heading out. Laney waved to her and said, "Your mom throws a great party!" in the artificially sweet voice she used only while standing at the front desk.

"I'll tell her," Lisa said, forcing a smile. She met Riley's gaze. "Can you take a lunch break?"

Riley glanced at her watch. She had hoped that work would give her an excuse for not having called back, but now that Lisa was at the clinic, the situation was even worse. She couldn't easily dismiss her with Laney watching, and there was no quiet place to talk. All of the walls were thin and too many ears could hear their tone if not every word. "Yeah, sure," she said, heading out the door.

Lisa followed her to the Italian restaurant next door. They sat down in a booth and ordered two half calzones to go. "I know you wanted to avoid me today, but the fact that you don't believe me about Jen is driving me crazy. I can't think about anything else. I'm freaked out that you are going to break up with me over this."

Riley nodded.

"What? That's it? You're just going to agree with me?" Lisa asked.

"I'm pretty sure we broke up last night," Riley replied, her voice several notches quieter than Lisa's.

"No, we didn't. You were mad that I hadn't told you what happened. So I told you. And now you know that nothing is going on, so we can figure out a way to move past this."

"Look, Lisa, I'm not going to kick you out of the house today. You can sleep in the spare room for as long as you need to. We'll be housemates for a while. You can do whatever the hell you want to do with Jen at her place."

Lisa slammed her hands on the table. She stood up, grabbed her coat, then turned back to Riley and said, "Nothing happened, Riley. Nothing."

Riley watched her walk outside. She stopped on the sidewalk for a moment with her hand covering her face, standing in nearly the same spot Riley had stood the night before. Finally, she turned to the left, toward the hospital and walked beyond Riley's view. When Gary finally arrived with their order, he seemed apologetic. Lisa's volume had left little to the imagination. Riley paid for the calzones despite Gary's offer for them to be on the house and headed out to her first home visit. Henry was one of her longest-running Saturday appointments. He wouldn't mind the calzone or the lunch company.

PART FIVE

Omissions

The shuttle driver got Riley from Napa to the Sacramento airport in under an hour, managing somehow to escape getting any speeding tickets in the process. Nearly two hours early for her flight back to Denver as a result, she made her way through the security check distractedly thinking of Ana. With plenty of time to spare before boarding, she walked the length of the terminal twice, then grabbed a slice of pizza for lunch. As she made her way back to her gate, she spotted Blair.

She was seated cross-legged near the gate for an Austin flight. Her laptop was plugged into an outlet and headphones were plugged into her ears. Riley watched her tap the keyboard keys. She hesitated a moment longer and then approached.

Riley waved when she was a few feet away. Blair startled at first, then grinned, pulled her headphones off and jumped up to hug her. "What the hell are you doing in this airport?"

"Long story," Riley said. "It's good to see you. You look great." Riley noted the changes that the past several years had had on Blair. Notably, her hair was longer and she'd lost weight.

Her round face was more angular. Of course, she had the same sky-blue sparkling eyes that had arrested Riley on their first meeting.

"How'd you end up with a layover here from the Seattle flight?" Blair asked. "Oh, I've missed you. What a nice surprise." Blair hugged her again. "My flight boards in ten minutes. I wish we had bumped into each other an hour ago. I've been wasting time watching Internet videos. It's so different being face-to-face. I like the haircut." She rubbed her hand up the back of Riley's head. "You got a close shave. Anyone mistake you for a teenage boy lately?"

"Not lately." Riley grinned. It was an old joke. "I've been walking back and forth for an hour. I don't know how I missed you before." It was really good seeing Blair in person. She felt a pang of guilt letting her think that she was in Sacramento on a layover, but telling her about Ana was more than a ten-minute conversation. "I'm surprised you're just now flying back to Austin. Work let you off this long?"

"I'm going to pay for it over the next few weeks with a crazy patient load, but yes, I got a full two weeks off. And I interviewed on Friday at a practice in Sac. The place is in midtown a few blocks from where we used to live. They liked me. I haven't decided if I'm going to accept their offer, but I'm thinking about it."

"That's great. Did you tell your parents? They're going to love having you back in town."

"I'm not going to mention it until I decide if I'm taking the job. Speaking of which, how's your job?"

"Fine. Sometimes I hate having a boss, but otherwise, I like the work."

"You should think about starting your own practice. You have the money to do it. Why deal with bosses if you don't have to?"

The gate attendant interrupted their conversation with an announcement about early boarding. Several passengers had already lined up next to the gate entrance. Blair unplugged her laptop and packed up her things. Riley clasped Blair's hand. She didn't want to let her go so soon. "I wish we had a little longer."

"Yeah, me too." Blair shouldered her bag. "Wait with me until I board? You never know how many years will pass before we bump into each other again."

They stood together, not talking, just holding hands. Blair's company had always been so comforting, and it was again, as if no time had passed. But there was no spark. Riley didn't long to kiss her. She just wanted to hold her close, for a long night, as they had so many times before, then say goodbye and meet again a few years later. As the last passenger in the waiting area boarded, Blair turned and kissed her. Her lips were soft and familiar. Riley let go of her hand and watched her disappear down the gangway.

A bitterly cold wind greeted Riley as she stepped out of the airport in Denver. The Christmas snow had disappeared, but the temperature felt even lower than before. Riley raced to get a seat in the parking lot shuttle. She had her gloves and hat on but couldn't stop shivering. She found her car and climbed in quickly. As she waited for the car to heat up, she noticed the coffee cup that Ana had left in her cup holder. Ana's lipstick was on the edge of the lid.

She listened to the evening news report as she drove home. It was the first time she'd heard the news in two weeks, and the announcer's voice conveyed the reality of being home in her old life. Her "old" old life, that is. The one she'd been living prior to the snowstorm that had shut down the airport and brought Ana into her present reality.

She texted Ana when she finally made it home, as requested, then walked into the kitchen. She immediately knew that Lisa had been there. There was an empty carton of milk in the recycling basket and a copy of the *Independent* open on the counter. She had dropped by, at the very least, or, more likely, spent nights there while Riley was away. Riley tossed the paper in the recycling basket. She headed upstairs and saw a light on in her bedroom.

Lisa was sitting on the bed. She had her iPad on her lap and closed the cover as soon as Riley walked into the room. "Hey, honey. You're home."

"Yeah," Riley said. "And you're in the wrong bed. Last I checked, you didn't sleep here."

Lisa watched Riley take off her clothes, making no effort to leave. Riley headed to the shower, too tired to make a scene. Lisa came into the bathroom while Riley was still in the shower. Riley watched her put the toilet seat lid down and take a seat. Riley closed her eyes, letting the water pelt her face.

"We broke up."

"Yeah, I remember. We broke up a year ago last December and then again in September. Am I missing a breakup in May too? Or did we just talk about breaking up and you slept in the guest room for a few weeks and then you somehow were back in my bed again?" Riley kept her eyes closed. She dropped her head and the water drenched her hair.

"I mean, Jen and I broke up."

Riley shut off the water and grabbed a towel. She dried off her face and her hair and then eyed Lisa. She realized now that Lisa's eyes were ringed with red. She'd been crying. Riley sighed. "I'm sorry to hear that."

"You never asked how things went in Alaska."

"Because I didn't care. And didn't want to know." Riley wrapped the towel around her waist. "How'd things go in Alaska?"

"Terrible. She got so drunk the first night that she was sick. Then we both got seasick on the second day, and it never really got better. It was awful, really."

"I'm sorry. Why is this important now? It's been four months." Riley wasn't actually sorry that the Alaska trip had been terrible. She doubted that Lisa believed her anyway. "Clearly you patched things up and moved on. And then what happened?"

"But that's the thing…We never did patch anything. It never really worked after the Alaska trip. We didn't click anywhere except in bed. And the thing was, I knew all along. It hadn't worked before, so why did I expect it to this time?"

Riley walked out of the bathroom. "Because she moved out here to be with you."

"Yeah, and apparently I was stupid or crazy for thinking that would change anything." Lisa got off the toilet and followed Riley back into the bedroom. "Anyway, I'm done with her. Once and for all."

"We'll see." Riley smiled. "One cold and lonely February night and I bet you'll be on the phone asking her if she wants company."

"Not likely. She'll be in Sacramento. She's moving back next week. She told me just before Christmas. It was one year, to the day, that you and I broke up. That first time anyway."

"Well, I just found out Blair is probably moving back to Sacramento too. Maybe we should hook them up."

"I'm not up for jokes tonight, Riley."

Riley dug out the flannel pajamas that she rarely wore. With Lisa watching her every move, she wanted to be wearing something. She pulled them on and sat down on the bed. Lisa moved to sit beside her, but Riley held up her hand. "You know you can't spend the night here. Not in my bed anyway."

Lisa stood awkwardly by the bed looking down at Riley. "I take it things are going well with what's her name."

"It doesn't really matter how that is going. I can't have you in this bed." Riley had no interest in talking to Lisa about Ana. She didn't want to admit aloud how well things were going, even to herself. "I am sorry it didn't work out with you and Jen. Really. I don't care anymore what happened before or if you are sorry or whatever, though I have to admit that in some small way I'm glad to hear you didn't have an amazing time in Alaska."

Riley sighed. Lisa had sat down on the edge of the bed and was wiping tears from the corners of her eyes.

"At this point, though, I'd like you to be happy. But I don't want you happy here. Not in my bed. If you want to sleep in the guest room or downstairs on the sofa, go ahead."

Lisa stood up slowly. She looked at the door and then again at Riley as if to test her resolve. "It's weird how things worked out, isn't it? You're so much happier, and meanwhile, I've started on meds for depression. And I was the one who screwed you over." She laughed cynically. "You don't have to tell me things are going well with your little femme crush. I can tell."

Riley turned off the light when Lisa left. She heard her use the downstairs bathroom and didn't hear the front door open or close afterward, so she guessed she was sleeping on the sofa after all. Riley settled under the covers. Ana's face came right to mind. She pictured Ana in the red dress she'd worn on New Year's Eve and the look she'd given Riley when they had finished dancing the last song of the night. Things had gone well, but three weeks was a long time to wait to spend a weekend together.

* * *

Riley circled the airport twice, averting her gaze each time she drove past the blue horse. At three stories tall and with flaming eyes, the horse would haunt her dreams if she didn't carefully avoid it. A fresh snowfall had covered the plains in blinding white. Against this backdrop, the horse appeared all the more sinister. She spotted Ana on the third pass through the loading zone. She had her sunglasses on and was staring at the line of cars. Riley parked and waved.

Ana's smile was infectious. She beamed. "I swear this has been the only layover I've ever looked forward to. Ever."

"It's good to see you too."

"No, Riley, what you meant to say was: 'It's really damn good to see you and I've been pining away for three weeks thinking of nothing but our time together,'" Ana said. She kissed Riley's cheek. "That's what you meant, right? You can drop the 'yeah, whatever' attitude. I see right through it."

Riley grinned. It was true that she had been thinking of little else for the past three weeks other than Ana's visit. She had even started to count down the days, but she wouldn't have admitted it. Riley grabbed Ana as she started past her with the suitcase. She rested her hands on Ana's hips and then kissed her, feeling a rush of excitement as their lips met. "It's really damn good to see you."

Ana pulled away. "That's better. Now pop the trunk."

Riley had canceled her afternoon appointments and rescheduled tomorrow's as well. Jeanette had raised an eyebrow but didn't pry further than to ask if she had a good reason. Riley had told her that she did, and they left it at that. Their working relationship had remained surprisingly unchanged despite the headaches Jeanette was having from Lisa moving back home with her trunk full of drama.

A week after Riley had returned to work, she'd gotten a message from Ana saying that she'd reserved Sharon's cottage. When Riley had called her back, she'd been vague about her plans but seemed to want to avoid going to Riley's place. She was determined that they drive straight to Sharon's. Now that Riley had Ana in her car, she was tempted to ask her to change her mind. She didn't want to wait for another two hours before she could take Ana's clothes off and pull her into bed.

"You sure you want to go all the way to the mountains? We could be at my place in a half hour."

"We've already got reservations. And I've been thinking of the last time we were in Sharon's hot tub together." Ana buckled her seat belt. "You aren't going to change my mind, so don't even try. And this time we'll have snow instead of a torrential downpour. You may have been thinking of what you wanted to do in bed, but I've been thinking of what I want to do with you in that hot tub."

"Okay, sold."

"I thought so." Ana smiled. "So, how did the drama with Lisa finally turn out?"

"Well, her stuff is mostly out of my house."

"Tom finally came for his furniture. We had a big fight over it. I told him he could leave the TV, but he couldn't drop in anymore to watch his games or whatever the excuse was and sort through my mail, check my phone messages or whatever he was doing to generally keep tabs on me. Apparently you left a dirty phone message on my home phone and didn't warn me."

Riley cringed. "I was wondering why you never mentioned that. I was just joking around…but, yeah, it was dirty. No worse than the messages I've left on your cell, though."

"Which are explicit enough." She set her hand on Riley's thigh and inched it up her leg. "I know you like to play games, but I had no idea you were the type to leave dirty messages. I kind of like it."

"My guess is that Tom wasn't impressed?"

Ana sighed. "I think he's figuring out that the ball isn't in his court anymore. In a way, it's good he heard the message. He needed a push."

They reached Sharon's place at dinnertime. Sharon had left her Christmas lights up and the Victorian looked like the set of an old Christmas movie. Sharon met them at the door with hugs. She smelled of cinnamon and cloves and pointed the way to a pot of mulled wine that she'd just finished setting out in the dining room.

"I've only got one couple other than you staying tonight, but I can't resist an excuse to make the wine. Deb likes it too."

Riley glanced over at her with this. "So you guys are seeing more of each other then?"

Sharon smiled. "She moved in last week. We have a lot of catching up to do." She waved her hand toward Ana. "But tonight isn't the time. I know you two have your minds on other things. Ana, I got your message about next month. It's no problem if you want the cottage, but you might consider a room in the main house. I doubt I'll have any other guests and we have central heat here."

"You've already got something scheduled here in February?" Riley asked.

Ana nodded.

Sharon looked from Riley to Ana and then raised her eyebrows. "You gals need to catch up as well, apparently." She went to pour the wine into two mugs and then hurried off to get the keys for the cottage.

"I had a feeling there was something you weren't telling me when we talked last."

Ana sipped the wine and then said, "I wasn't quite ready to tell you. I'm not sure I am now either. There are a lot of details I still need to work out. Can I just say that, yes, I'll be in Colorado in mid-February?"

"I want to have time to get some days off if I can."

"I am only coming for a short trip. And I might not be alone."

Riley didn't look at Ana. She was thrown by the idea that Ana might come here with someone else—of course she could—and glad when Sharon returned at that moment, jingling the keys. "I already fired up the woodstove. It should be toasty in there for you two. And the tub's hot as well. But you might have to dust some snow off the cover."

The cottage was warm as promised. Ana hung up her coat and a few things from her suitcase. She placed everything in neat order before glancing at Riley.

"You're upset, aren't you? I really was planning on telling you. Just not tonight." She brushed her hand up Riley's arm. "I've been thinking of all the other things I'd like to do to you. But we can talk. After would be better."

"I don't like secrets."

"I noticed. Your jaw clenched right up." Ana's hand dropped off Riley's shoulder. She went to the bed and kicked off her shoes. She leaned back and stretched across the pillows.

Riley had lost the urge to take Ana to bed first thing. She didn't like the feeling that something had come between them and had lost her footing when she noticed Ana's set expression as Sharon spoke. The feelings of distrust that so often had come up in conversations with Lisa resurfaced with an unsteadying rush.

"Come here," Ana said.

Riley took off her coat and hung it over the chair. She stood next to the stove, her hands close enough to the heat to be uncomfortable. "I'd really like you to tell me what's going on first."

"What if it is a good secret that I don't want to share with you because I want it to be a surprise? Loosen up. You're too serious sometimes."

Riley went over to the bed. Ana was propped up on the pillows, but her legs dangled off the bed. Riley moved them apart and stood between them. She stared at Ana for a long moment, feeling a pulsing energy between her own legs. "I generally don't like surprises any better than I like secrets."

Ana stuck her tongue out and licked her lips suggestively. She slipped off her blouse and bra. "I want to think about something else for the next hour or two. Maybe you should as well."

"I don't know if I want to."

"Really?" Ana slowly sat up and began unbuttoning Riley's shirt. Riley watched her but didn't make a move. Ana continued, "I'm suddenly remembering how much of a pain in the ass you can be." She finished with the last button but didn't pull the shirt off. She leaned back on the bed and undid her pants, then lowered them past her hips and licked her fingertip. "But I also remember that you are terrible at keeping your hands to yourself."

Riley watched Ana's hand slip beneath her underwear. Ana's eyes were closed and her hand moved back and forth over her groin. Riley gazed at Ana, nearly naked and stretched across the red plaid quilt in a diagonal line. She was so damn beautiful. But it had been a long three weeks. Riley decided maybe she wasn't good at long distance, especially if her experience with Blair was any indication. Her body wanted Ana, but the time apart, and the mere mention that Ana was planning to come to Catori with someone else, brought up all of her old insecurities. She didn't feel close enough to make love to her yet. It was only going to be sex.

"Don't get cold feet on me now," Ana said, propping herself up on an elbow. "I'll tell you everything over dinner. I promise. But I want you now."

Riley let Ana pull her back onto the bed. She had brought toys; a dildo and a harness along with her favorite flavored lube were packed in the overnight bag she'd brought. But she wasn't in the mood for that anymore.

Ana pushed Riley onto her back and leaning over her, asked, "What are you thinking about?"

Riley stared at Ana for a moment, then turned to look out the window. Ana's hand brushed against her cheek.

"Don't," Ana whispered.

"Don't what?"

"You're pulling away. I've told you before—you have no poker face." Ana kissed Riley's cheek, then turned Riley's head so they were face-to-face again. Their lips were only inches apart. "Tell me." Ana waited for Riley to answer. When she didn't, Ana leaned close and kissed her.

The feel of Ana's lips, the faint scent of her body lotion, and then her hands caressing Riley's chest blurred everything else in a dizzying rush. She was already wet. Ana moved on top of her as soon as Riley returned her kiss. Ana's need was impossible to miss. Riley tried to sit up when Ana moved between her legs, but she pressed her back down again. She shifted lower still until her chin rested on Riley's groin. She glanced up at Riley, as if second-guessing herself.

Riley reached for her, massaging Ana's shoulders and back. She closed her eyes when she felt Ana's tongue slip over her clit but kept her hands on Ana's back, trying to follow her moves and then losing track as Ana's tongue brought her closer and closer to a climax. She came hard and quick, hardly recognizing her voice when she cried out.

She shifted away from Ana's lips the moment she came, taking no time to catch her breath. Ana had shifted off her and moved up to the pillows next to her. Riley climbed on top of her. Her orgasm had only increased her need for Ana. She thought again about the toys she'd packed but decided she wanted to feel Ana, skin to skin. Ana was dripping wet and Riley's fingers slid right in.

Riley lay on her back, listening to Ana's breathing, hearing it slow down, then felt Ana's palm spread over her belly. Ana lay against her side, her breath warm on Riley's neck, and neither of them moved for a long while. Riley got up first. She went to the bathroom and when she came back to the room, Ana was sitting up on the bed. She'd put on Riley's shirt but hadn't buttoned it, and her breasts were peeking out.

"I don't think I can wait until dinner," Riley said. She found her overnight bag and pulled out a flannel shirt and a clean pair of underwear. She dressed while Ana watched. "I've had too many bad experiences with women and secrets."

Ana pulled the corner of the quilt up and over her legs. She sat cross-legged on the bed, her gaze now fixed on the flames flickering behind the glass in the woodstove.

"Joe wants out. It's a franchise, so the whole thing is complicated. The thing is, he has a good deal here, but he mismanaged the place right from the start and now he has IRS issues that are just a nightmare."

She paused and looked up at Riley. "I know I could have had that place making money for him. A lot of money. But he wouldn't do anything I suggested. And the corporate folks are pissed because they wanted him to sell out years ago and now there's this IRS headache to deal with on top of everything else. I want to buy him out and run the thing myself, but I don't have enough saved. So I asked Tom to be a partner in the business. He's got the money and he's willing to let me take this on and stay out of my way."

"Wait. You're thinking of managing all of this from California?"

Ana shook her head. "I'm thinking of moving here. Sharon and I have talked. If this all pans out, I'll rent the cottage until the busy season starts in June. I'll be in and out, of course, since I'll still have to do the consulting stuff on the side. I don't think I'll have the winery up and profitable until the end of May, at the earliest, but I want to be doing this full time for a while. A few years, probably. Before I can hand things off to someone I trust. Then I'll go back to consulting. It's a big leap, but I know it could work. And I'll be in Colorado."

Riley sat on the edge of the bed. "You aren't thinking of doing this just to be in Colorado, though, right?"

"No. If that were the case, it would be a hell of a lot easier if I simply bought a townhouse next door to yours."

"And Tom has to be the one with the money?"

Ana reached out and touched Riley's hand. "You're going to have to relax about Tom. Nothing's going on with us. I know it is hard, especially when we are in different states, but you're going to have to trust me."

"But when you said you might not be coming here alone, you meant that Tom might be with you, right?" Riley stood up. "Why did you ask Tom? You could have asked his aunt. He doesn't have to be the one with the money."

"His aunt doesn't like investing in anything she can't manage herself. And if you know of someone besides Tom who happens to have a hundred thousand dollars lying around that I can use as capitol, let me know."

"I might."

"How's their credit? 'Cause I'm not getting a loan with my score alone."

Riley hesitated. "If I'd known you were thinking of doing this…"

"Why would that have changed anything?"

"I don't know. Maybe if I had known before, I would have come up with someone else to be your investor."

"Well, until you find that someone, you are going to have to get over being jealous. Tom isn't my boyfriend anymore."

"I'm not jealous," Riley said, fighting the urge to raise her voice. "I just don't want him to still be a part of your world if I'm going to be a part of it. That's it. I need you to pick. I don't care either way."

"You don't care either way? Bullshit, Riley. You do care. And I have picked." Ana sighed. "Can you hand me my clothes? I think we both need dinner."

Several times during the meal, Riley started to explain why she had issues with Tom, but she stopped herself each time. She didn't want to talk about everything that had happened with Lisa, and yet she doubted Ana would understand why Tom's involvement in any significant aspect of Ana's life was such a deal breaker without the whole story. She almost said that her relationship with Lisa had probably left her damaged goods, but she stopped before the words came out. She didn't want to talk about Lisa at all and she didn't feel damaged. She'd just lost her naiveté.

They left the restaurant without having discussed Tom or the winery at all. Ana clasped her hand, and they walked down the main street of town, skirting the river, now more the size of small creek with frozen patches and snowy banks. They passed the footbridge leading to the section of town that had flooded months ago. The once flooded restaurant showed no sign of damage now. Ana pointed to the sign for the winery. A red Closed sign hung over the main sign.

"Joe's buried himself so deep. They should be open on a Friday night. They've been in the red so long that they have given up entirely. I think that he and his wife are only making wine so they have something to drink at this point."

"Why this winery? The town's nice, but this river could easily flood again next year. Why take a chance on a place that is set up to fail?"

Ana opened her mouth to say something, then clamped it shut and shook her head. "I don't think I need to sell you on my business plan."

"Maybe you should try."

"Maybe, but I'm still trying to get over being mad at you for our argument earlier." Ana shook her head when Riley met her gaze. "And for being so under my skin that I have already put my condo up for sale. The crazy thing is, sometimes I feel like we barely know each other."

Riley stared at the footbridge, weighing Ana's words. Ana had walked twenty paces ahead but stopped now and looked back at her. The building that housed the restaurant and winery was a lovely piece of real estate. She had never considered investing in a business, but it wasn't unrealistic. Not for Ana. The problem was Tom.

She caught up with Ana and slipped her hand in hers. They passed Cheddar's, but the café was already closed for the evening. A few of the other storefronts in town were shuttered for the winter months, but most had just posted reduced hours through the slow season. By late spring, the streets would again be bustling with the tourist crowd.

They reached Sharon's place and headed up the stairs to the front porch. The back path to the cottage was unlit and covered in icy snow, so they took the route through the main house. The house still smelled of mulled wine. Sharon and Deb were on the sofa in the living room.

Sharon waved when they came in. "There's still some wine if you're interested. And if you're looking for company this evening, which I doubt, pull up a chair."

"Mind sharing?" Ana asked Riley, as she filled a mug from the pot that was keeping it warm. She turned to Sharon and continued, "I think we're calling it an early night. But thank you."

They passed the hot tub on their way to the cottage, and Riley cracked the cover enough to reach her hand inside. The water was hot, as promised. "Skip the suit?" she asked, already unbuckling her belt.

"Not a chance. Come on, Riley," Ana said, unlocking the cottage door. "You never know who might decide to come outside."

"There's only one other couple staying here. What are the chances that they decide to use the hot tub when it's freezing out?"

"Get your suit."

Riley awoke the next morning shivering. The wood had burned out overnight. Ana had pulled the quilt up around her and then rolled to one side, leaving Riley half covered. Riley got out of bed and dressed quickly. She set about restarting the fire in the stove with the logs Sharon had left, wishing she'd thought to add logs before they'd gone to sleep. It took some work, but before her fingers had frozen stiff, she had a weak flame working on the tendrils of kindling. Ana slept on, with every bit of bedding wrapped around her body. Riley added more wood, bit by bit, until she could feel the warmth of the fire radiating past the small stoop where she sat.

By the time the fire was burning brightly, the first rays of sunlight had seeped past the edge of the curtains. Ana woke not long after. She glanced about the room until she spotted Riley, still seated between the stove and the wood.

"We need to talk," Ana said, her voice still groggy with sleep.

"Okay, what sort of conversation do you have in mind?"

"I want to figure out how this is going to work. I'm only going to be in this cottage temporarily. Once I have the winery renovated and find the right employees, I won't need to be in this town. But after last night, I'm not sure you want me in Denver like I was planning."

Riley broke the branch she had in her hands in half. The snap was satisfying. "Gonna move on the winery before or after we figure out where we are going with this relationship?"

Ana sat up in bed. She shivered and pulled her blankets up over her shoulders. "You've been doing some thinking too, haven't you? How long have you been sitting over there?"

"The fire burned out and you stole the blankets." Riley shifted closer to the stove.

"Sorry."

"I want to know why you want to do this. Are you going after this winery because you really want your own turn at running the business? Or are you just looking for a reason that makes moving to Colorado make sense?"

"You don't think I should move here for someone I barely know, do you?"

"I don't want to be on the other end of that mistake." Riley studied Ana's face. She couldn't read her expression. Riley stood up and stretched, her legs and arms stiff from sitting on the low stepstool and from the cold creeping under the door. "Well?"

"My answer is both. Yeah, I want my own shot. I want to prove I can turn that place around…And maybe part of it is that I want to show Tom and Madam Bea and all of the rest of his stick-up-their-ass family that I have what it takes. Maybe I am tired of people thinking my looks are what seals the deals."

She sighed. "But I damn well wouldn't have picked this mountain town in the middle of nowhere to do so. In fact, I had been looking at another winery in Santa Barbara. But then I met you. I know it's possible that I'm making a mistake with you." She reached out her hand when Riley came to stand next to the bed. "Am I?"

"Too soon to tell." Riley clasped Ana's hand. She brought Ana's hand up to her lips and kissed it lightly. Ana patted the bed. Riley sat down, letting Ana wrap the quilt over her shoulders and pull Riley close to her. "If you move to Denver, you'll be an hour and a half away from the winery. And I can't move to this little mountain town in the middle of nowhere and expect to keep my job. Or even establish a viable practice."

"I'm not suggesting you should move at all. The way I drive, I can make it to Denver in an hour."

"How much have you discussed with Tom?"

"He's ready to sign the papers. Joe initially approached him about selling. Tom and I shot a few ideas around with Joe, but he was done and we both figured that out pretty quick. The flood tipped the scales against him. It didn't help that he refused to follow through on any of the suggestions we made from the beginning. Tom was actually the one who said I should take over. I know he didn't think that I would seriously consider it. But we talked and he was interested in a partnership."

"Of course he was."

"Riley, he's my *ex*. We're done."

"But he'll still be a part of your life if you go through with this, in more ways than now even. And you admitted that you feel you still have something to prove to him."

"I can promise to you that nothing will happen. But that won't be enough, will it? You're going to have to figure out a way to handle the fact that he'll have a part in this deal."

"I don't want to." Riley paused. She didn't want to talk about Lisa, but she couldn't avoid it now. "You know, what happened between Lisa and me would have happened probably anyway, eventually, but it was her ex that turned things. They worked together and said they were just friends, of course, but whenever we'd have a disagreement, Lisa would be on the phone with Jen. When I worked late, she spent the evening with Jen. They texted all the time, saw each other at work…It wasn't long before they were sleeping together again. I guessed it would happen from the beginning, but Lisa denied everything. It went on for months. I was jealous of Jen, I knew that they were becoming too close, but I didn't want to admit what was happening."

Ana didn't say anything. She placed her hand on Riley's thigh and leaned against her. After a moment, she started rubbing Riley's shoulders, then shifted behind Riley and started working on her neck and back muscles. Riley slowly relaxed as Ana's hands worked on the tight spots. Ana pulled off Riley's shirt and continued the massage, pressing Riley onto her stomach across the length of the bed. A low whooshing sound came from the stove followed by an occasional snap, but the cottage was otherwise quiet. Ana finished the massage and pulled the blankets up to cover Riley. Riley rolled onto her side and Ana lay down next to her. Their lips met and Riley didn't want to stop kissing her. Ana pulled away, finally, placing a fingertip on Riley's lips as they parted.

"Tom doesn't have to be a part of anything in my life. I can still sell my place in Napa, keep the consulting job and rent an apartment in Denver."

"No. I can see how much you want the winery. I think you could turn it around if anyone could."

"It pisses me off that you won't trust me. Can I call up Lisa and tell her off?" Ana grinned. "But, you know, I wouldn't want your ex to be your business partner either."

"And without Tom...you wouldn't get your shot at running the winery. And I'd be the reason you never took the chance when you had it."

"I'll have other chances. Maybe in a place without the flood risk."

"I don't believe that you would actually drop this."

"It's been my obsession since the flood," Ana agreed. "And you were only partly to blame. Like I said, I had my eye on the Santa Barbara place before this one. But in some ways, I think this place could be even better."

"What about Madam Bea? You said she runs the investments for the family anyway."

"I'm not getting into any deal with her that I don't absolutely have to. I trust Tom. He's my ex, but he is a good guy. I can work with him, and I know he won't turn around and double-cross me."

"You did dump him, you know. He might be different now."

"It was mutual."

* * *

Riley took Ana to the airport and then headed into work. She found a sticky note from Jeanette on her desk. Jeanette had left early but was returning that evening and wanted Riley to wait for her. Riley folded the note in half and glanced at her schedule. She had clients until eight o'clock; Jeanette had added her name to the end of the schedule.

Jeanette showed up as Riley was locking the door behind the last client. She unlocked the door and held it open for her. Jeanette held up a plastic bag with two Styrofoam containers inside. "Chinese. I looked at your schedule earlier and knew you weren't going to have time to eat."

"You're right and that smells delicious."

"Good," Jeanette said, heading toward her office.

Riley locked the front door and turned off the lights. She went to the break room and grabbed two water glasses and forks. Jeanette handed her one of the containers when she sat down. "Chef's Special with rice."

"Sounds like dinner."

Jeanette let Riley eat several bites before starting with, "I called Sharon yesterday. I had plans to spend next weekend at her place. I didn't know you were there. She mentioned you were with someone."

Riley set her fork down and took a sip of water. "Lisa knows."

"I'm sure she does. She keeps tabs on everything you do. That isn't what I was getting at. Sharon said this woman was from California."

"I'm not moving, Jeanette."

Jeanette nodded. "That was pretty much what Sharon said as well. I just don't want to find out through the grapevine that I'm going to need to replace you. To be blunt, you see more than half of our clients and there are three of us dividing up the workload. You can do the math."

"In other words, I'm working too hard and we should tell Laney to ease up on my schedule?"

"In other words, I can't lose you unexpectedly. Right now, you're the only one willing to work nights, and although I don't think it is a good idea, you sign up for nearly every weekend. I'm worried you are going to burn out, Riley." Jeanette sighed. "Anyway, I need to know if anything is going to be changing in your life. Before you tell your new girlfriend, tell me."

"You're not going to lose me unexpectedly, Jeanette. But if things work out, down the line I'm going to ask for weekends off."

Jeanette nodded. "Tell Laney to start scheduling you now for only one weekend a month. You need some time to yourself."

"How's Lisa?"

Riley had never asked Jeanette about Lisa. She felt strange asking now, but since Jen had broken up with Lisa, her feelings had shifted. She wanted to know that Lisa was doing okay, but her feeling of compassion didn't extend much beyond that.

Jeanette rolled her eyes. "Don't get me started. You don't want a roommate, do you?"

"You or Lisa?"

Jeanette laughed. "At this point, I don't really care. I'm one step away from evicting her."

"You won't do that and she knows it."

Jeanette nodded. "You're right, of course. But sometimes I'd like to at least threaten it."

"It won't do any good. I won't tell you how many times I've tried to stop her from coming over to my place. I'm going to need to change the locks, I suppose. At least she's stopped spending the night."

"She told me she's thinking of moving to California. Again. Jen lost her job at the hospital here, and I guess she knew it was coming. Lisa told me that Jen had already applied to a few places in California, without Lisa's knowing until well after the interviews. Sounds like the same hospital in Sacramento where she used to work is taking her back. And, as I'm sure you know, Jen broke up with Lisa and then they were back together the next week. I've had it up to here with her drama."

Lisa had told Riley only part of the story, of course. "Well, if she moves to California, you'll get the house back to yourself."

"You're right. I'm not discouraging her from moving." Jeanette paused. "But I would discourage you. I'd like to tell you that you aren't allowed to leave, but that isn't in the contract, unfortunately."

Riley smiled. "You could, however, give me a terrible reference if I try to get a job somewhere else."

Jeanette arched her eyebrows. "I like the way you think," she joked. "So, tell me, how likely is it that this woman you're seeing would move here?"

"It's up for debate."

"But you're definitely not considering moving there."

"I'm not going to move for a relationship. Not again, anyway. Besides, I like it here. Are you going to eat?"

Jeanette opened her container. "I've been too nervous to start. You're sure I don't have to start looking for your replacement?"

"It's probably never a bad idea."

Jeanette glared, pointing her chopsticks at Riley. "You better be kidding."

Riley grinned. "I'm staying here, Jeanette. I promise you'll be the first to know if I ever change my mind about that."

They turned their attentions to the cases that they had seen that day and to devouring the Chef's Special. Between bites, Riley remembered the wine from the winery that Ana had given her that morning. She went out to her car and found the bottle of peach sauvignon. Jeanette nodded approvingly when she held it out to her.

"Might as well pop that open now. I don't want to go home yet. Lisa will be waiting up for me. She knows I'm meeting with you tonight. The Chinese food was her idea. Well, she told me you liked Thai, but the place she wanted me to go to was closed tonight. So you got Chinese instead."

Riley softened at this. Thai food was their standby. Lisa had always picked up an order of pad thai from their favorite restaurant downtown whenever either of them had a rough day. Riley never could be mad at her for long. "Chinese takeout is perfect. Thank you."

Riley missed a call from Sharon while she was in an appointment. Sharon's voice message began with an apology. She'd told Jeanette about Ana. Riley smiled when she heard this. Sharon couldn't keep anything to herself. But if she was trying to warn her, she was a week and a half late. Riley guessed it was more an apology than a warning. In the next breath, Sharon was asking Riley to make another trip to the mountains. Deb had slipped on ice and done something to her knee. She'd seen a doctor but wasn't improving. Sharon wanted Riley to take a look and the rest of her long message was difficult to follow. Riley called her back and was soon making plans to drive up that afternoon.

Sharon greeted her at the door with a big hug. "She isn't an easy patient. I doubt you'll be able to convince her to do anything differently than the way she wants to do it."

"You said she was scheduled to have an MRI yesterday, right? How'd it go?"

"Fine, but of course we won't know anything definitive until probably next week. They didn't talk to her about the results. I don't know the details of her initial visit with her doctor, but Deb made it sound like they think it is only a flare-up of her arthritis, something that should respond to medication. But it's been five days now and there's no improvement. She won't stay off of it, of course."

"Where is she?"

"In the kitchen."

Deb was hobbling from the dishwasher to the cabinets on the other side of the island with a stack of dishes in one hand and a cane in the other. "Riley," she said with an upbeat voice. "Sharon coerced you yet again into helping me. I wish we were up in Williams Canyon working instead."

"Not right now. It's five below with wind chill."

Deb heaved the plates up into the cabinet. "I haven't been outside today. I'm a little stir-crazy." She maneuvered back over to the dishwasher and started stacking up bowls.

"A little?" Sharon continued, "Deb, I can put the dishes away. It will give me something to do when you go lie down on the sofa."

Riley took the bowls out of Deb's hands. "Well, I'm sure you are fine, but why don't I take a look since I'm here anyway?" Riley put the bowls in the cabinet next to the plates.

Deb grabbed a dish towel and dried her hands. She looked at Sharon and something unspoken passed between them. Deb nodded and hobbled out into the sitting room.

Deb settled herself on the sofa, and Riley sat down on the coffee table opposite her. Deb tugged her pant leg up past the knee, cringing with the movement, and then gingerly touched the spot. "Damn it. I hate getting old."

"Twenty-year-olds wreck their knees all the time," Riley countered.

"But if I were still twenty, the rest of me wouldn't feel like a sixty-year-old. One injury and everything else seems to fall apart too."

"Falls apart? Yeah, right. The reason you feel like crap is that you aren't willing to give yourself a break and let this thing heal."

"All right, I'll stop the pity party." Deb jabbed Riley's shoulder. "Look at my leg and let's get this over with."

Riley took a closer look at the injured knee and whistled softly. "Damn, that is swollen."

Deb sighed. She touched it gingerly and then leaned back on the pillows. "I need to stay off it, don't I?"

Riley nodded. She had brought in a duffel bag of her things. She got out an ice wrap, placed pillows under Deb's knee and elevated the leg, then positioned the wrap over a towel on Deb's knee. "Twenty minutes on the knee every two hours, all day. At least six times a day. And no walking unless you have to pee for the rest of the weekend. Are you taking an anti-inflammatory?"

Deb nodded. "And a muscle relaxant. But it makes me too sleepy."

As Sharon watched from the hallway, Riley went through exercises that Deb could try while still on her back. When she was finished, she noticed that Deb's eyes were half closed. "Try and take a nap. I'll take off the ice pack when your time is up."

Sharon had her arms folded. She turned back to the kitchen and Riley followed her.

"I know it's probably nothing, but seeing her lying on the sofa like that brings back all of these memories of Cherie."

"She'll be fine, Sharon. She likely tore her meniscus and maybe the ACL as well. But there's surgery for that, and she's tough, as you know. With the right rehab, she'll be hiking up those canyons again in no time."

"Yeah, I know I'm overreacting. I almost called you back to tell you not to come, but she found Cherie's old cane and was using it to hobble around and I just about lost it." Sharon's voice faltered. "Cherie used the cane when she'd gotten too weak."

Riley placed a hand on Sharon's shoulder, then pulled her into a hug when she shook with soundless tears.

Sharon convinced Riley to stay for dinner after they got Deb upstairs to the bedroom and situated with her leg up and the television in view. It started to snow not long afterward, and Riley agreed to spend the night in one of the guest rooms. Sharon only had four guests for the weekend and clearly wanted the company. Deb had spent most of the afternoon napping and was soundly snoring after they'd brought up her dinner.

Sharon made tea and handed Riley a cup. They sat in the sitting room with the fire crackling and Sharon's jazz music playing on the lowest setting. "Ana is serious about the winery."

Riley sipped her tea. "Do you think it was mismanaged or that it just didn't fit here?"

"Mismanaged. No question about it."

"I think Ana can turn it around, but I keep thinking that she's making a mistake. I don't think this town is really the best spot to invest in at all, not after the past two summers anyway."

"You know how I feel about that. We had a tough time after the fires and then the flood, but the tourists won't stop coming.

Give it five years and this place will be better than it was before. We've had more publicity in the past two summers than we've ever had." Sharon paused. "Of course, the more important question is, should she invest in this relationship with you? She picked this winery mainly because it's within commuting distance of Denver."

Riley nodded.

"I would trust Ana to get any place up and running at its full potential. And I do think that this town could use a little more class. She'll bring that." Sharon took a sip of her tea and grimaced. "I let the tea steep too long. It's bitter."

"And then there's her ex, who will be part of the deal."

Sharon eyed her over the mug. "And you aren't ready for her to be taking this on with her ex? She told me that she was getting a loan but needed his name on the paperwork and his money to back up the loan, of course. How involved do you think he will be?"

"That's what I don't know."

"And you didn't tell her that you have money, did you?"

Riley shook her head. "I considered it. But then, how would that sound? 'I'll invest in this winery of yours, not because I think it is a good idea, but because I'm jealous of your ex's involvement in it.'"

"And she'd ask questions you aren't ready to answer."

"Maybe that is the main reason I didn't say anything. You might have caught me." Riley shrugged. Sharon knew about Riley's finances only because of the troubles the inn had run into after the floods. Sharon had so many cancellations afterward that she hadn't made her usual numbers for the late summer and fall season. And she'd gone into the year on a tight budget because of the prior year's fire. Riley had figured things would be tight and had asked Sharon if she needed any help, short term. Sharon had refused but asked enough questions to finally get Riley to discuss her financial situation.

"Maybe she wouldn't care."

"The problem is, it gets in the way of everything else. We barely know each other. I'm not ready for that part of my life to change how we go forward."

"That is one problem I've never had to deal with, for better or worse. You don't usually tell your girlfriends?"

"Well, not right away. I never told Lisa."

"She didn't ask?"

"No. I paid the bills and kept my investments to myself. It never came up. She never even met my parents. There was a lot Lisa never asked about. But I think she suspected I had extra income…How would it sound to Ana if I brought it up now? I've never figured out how to casually mention a trust fund. And I don't know if I want to fund the winery just so Tom isn't part of her life."

"You definitely need to find a different way to word that if you do decide to tell her." Sharon laughed. After a moment, she said, "Ana is a risk for you in other ways already."

"What risk am I taking with her if I don't get involved in the winery?"

"Don't try and cover up for me, Riley. I know you already love her. You fell in love that first weekend you two were out in the cottage. She is easy to love, isn't she? And this isn't like your feelings for Lisa, who might have hurt you, but you could have taken that or left it and she probably knew that all along. Ana isn't someone to be with so you can pass the time. Once you really have Ana, you aren't going to want to lose her."

Riley considered Sharon's comments about Lisa. It was true that she already had more invested in Ana than she had ever had in Lisa. "Maybe I'm in too deep already. Maybe it's too late to consider the risks. What about Deb? You made the leap you thought was too much of a risk after all. She moved in."

"I'm glad Deb is here." Sharon glanced up at the stairs. "We're good for each other. This business with her knee makes me realize that all the more. But she's convenient. I like her company and she seems to like mine. Neither of us are taking a big risk with this. We both gave our hearts away a long time ago. With Ana, you have more to lose."

"What would you do?" Riley stood up and stretched. She went over to the fireplace and felt Sharon watching her. "Would you step aside and let her go into a partnership with her ex?

Would you try and argue her out of the winery deal? Would you tell her your dirty little secret, that you're a trust fund kid? Or would you just let her go now, before she gets bored and moves on to someone else?"

"You're not really asking that last bit, are you? She likes you, Riley. You don't have to question that part."

"Am I crazy to worry about how the winery will change things?"

"I think it's up to you how it all plays out." Sharon finished her tea and leaned back on the sofa. "When she was here in November, Ana stood just where you are right now, telling me how upset she was that you'd left that day. I gave her your address, but I knew she wasn't going to drop in on you. She has too much pride."

Riley let this last thought sink in. "I'm going to go for a walk."

"You realize it's snowing. And probably minus eighteen by now."

"But you have a hot tub." Riley was already going to the coat closet to get her jacket and mittens. "I need to stretch my legs. I'll jump in the hot tub when I get back."

"I'll leave a towel at the back door."

Riley walked outside. The wind swirled the snow and the porch lights reflected off the flakes, making each one shimmer. The air was too cold to breathe; Riley pulled the collar of her jacket up to her nose to create a buffer. She'd borrowed a wool cap from Sharon and pulled this down over her ears.

It wasn't a long walk to the winery. There were cars parked along the main street, but no one drove past and the sidewalks were empty save for the rapidly falling snow. The wind erased any footprints that may have been left by other pedestrians. The restaurant by the winery had a small crowd of diners, none of whom appeared to be in a hurry to leave.

Despite the Closed sign hanging in the window of the winery, lights were on inside. Riley could see Joe at one of the tables. He was typing on a laptop computer and had a bottle of wine uncorked by a pile of papers. He took a sip from the bottle and then went back to his typing. Riley went up to the window and knocked on the glass. She doubted he would recognize her, but he squinted for only a moment and then went to open the door.

"It's a little cold for a stroll," Joe said. Wine was thick on his breath.

"I'm on my way to a hot tub. Taking the long route. I don't know if you remember me?" Riley paused, waiting for Joe to nod. He did so and she continued, "I heard the flood did you guys in. Ana told me you're looking for a buyout."

He sighed. "It was the last kick. Thank you for your help that weekend anyway." He sat back down at the table. "I'm ready to be done with this mess. We're moving out of the flat upstairs next weekend. I've got a couple keeping this place open four nights a week until Tom takes it over. Between you and me, I don't think he's going to run the place any better." He took a gulp of wine. "Ah well, let him try. Do you want something to drink?"

Riley shook her head. "If you could go back and do it over from the beginning, what would you have done differently?"

"Probably I should have hired someone better looking than me or my wife to serve." He smiled. "And we had a master sommelier come in once and go over the menu. He recommended some changes and a wine and food pairings list that I never implemented. I didn't follow through on any of his suggestions, in fact. Then, of course, the tax audit could have gone better. I should have hired an accountant at the start."

"It would be easier to blame everything on the insurance company. Or the flood."

He laughed and took another sip from his bottle. "Cheers."

Riley chatted with Joe about the weather and then, as they both watched the snowfall grow heavier, Riley decided to head back to Sharon's. She walked back to the B & B with her head down. The biting wind had worsened in the brief time she'd been inside the winery and the accumulating snow was past the top of her boots. She reached Sharon's front steps and trudged up, gripping the rail the entire way. Sharon had left the front door unlocked, but a sticky note instructed Riley to lock up once she'd come inside. Riley stripped off her gear, the wool cap, mittens and down coat. The coat, a Christmas gift from her parents, had already earned her seal of approval. She went to the kitchen and filled a glass of water, then found the towel Sharon had left for her. She hurried outside to pull back the hot tub cover, disturbing a foot of snow as she did, then stripped off her clothes and climbed into the steaming water.

* * *

It hadn't snowed for well over a week and what was left from the last storm had long since melted. For several days, the forecast had sounded more like a spring weather report than a midwinter one.

Riley stood on the footbridge across from the wine shop. A group of boys wandered past wearing T-shirts and tossing a ball between them as they walked. Riley had already taken off her coat and was warm in only a long sleeve shirt with the sun on her back. Ana appeared, finally, at the entrance to the wine shop. She shook hands with Joe and then made her way over to Riley.

"Joe's paperwork is all in order. Unbelievably. Ready for our meeting?"

Riley nodded. "You brought a briefcase?"

Ana patted the case. "This is my thing, remember? Your job is to play the part of the bank, listen to my business plan and decide if you want to give the financial backing to it. I've got Tom's credit, and I need his hundred thousand to qualify, but I want my own loan. I've got to be able to convince the bank that this is a good idea. But I actually think you are going to be harder to convince."

"Me?"

"Unless you've let go of the part about Tom being my partner on this since I last saw you."

Ana's bank meeting was set for the following morning in Denver. Originally, Tom had been going to join her for the meeting with Joe and for the bank meeting as well. When his plans changed and Ana invited Riley to join her, she didn't ask for details. In Tom's absence, Ana had asked Riley to listen to her give a practice run-through of their business plan before the bank meeting. Riley agreed, partly because she hadn't let go of the idea of telling Ana that she could invest in the winery herself. They crossed the street and headed into Cheddar's.

Scott greeted them with a smile. "It's been a while. Good to see you two here. You must have heard Colorado was having an early spring."

"Couldn't ask for a nicer day. Doesn't even feel like February," Ana replied.

Riley hadn't spoken with Scott since the night she'd seen Tom kiss Ana. So much had happened since then. He tapped his pencil on a small notepad. "What can I get for you?"

"I'll take a chai tea," Ana said.

"Of course," Scott said. "And Riley, what would you like?"

"That brownie. I'll have a coffee as well."

"Pick a table. I'll bring it over in a minute," Scott said.

Ana chose the table by the window. She popped open her briefcase and took out a file. "You sure you want to hear all of this? It wasn't just your excuse to get together, was it?"

"I want to hear it. And it was my excuse. But you still have to convince me this is a good idea. How is it going to be different from Joe's attempt?"

Ana pointed at the first page. "Well, some things aren't going to change. I'm keeping the same name, same design on the sign and everything. That is part of the deal with the franchise. But I'm definitely going to redesign several things. The web page, for instance, needs more than a picture of a wine bottle and the contact information. The interior of the place needs a facelift."

She flipped the page. "The metal chairs are going to go. I've got plans to renovate so there is a more relaxed feel to the place. Relaxed, but in good taste. And I have a budget here for that."

She flipped the page again. "Okay, now we get into some numbers for the bank to look at. For the bank loan, I'll have to show Tom's money as collateral; we've set up a partnership and terms for this. I have no intentions of using his money unless I run into some trouble. I'll still have my income from consulting, and I'll have the loan to cover everything else so that there aren't any weird money issues that come up with Tom's role in this. I've looked into the options." She paused when Scott brought over the brownie and their drinks.

Scott winked at Riley. "Enjoy," he said, setting the plate with the brownie in the middle of the table. Oliver was in the kitchen washing dishes, and as Scott returned he leaned over his shoulder to whisper something.

Ana caught Riley's attention. "You're distracted already."

Riley looked down at the page and at Ana's hand, her finger still pointing to the top line. "I'm not distracted. Go ahead."

"Okay." Ana scanned the page and pointed out the important terms of the loan, flipped a page and then started into the plan she had for expanding the food and wine offerings, pairing some wines with small plate appetizers or desserts for a set price, and then the marketing campaign. Joe had resisted doing any advertising beyond the small paper with a circulation limited to the residents of the town. When she finished, she leaned back in her chair. "You aren't going to say anything, are you?"

Riley picked up the file. "In my role as the bank? I think the plan looks solid."

"And in your role as my girlfriend?" Riley twitched at the term, but got her expression under control, she hoped, before Ana noticed. Ana broke off a piece of Riley's brownie. "You aren't going to answer me right away, are you? I'm learning that you take your time with everything. I need to get used to that."

"Not everything, just the important things."

Ana shrugged. "I like that you don't say things that you don't actually mean."

Like "*I love you,*" Riley thought. She set the file down and looked over at Ana. She hadn't said anything when Ana pecked her cheek with a kiss and said, "Love you," right before she dashed into the airport the last time they'd seen each other. Ana had almost missed the flight. She had texted Riley as she was boarding with two words, "Next time?" She'd only had a three-hour layover and it wasn't nearly enough time together, but they had this long weekend planned for only a few weeks later.

"How's the brownie?"

"Good. I like the crispy edges," Ana said, breaking off another corner piece.

"Perfect. I like the moist middle."

"I could have guessed that."

Riley sipped her coffee and watched Ana take chunks from all around the edge of the brownie until there was a stamp-sized circle left. Riley reached for this, popping it in her mouth in one bite. "I like it. Not as much as I like you, but it's pretty close."

"I feel that way about chocolate in general."

Riley finished the last sip of her coffee.

Ana stood up. She stretched her arms and looked out the window. "Want to walk with me?"

They walked along the road above the river, following the snaking course of it and stopping frequently to notice how low the water level was compared to the flood marks from months ago. They reached the place where the river tunneled under the road and stopped. Ana leaned on the wrought-iron fence that bordered the river bank. The water coursed ten feet below, the sound of it subdued from the roar it once was to a shushing background noise.

"I'd sign on to the bank loan. If I were one of the loan guys, that is. And I'm going to be okay with you and Tom working together."

Ana gazed at the water. "I thought you were going to grill me about flood insurance. I had this whole argument ready." She turned toward Riley. "But then you don't do what I expect half of the time."

Riley slipped her arms around Ana's waist. "I love you."

Ana brushed her hand across Riley's cheek. "I love you too." She stared at her for a moment, then leaned close and kissed her. Ana smiled. "You made me wait for that one."

They drove back to Denver that evening. Ana fell asleep as soon as they got on the freeway, woke briefly to apologize for falling asleep and then fell asleep again. Riley parked in front of her house and gently nudged Ana awake. She jolted at Riley's touch, then rubbed her eyes. "We're here."

"I slept the whole way?"

"You did," Riley said, unfastening her seat belt. She started to get out of the car and then sank back into her seat. "Damn." Lisa's car was parked across the street.

"What is it?"

"Lisa's here." Riley turned to look at Ana. "I swear she hasn't been by in a month. I don't know why she's here now."

Ana looked up at the house and Riley followed her gaze. The light was on in her bedroom window. "Do you want to go in alone and talk to her?"

Riley shook her head. She pulled out her phone and called Lisa's number. Her call went right to voice mail. "There's no reason you should wait out here. Let's just go in."

Ana reached for Riley's hand. "What if she's up in your bed waiting for you?"

Riley sighed. With Lisa, that was a real possibility. "Then I will definitely want you as my backup. I swear she hasn't been over here. At least, not while I've been home."

"Did you ask her to give your key back?"

Riley shook her head. "Guess I should, huh?"

"Tom hasn't given me his key back yet either." Ana opened her door and glanced back at Riley. "See, there is something appealing about moving to a completely new place, isn't there?"

Lisa had left the television on downstairs. The sound of canned laughter filled the room. Riley found the remote and turned off the show. The house smelled of microwave popcorn, and a half-eaten bag was on the sofa. Riley grabbed this as she headed toward the kitchen. She tossed it in the trash and scanned the mess on the counter. Lisa had also made a frozen pizza and eaten a quarter of it. The remainder was on the kitchen table. Ana walked over to the table. She touched the pizza crust. "It's cold. She's been here for a while."

"Thank you, Sherlock," Riley said drily. She looked up the stairs, debating the idea of suggesting they get a hotel for the night.

"Why don't you go up alone and if I don't hear you after five minutes, I'll come save you," Ana said, clasping Riley's hand. She pulled her close and kissed her, then smiled. "Tell her your bed was already reserved."

Riley sighed. She let go of Ana and headed upstairs. Lisa was asleep in her bed, snoring softly. She had left the bathroom lights on, but the main light over the bed was off. Riley sat down next to her. She placed her hand on Lisa's naked shoulder and gave her a light shake.

Lisa's eyes fluttered open and then shut. "Oh, hi."

Riley dropped her head to her hands. Lisa's sweet face was easier to appreciate when she was asleep than when she was awake. Riley stood up after a moment and went to turn off the bathroom lights. She picked up her phone and searched for a hotel, called the number to reserve a room, and then headed downstairs. Ana was putting the pizza in the refrigerator.

"How would you feel about spending the night with me at a hotel downtown? My parents stayed there when they came into town a few months ago just to try it out. My mom likes trendy boutique places that rarely advertise and read about this one in some online thing. I called and they have a room available."

"Wait. You want to get a hotel room instead of kicking her out of your bed?"

Riley sighed. "I thought you probably wouldn't like the idea."

"No way, Riley. She can't spend the night at your place anymore."

"She hasn't been here. This is the first time, I swear. I'm guessing that her mom told her I was going to the mountains and she figured I'd spend the night there." Riley noticed Ana's set expression and continued, "Look, I can't do it. She's sound asleep."

Ana grabbed her things without saying a word. She headed for the door. Riley followed, thinking of Lisa upstairs in her bed and the fact that for a moment she'd longed to crawl into bed with her. The impulse had caught her off guard. She locked the front door and went to the car. Ana was already standing next to the passenger door. She didn't meet Riley's gaze.

Riley unlocked the car door. She noticed Ana's hesitation. "It's a nice place. You'll like it."

Ana sat down in the passenger seat but grabbed Riley's keys as she started to turn the car on. "You still have a thing for her, don't you?"

Riley leaned back in the seat. "She hasn't been here in months, I promise you. We haven't slept together since I don't know when. I have no idea what she's doing in my bed tonight, but I have nothing to do with it."

"Tell me yes or no, Riley."

"Nothing is going on with Lisa and me." Riley slapped the steering wheel and a honk squeaked out in response. Riley thought again of Lisa's sleeping face, the curve of her neck and the bump in the blankets where her naked shoulder had pushed them up. Was she telling Ana the truth? "I couldn't go back to her after everything. Too much happened that ruined anything good that we had."

Ana waited a long minute before responding. She had Riley's keys still in her hand. She clicked the tiny penlight on and off a few times, sending a beam of light through the windshield. The glow was too weak to penetrate further. "You realize that you didn't actually answer my question, right?"

"My answer is no. I'm not holding a torch." Riley knew she couldn't be in a relationship with Lisa again. If she thought about it long enough, she didn't want to cuddle with her either. Riley couldn't deny that in some ways, she was still attracted to Lisa, sometimes. But she knew the impulse she'd felt in the room wasn't one she would actually follow through with, regardless of Ana.

"Then go send her home. She doesn't belong in your bed anymore. And I'm not going to a hotel with you while she's sleeping up there. When I fly out tomorrow, I don't want to be thinking of how you are going back home to her."

"I'm going straight to work after I drop you off."

Ana dropped Riley's keys into her purse. "No hotel."

Riley knew by her tone that Ana would not change her mind. She climbed out of the car, again, and then asked for the keys. Ana fished them out. "You're staying here?" Riley asked.

"I don't even want to say hello to her. I don't need to be a part of this."

"You're right," Riley said. She closed the door and went back to the house. When she got up to her bedroom, she switched on the overhead lights. Lisa made no response. Riley found Lisa's clothes, strewn about the floor and pulled the blankets back. Lisa shivered and brought her knees up to her chest. She rubbed her eyes when Riley started putting on her socks.

"What are you doing? It's late."

"You can't stay here, Lisa."

"My mom has guests tonight. It's just for one night, Riley."

"Your mom has a guest room. They aren't staying in your room, are they?"

"They're using my bathroom."

"So don't shower." Riley finished with the socks and found Lisa's underwear next. She inched them up to Lisa's knees and then started with the pants. "Why is it so much harder to get someone else dressed? It's so easy to get someone undressed."

Lisa rolled over and kicked off her pants. "Just come to bed, Riley. Don't give me a hard time about one night. I've missed you and I wanted to cuddle. You weren't here. I made pizza thinking you'd be home soon, but it got late and I was tired." She reached for the blankets, pulling them up to cover her chest.

"I don't want to cuddle with you, Lisa. Ana's down in the car waiting. You have to go."

Lisa opened her eyes at this. "Your Trixie is here? So you're kicking me out because the new girl is waiting for the spot. Nice, Riley. Tell Trixie this bed is taken. I'm sure she could get paid to sleep with someone else."

Riley gritted her teeth. Lisa called everyone she didn't like to work with a Trixie. Even male nurses were sometimes given this title. The beauty that she'd seen in Lisa's sleeping form was gone. Riley stood up. "You've got five minutes, Lisa. Get dressed and leave."

Riley went back outside to the car. She climbed in without saying a word to Ana. Several minutes later, the light in the bedroom turned off. Riley sighed. Ana reached out and took her hand. "I know you feel like an asshole making her leave, but she broke the rules you gave her."

Lisa emerged finally. She glanced up and down the block, then spotted Riley's car and stared at them for a moment. She crossed the street and climbed into her car. A moment later, the lights flashed on and her engine roared. Riley looked over at Ana. Her jaw was set, and it was clear she was still upset.

"Maybe we should go to that hotel," Ana said.

"What? You're joking, right? I kicked Lisa out so we could stay here, and now you want to go to the hotel?"

"No, you kicked Lisa out because she had no reason to be in your bed." Ana shook her head. "Don't make this thing my fault." She motioned to Lisa's car. "The fact that your ex hasn't let go of you isn't my issue, it's yours. I don't like the idea of crawling into the same bed she warmed up."

Finally Lisa pulled out of the parking space. She made a U-turn in front of Riley's car and then hit the gas. The old Toyota's tires spun on the gravel. A moment later her car disappeared down one of the side streets. "It isn't like she was doing anything up there. She was just sleeping."

"What if it had been Tom in my bed?"

Riley gave a reluctant grin. "You got me. I'd be pissed. And I'd want clean sheets."

"Thank you." Ana sighed. "And yes, you're going to change the sheets."

Riley nodded.

"I got a text from my Realtor while you were up there. Someone made an offer on my place." Ana looked at Riley, as if waiting for a response but then continued, "It's a good price. I have to look everything over, but it sounds solid. I'll probably take it."

"I didn't know you had listed it already."

"It went on the market on Wednesday. I didn't think I'd get an offer this soon."

"I know you have it set up with Sharon that you are going to rent the cottage, but you could just as easily stay here for the next few months. It will take a while to get the bank approval and do the transfer...My place is closer to the airport and you can keep doing your consulting work until you're ready to be at the winery full-time."

"You're asking me to move in with you after we've been dating for how long? You are still edgy when I call you my girlfriend. Yeah, I noticed."

"I'm not edgy. And if you are living here, you'll see that Lisa isn't part of my life anymore." Riley paused. The real reason she wanted Ana to move in was harder to state out loud. She hesitated and then spit it out. "I think we need to see if our real lives, work, everything else, can fit together. Since we've met, one of us has always been on vacation when we've been together. I want to know if you still like me when I'm there every day."

"You're worried that I'm going to get bored with you?"

"Maybe."

Ana sighed. "So what happens if living together doesn't work out? What if it's just the thrill of getting to know each other that has made this work? Will we wake up one day and realize we are in two different worlds even if we live in the same house?"

Riley stared at Ana without answering. All of Ana's questions had been circling round in her mind for days. This was what she had to know before she could commit. Falling for Ana was easy. But could they last? Lisa's prediction of Ana tiring of her in a few months still preyed on her mind. She'd also wondered if she would tire of Ana. Would everyday life push their relationship the same direction as had happened with all of her previous relationships, to a place where she used the word love to mean little more than a complicated friendship?

PART SIX

Truth or Dare

Ana was awake, sitting up in bed and staring out the window. Snow was falling and the crystals were so small they looked like sugar when the wind picked up. Riley reached for her, but Ana made no move toward her. Riley closed her eyes, thinking she could slip back asleep if she didn't glance at the clock. It was too late in the season to enjoy a snowy day. By the time April rolled around, she was completely over winter.

"Do you have plans for Easter?"

Riley stretched and rolled on to her side. It wasn't likely she'd fall back asleep anyway. She propped her head up on one elbow. "When's Easter?"

"Next weekend." Ana picked up Riley's phone. "You know, I have never looked at your phone. I haven't checked your email, peeked at texts, scanned your appointment schedule, nothing."

"Unusual for you, I take it?"

"Maybe." She tossed the phone to Riley. "But I like not knowing."

Riley rubbed the sleep out of her eyes. She clicked on her calendar. "I'm not working. And that will be my third Saturday off this month. I have to admit, I love not working weekends."

"You do know that Easter is on Sunday, right?"

"Yeah, I know, but when I'm doing something with you, I need to plan on it taking all weekend."

"You make me sound high maintenance." Ana stretched on the bed. She picked up her own phone and scanned through her messages. Riley watched her click over to her email and scan through this as well. She looked over at Riley. Finally, she set the phone down and said, "I'm going to Lodi for Easter. I was thinking maybe you could come with me."

"Wait a minute…Are you asking me to come meet your family?"

Ana folded and unfolded the top hem of the sheet. She eyed Riley but was silent for a long minute. "It sounds crazy when you say it out loud. Maybe it's a bad idea. Maybe I want to think about this a little longer."

"Too late. You already invited me. I'd love to come."

"I'm probably going to change my mind. Why would I want to torture you with my family?" Ana got out of bed and went to the bathroom. She had the habit of leaving the door open and continuing their conversations while she peed. "Don't buy your ticket yet. Give me twenty-four hours to decide that I am totally insane for even suggesting this."

"Why wait twenty-four hours? I like the spontaneous you who throws caution to the wind. Better than the creepy one who looks through her girlfriend's phone." Riley climbed out of bed and pulled on a pair of underwear and jeans. She went to the window and opened the drapes. It had snowed overnight, and her car was covered in several inches of white.

Ana came out of the bathroom and stood by Riley. "My family is crazy, you know."

"I only know what you've told me, and they don't sound all that crazy."

"Clearly I should have elaborated. I've got some stories," Ana replied. She brushed her hand up Riley's arm, then leaned close to kiss her neck.

"I'm going to ask them for stories about you," Riley taunted. "I bet your sisters have a few good ones that you'd never tell."

"See? I take it back. You can't come."

Riley grabbed Ana and spun her around. "Too late. You asked and I'm coming."

"Aren't you late for something?" Ana asked, pulling out of Riley's arms. She arched her eyebrow when Riley reached for her again. Ana slipped past her grasp and went to the closet. She pulled out the overnight bag that she kept packed and always in the same place in the closet. "You're meeting me this evening at Sharon's, right?"

"Yeah, I have appointments until five. I'll head out after that. Depending on the roads, I should be there after you've changed your mind twice about me coming with you for Easter."

"Or three times," Ana replied. She smiled, but the expression on her face was somehow somber.

* * *

Riley finished up with her last client and slipped out of the office without checking the reception desk for messages. The sun was dipping low on the horizon and stubborn patches of snow glared in the light. Riley had made the drive to the mountains enough now that she had every route timed. More often than not, Ana would drive to the winery first, Riley would meet her in the evening and they'd spend the night in Sharon's cottage before driving back to Denver the next morning. This had been the routine, at least, for the past month. Ana had to travel for the better half of each week, but she planned her trips so she was back in Denver by Thursday or Friday and they'd had nearly every weekend together. Since her conversation with Laney about scheduling, Riley'd had only one weekend of appointments each month and fewer evenings as well. Laney complained about the hassle of fitting in the regular clients, but Riley had no complaints at all with the lighter schedule.

Ana had moved in with Riley shortly after she'd heard that her condo had sold. She'd only brought three suitcases and the overnight bag. The rest of her things were in storage in California. Riley had been partly relieved that Ana had only come with suitcases. It made the move feel like a low-pressure trial. Ana had given no hint, though, about when she planned to bring out the rest of her things, and Riley had begun to wonder how long the trial period would last.

Riley parked in Sharon's nearly empty lot and cut through the backyard to the kitchen. She tried the door and found it unlocked as usual. Deb was in the kitchen, her leg in a brace and a frying pan in her hands. She had a red plaid flannel shirt on with the collar turned up. She raised the frying pan, greeting Riley.

"Your gal isn't here yet. Sharon's in the front room chatting with some guests. Hungry?"

Riley shook her head. She was hungry, in fact, but she'd had Deb's food one too many times. Deb cooked like an old bachelor, lacing things with extra salt instead of spices and adding ham or crumbled bacon to nearly every recipe, including spaghetti. Somehow, Sharon didn't seem to mind. "How is rehab going?"

"I do the exercises they tell me to do. Maybe not every day. I haven't had much pain, though, since the surgery. And the hot tub helps."

"Do the exercises every day," Riley said. "You aren't going to be climbing up the side of William's Canyon this summer unless you are serious about the rehab. It doesn't take that long."

The door to the dining room swung open and Sharon popped in. "I'm going to be upstairs setting up the Purple Room. Just took a reservation for the next three nights. Can you answer the door if anyone knocks?" She paused long enough to see Deb's head nod, then turned to Riley. "Want to give me a hand with the sheets? I had a late checkout this afternoon and didn't quite finish with the rooms."

Riley followed Sharon upstairs, her arms filled with folded sheets and towels. The Purple Room, the largest in the house, was equipped with a king-size mattress, a sitting area and enough space for a full-size cot as well, if requested. The attached bathroom had a Jacuzzi tub and a view of Pikes Peak from the window above it. The towels were dark purple, as was the duvet, but the rest of the room was decorated in a woodsy fashion with pine furniture and photographs of mountains and rivers.

Sharon had bedmaking down to a science, and Riley did little more than hand her the requested linens. When they'd finished with the room and were preparing to leave, Sharon hesitated. She stood in the doorway and then turned to Riley. "I've been waiting for a chance to catch you alone so I can ask… How are things with you and Ana?"

"Good, I think." Riley paused. "She invited me to come to her family's Easter out in California."

"And?"

"I think I'm going."

"You don't sound all that excited. Not quite ready to meet her family?"

"I want to meet them. She's told me enough stories that I'd like to put faces to the names, at least. But she isn't out to her family."

"And that's going to change when she shows up with you. She's not going to give them any warning?"

"I'm still not sure that she won't change her mind about taking me along. Chances are probably good that I'll be spending Easter in Colorado wondering why I didn't pick up an extra shift."

"Well, even if she does, the fact that she's even considering it tells you that she thinks things are going well enough between the two of you." Sharon went out into the hall and opened a cupboard. She handed Riley two individually wrapped chocolate mints. "One on each pillow, please."

Riley placed the chocolates and then straightened the shams. "The thing that is bugging me is that things are going well. Almost too well…I've never been with someone that I am so excited to see every time she walks in the door. I think about her more than I've ever thought of someone. It's distracting. Every time she leaves on one of her work trips the house feels so empty, I almost wish she wouldn't come back because I know she'll have to leave again and I hate the days that she's gone so much. That sounds crazy, doesn't it?"

Sharon laughed.

"At the same time, I can't wait for her to come home. And in the back of my head, I'm waiting for her to tell me that she's getting back with Tom. I've started to worry that I'm falling too hard."

Sharon placed a hand on Riley's shoulder. She didn't say anything, but her expression made it seem that she understood. Riley thought of their first conversation, two years ago, about falling in love. At the time, Riley hadn't thought she was in love with Lisa, at least not the way Sharon talked about how she'd fallen for Cherie. She had doubted that she'd ever feel the way Sharon had described. Now she knew the joy and pain of the highs and lows that came with really loving someone, and she wasn't certain she'd ever be the same.

"Sharon," Deb called up the stairs, "there's a couple here. They don't have a reservation, but I told them I think we have room."

Sharon glanced at Riley before she turned to head downstairs. "Stop overthinking this. Just slightly terrified is how you are supposed to feel."

Ana met Riley in the front living room. She leaned over Riley's book and kissed her. "I shouldn't distract you from that story. It's probably more interesting than anything I have to say tonight."

Riley set the book down. "Long day?"

Ana had changed out of her slacks and into a pair of sweats. "I want to order takeout. Or maybe delivery. Pizza?"

Riley reached for her phone and found the number for their favorite pizza place in town. "Anything's better than Deb's cooking." Deb and Sharon were in the kitchen eating, and their muffled voices filtered through the swinging door.

"I met with the chef I was ready to hire. He looked so good on paper, and he nailed the phone interview. He isn't going to work out. Showed up stoned. Who does that?"

"It's legal in this state."

"Don't even start," Ana said, frowning. She waited for Riley to talk with the pizza guy, then added, "I want olives."

Riley finished the order and then reached for Ana. She pulled her into a hug. "What about the gal Sharon knows? She doesn't have the fancy degree from a French cooking school, but she made really good little quiches. Sharon says she can make almost anything."

"Yeah, I'm sure she can. And I didn't miss the fact that you flirted with her for a good twenty minutes. I'm not surprised you remembered her quiches."

"I wasn't flirting with her. There is a slight chance that she was flirting with me. I'll give you that."

Ana arched her eyebrows. "Mini-quiches were fine for Sharon's party. But yes, I'd really like someone from a fancy French cooking school. They need to know how to pair food with the wine. And I want people to be excited about the menu. I need this to be several steps above a cheese and cracker platter. I want people to think about coming to the winery because of the wine and also because the menu sounds good enough to eat. For that, I need a real chef."

"Okay. Anyone else on your short list?"

Ana shook her head. "I'm reposting the listing. If I don't find anyone by May first, I might have to consider the quiche girl." She pointed a finger at Riley's chest. "Maybe. Depends on whether I want to deal with her flirting with my girlfriend when I'm not looking. At least I already have the servers lined up, assuming none of them decide to flake before their start date. The chairs arrived today. They look good. I got the window guy scheduled for Monday. Things are coming together." She reached for Riley's hands and positioned them on her shoulders. Riley fell into the massage routine. Ana's neck and shoulders were always tense, but she loosened up easily.

The bank had approved the loan, and Ana had already finished most of the renovations on the winery. Joe and his wife had moved out of the apartment with the plan to stay in town, but their forwarding address was Kansas. They had taken with them more cases of wine than the transfer allotted. Ana had noticed the discrepancy but decided to write the cases off as a loss rather than chase Joe down in Kansas. The accountant, who had longed to wash his hands of any dealings with Joe, agreed. By mid-May, Ana planned to have a reopening party. She had invited all of Sharon's friends, which was a little more than half the town, Riley guessed. Tom was scheduled to come as well, of course.

"So. I'm not going to change my mind. I want my family to meet you."

"Are you going to let them know beforehand that you are bringing someone?" Riley asked.

"No. They just get to be surprised. I can't make that phone call without getting too many questions I'm not ready to answer. Not over the phone, anyway."

"You think it is going to be easier in person?"

Ana looked up at Riley. "Probably not. But with the right drink, maybe."

"Okay, let's do this. Can we buy the tickets now?"

"I won't change my mind. Where else would I want to be next weekend but in Lodi—with my girlfriend?"

Riley grinned. She wanted to tell Ana how happy she was about the trip but didn't want to add any more layers to what was already a pretty complex situation. In some ways, this felt more important than Ana deciding to move in with her. Even though she knew Ana had told her that she hadn't brought any of her past partners home to the family, the fact that she wasn't out to her family had made Riley question whether or not she wanted their relationship to be long-term. She wanted to admit that she'd told her parents many things about Ana and that she wanted them to meet her as well. But with Ana being closeted to her family, it didn't feel right to talk about her own.

"Lodi for Easter. Why would you want to go anywhere else, right?" Ana added, her voice becoming distant. Riley was finishing the massage when a knock came at the front door. One of the guests had forgotten his key. Sharon and Deb came out to the front room then and started chatting with the guest about the local restaurants. Not long after, the pizza arrived, and Ana and Riley headed to the cottage. Riley had mastered the woodstove, finally, and could usually get a good fire going even before Ana had unpacked. The place now felt like a second home.

* * *

The car rental line was long, and the guy working the front desk looked like he hadn't slept in two days at least. He took off his glasses and rubbed his face every few minutes and seemed to be annoyed by every customer that stepped up to the counter. Riley had left all of the details of this trip up to Ana, so she found a seat with a view of the parking lot and sat down with their luggage. She dozed until she heard Ana's voice.

"No, I reserved a standard." Ana held up her printout. "Nissan Altima or similar, see?"

The man at the counter shrugged. "We have the reservation for an economy, Ms. Potrero. I can show you my screen. That's the Kia Rio. You can pick the color. We have red or silver." He took off his glasses again and rubbed the bridge of his nose. "What would you like, ma'am?"

"A Nissan Altima or similar. I don't care what your screen says," Ana said, her volume increasing. She shoved the paper across the counter and jabbed her finger onto the page. "This is my reservation. You need to figure out a way to make this work."

"I'm sorry, ma'am, but as you can see, we have had a number of reservations. We've been very busy. The only car I can offer for that price right now is the Kia. You can pick the color. The red is very nice."

"I would like to speak with your manager, please."

Riley didn't need to look at the expression on the man's face. Ana's tone had changed, and her volume had dropped suddenly. Riley had heard that change in her voice before and knew well enough that the man at the counter wasn't going to get anywhere if he tried another of his standard placating lines. She couldn't see Ana's expression, however. The man at the counter tapped his pen against the edge of the keyboard and then turned to head into the back room. He was gone for no more than two minutes when he reappeared with another man. "This is my manager, ma'am."

"We have no Nissans at this location," the manager said.

Ana nodded. "Or similar."

The men exchanged a glance before the manager said, "Well, I do have a Dodge Charger available, but there is an additional fee, of course."

"No additional fee. I'll take the Charger for the quoted price."

"Ms. Potrero, the Charger is a full-size vehicle," replied the guy with the glasses.

Everyone in the line seemed to be glued to the scene at the counter. No one was checking their cell phones or shifting their feet with irritation at the wait. Ana stared at the manager. He shifted his eyes from Ana to the computer screen and to the line of waiting customers. Finally, he stepped up to the computer screen. A moment later, he handed Ana the paperwork and a set of keys. "Brian will be happy to show you where the Charger is parked."

"I'm sure he will," Ana said.

Riley cringed at the tone. She wanted to explain to Brian that it had nothing to do with him or the car. She picked up their two bags and didn't make eye contact with Brian. Ana was two steps ahead.

Riley waited until they had pulled onto the highway before glancing over at Ana. "You want to talk?"

"About what?"

"I don't know, the weather?" Riley took off her ball cap and ran her fingers through her hair. She stared out the window. Ana had been in Atlanta for the work week. She'd been in Denver less than twelve hours before their flight to Sacramento. Riley had picked her up at the airport after work late on Friday night. They had said barely two sentences to each other before they were back at the airport the next morning.

Ana swerved into the fast lane. "What is it?"

"What do you have against Kias?"

"The car? Have you driven the model they wanted to pass off on me?" She didn't wait for Riley's answer. "I have. There's no room in the trunk or the back seat. Anyway, I'm a platinum member with them, and I've never had to deal with crap like that. That guy needs to be fired."

"We have two little bags. What are you planning on doing with all of the room in this car's back seat?"

"I don't know. Any ideas?" Ana shook her head. "You have no idea how many rental cars I've driven. The point was, I've given them a lot of business and I expect certain things from them or they are going to lose me as a customer. At several of the airports I don't even have to wait in their damn line. That guy had no clue."

"You know, forget about it. I don't want to talk about rental cars," Riley said. "I want to talk about what we aren't talking about."

"You're going to have to give me a little more to go on there. What aren't we talking about?"

"Why didn't you want to tell your sisters that you were bringing someone for Easter? I can understand not wanting to tell your mom, but why not anyone else in the family?"

"If I tell one, I tell them all. Anyway, I don't want to talk about it. They'll figure out I'm with a woman, and we can skip the conversation. Let's drop this."

"You are about to come out to your family, and you don't want to talk about it at all?"

"Not really." Ana glanced at Riley, then eyed her rearview mirror. "So? What do you want me to say?"

Riley switched on the radio and found a station playing pop songs. Ana reached over and turned up the volume.

They drove another twenty miles before Ana said, "I haven't thought about anything else all week. I texted you every night I was in Atlanta to say that I had changed my mind and wanted to skip Easter after all. I even found a hot springs resort two hours from Denver and made a reservation for us. Of course I never sent the texts. I canceled the hot springs reservation yesterday afternoon."

"Regretting that decision?"

Ana nearly smiled. "So, the truth?"

"Yes, please."

"I'm scared."

"What are they going to do?"

"On Easter? Probably nothing. They will wait a few days. I bet my mom will latch on to you right away. She'll try and feed you everything. Don't let her get you drunk. And I guarantee she won't say a word to me about the fact that I'm with a woman."

"Good. We can skip a big family fight then."

"She probably won't talk to me at all. Which is worse than a slap on the face, at least in her mind. But she will get shit-faced drunk. Isabel, on the other hand, is going to say something later. She likes drama. She also likes to drink. And Sabrina would usually be on my side, but she will probably be too pregnant to give a damn about anything. Her due date is May tenth. And her baby-daddy, Johnny, is supposedly out of jail, so he'll probably make an appearance. Rick, Isabel's husband, hates Johnny. Something happened between Johnny and Isabel years ago and Rick won't let it go…so, that will be interesting. And there will be four kids running around on sugar highs from Easter candy."

"And how close is the hotel to your mom's house?"

"Don't even think about bailing," Ana replied. "Aren't you glad I waited to tell you all of this until now?"

"Maybe no one will care that you are with a woman. Maybe they will all have more important things to be thinking about like the coming baby. Or staying out of jail. Or Easter egg hunts."

Ana laughed. "Did I mention we all have to go to Mass together on Sunday? And the priest knows us by our first names. My mother will introduce you. Count on it."

"You're worth it."

Ana glanced at Riley. She started to say something and then seemed to change her mind. The radio disc jockey's voice came on and as soon as the ads started, Riley switched the station. She found another station playing more of the pop songs Ana liked.

"I am scared of what they will say. And I'm more scared of what they won't say. Then again, part of me doesn't give a damn what they think. But I really want them to know I've found someone. Anyway, whatever." Ana wiped her eyes before the tears fell. She focused on the highway. Several minutes later, she said, "I can't believe I'm really putting you through this. I'm going to owe you after this. If I survive, that is."

"I'm sure you will think of some way to make it up to me."

Ana shook her head. "Don't count on it this weekend."

* * *

Ana called her mother late Saturday night after they had gone to dinner at the restaurant by the hotel and watched a movie in their room. She told her mother that her flight had arrived late and she wanted to skip the early morning Easter egg hunt. She planned to meet up with everyone at the church instead. Riley could tell from Ana's end of the conversation that her mother wasn't happy with the change in plans. Ana ended the call quickly and without mentioning that she wasn't alone. She had spoken barely a word to Riley since they'd arrived in Lodi.

Ana slept in, or pretended to, Riley suspected, on Sunday morning. Riley went to the hotel gym, which was little more than an air-conditioned room with no windows, a rack of weights, a stationary bike and a treadmill. She worked out for over an hour only because she had nothing better to do. Ana was still in bed when she returned to the room to shower.

Riley had brought the blue linen pants that her mother had insisted she wear to a cousin's wedding years ago. She ironed her white dress shirt and slipped it on, then tried the pants. They still fit, though the butt felt a little snug. She blamed that on the muscles she developed in the weight lifting class and decided not to tuck in her shirt. Finally dressed, she sat down on the edge of the bed. Ana didn't move when she rested her hand on her shoulder. "Do you want to get breakfast before we go meet everyone?"

Ana shook her head.

"Well, I'm hungry. I'm going to take a walk and see if I can find anything."

Ana opened her eyes halfway. "Take the car. The keys are on the dresser."

"You want me to pick you up anything? Bananas are easy on even a nervous stomach."

"I'm not nervous."

"Clearly," Riley said, getting up to grab the keys. "I'll get one anyway, in case you change your mind."

Riley returned a half hour later and found Ana in the shower. Ana ate one bite of the banana and then set it aside. Still naked, she started drying her hair and was so much in her own world that she didn't hear her phone ringing. Or decided, perhaps, to ignore it entirely. Riley picked up the phone and went over to where she stood, staring at the bathroom mirror. She held out the phone. Ana glanced at the screen and shook her head. Isabel's name was on the screen. The call finally went to voice mail. Riley set the phone on the counter by Ana. She had learned to give Ana at least an hour to get ready if they were going out and she doubted today would be any different.

Riley turned on the television and ate the yogurt and granola bar she'd bought at the gas station down the road. When she'd asked about a place to get breakfast, the hotel clerk had given directions that included a description of every place within five miles. Riley hadn't paid close enough attention at the beginning of his spiel and didn't want to hear the directions to the closest place twice, so she'd driven around until she found a gas station with a food mart.

When Riley volunteered to drive to the church, Ana only nodded. She gave monosyllabic directions or simply pointed the way. Riley parked in the lot behind the church and reached for the door handle, hesitating when she realized Ana's seat belt was still fastened. "Still want to do this? I'm fine going back to the hotel and watching movies. You can pretend you came alone."

"There's my mom's car," Ana said. She pointed to a faded green Ford Focus one row away. "She's probably already inside doing her rosary. She likes appearances more than anything else." Her sisters pulled into the lot one after the other, and Ana pointed first to Sabrina's car and then to Isabel's minivan. She named each person as he or she climbed out, including all four of the children.

Once everyone had disappeared into the church, Ana unbuckled her belt and opened the door. Riley followed her inside the church. The pews were already crowded and there were more than a dozen people standing at the back. Ana dipped her finger in a bowl of holy water, touched her forehead and made the sign of the cross. Riley's family had never gone to church. She'd been inside more than a few, but only when she had traveled abroad and then only to admire the stained glass, a certain statue or the architecture of the building.

Riley hoped they'd stand in the back, but Ana made her way along the side of the pews until she was midway to the front and had found the pew where her family was sitting. Room was quickly made for Ana next to her pregnant sister by pushing the four children closer together. Riley sat down on her other side, conscious that the eyes of everyone in the pew were on her as she did so.

The Mass was difficult to follow. Riley only paid attention when people stood up or kneeled. She followed suit, keeping her eyes on Ana's folded hands the rest of the time. When the rest of her family filed out of the pew to get the flat circles of bread and a sip of wine, Ana stayed behind with Riley; they had to step out of the way as everyone returned to the pew.

It wasn't hard to pick out Ana's mother. Neither Isabel nor Sabrina looked anything like Ana. But Ana's mother shared many of Ana's features. They had the same shape to their nose and lips and the same shade of amber brown eyes. When she passed in front of Riley on returning to her seat, she smiled and it was Ana's smile. Her mother also had the unmistakable air of someone who had been quite beautiful in her day. She carried herself as if each of the three hundred or so parishioners was looking directly at her.

When Mass was over, everyone filed out of the church behind the priest and the altar boys. The procession ended in a garden area in the front of the church. Folks quickly dispersed on the lawn there, milling about the front door or queuing up in a haphazard line to shake hands with the priest. Ana's mother came right up to Riley and extended her hand. "I'm Mrs. Potrero, Ana's mother."

"I'm Riley. It's nice to meet you."

"Ana never brings anyone. What a wonderful surprise." She leaned toward Ana and kissed her cheek. Without missing a beat, she then directed their group over to the priest.

Ana shook hands with the priest right after her mother, as if she hoped to get the task over as soon as possible, then moved off to the side of the courtyard. Ana's mother introduced Riley. The priest squeezed her hand but seemed to look right through her. Riley went over to where Ana stood, though not close enough to draw attention. Ana was silent, watching her mother closely and fidgeting with the loose ring on her index finger.

Next Ana's mother introduced Johnny to the priest. He had tattoos from the edge of his collared shirt up to his ear lobes. Riley found herself staring at the ones on his lobes, trying to turn the letters into a coherent word or even code and failing, partly because Johnny kept glancing over his shoulder as if he thought someone was tailing him.

Sabrina followed behind Johnny, letting the priest brush his hand in blessing across her swollen belly and barely managing a smile in return to his murmured words. Isabel filed her four children by in a line then, wiping noses and straightening bows before each one was paraded past for a head pat. Lastly, Isabel and Rick passed in front of the priest. He smiled and took their hands in his and spoke a few words with a bowed head.

When the priest had finished with their group and moved on to the next family, Ana's mother leveled her gaze on Ana. Riley felt her straighten. The wordless exchange between Ana and her mother made Riley long to be anywhere but between the two women.

Ana turned to Isabel and quickly introduced Riley, then, when Sabrina came up to their group, finished the brief introductions.

Johnny was standing off to the side by himself and scarcely looked their direction. Ana hadn't called Riley her girlfriend. She hadn't specified any term, actually—friend or otherwise. She'd only said her name. Judging by their expressions, Riley guessed that each sister had questions on the tip of her tongue, but no one said anything.

Isabel turned to her mother and said, "The kids will be running in traffic in about five minutes if I don't get them back into the van. I'll see you at home." She called to each of the kids and then set her husband after the boy who was a hundred yards away from the rest of the pack.

Sabrina was standing next to Johnny, bracing the underside of her belly with one hand and staring at Ana. Johnny had his cell phone out and was staring at it. Riley was wondering what silent conversation was going on between Ana and Sabrina when Sabrina stepped forward and said, "It's so nice to see my sister bring someone. Did she warn you about holidays with our family?"

Riley glanced at Ana. Before she could answer, Ana's mother said, "Why would Ana need to warn anyone about having Easter with her family?"

"No reason, Mama." Sabrina winked at Riley and said, "If I weren't feeling like my belly was going to pop, I'd give you a hug." She smiled at Ana and then reached for Johnny's arm. "Anyway, I have to pee. We'll meet you at home?"

Sabrina led Johnny back into the church with an urgency that made him finally pocket the cell phone. Ana cleared her throat, and her mother's gaze turned back to her.

"Can we pick anything up from the store?" Ana asked. "Do you need anything else for the meal? Or drinks or anything?"

"It's Easter," Mrs. Potrero replied.

"I know it's Easter, but the stores are still open."

She waved her hand. "Riley, do you know that Ana hasn't been able to come here to see her niece or nephews since Christmas? And she had to miss the Easter egg hunt when she could have spent time with them. She's a busy businesswoman,

I know. Always working hard and staying so busy. And now she wants to go shopping on Easter." She leaned close to Riley and said, "I don't know how much time she spends with you, but I can guess you'd like to see more of her, wouldn't you?"

Ana's hands tightened into fists, but her arms hung at her sides. She shook her head. "I was only offering to pick something up if you needed it."

"I'll see you at home, Ana. We have everything we need."

Riley didn't offer to drive the rental car back to the airport. She just took the keys. Ana had climbed into the passenger seat wordlessly. The first half hour, they listened to music, then Ana switched off the radio. She stared out the window to the dark fields beyond the highway lights. Not long after her first drink, Mrs. Potrero had insisted Riley call her Terese and she'd kept Riley at her side for most of the afternoon and evening. The stories she'd told about Ana ranged from missed lines at a grammar school play to a high school boyfriend fiasco involving three boys that had all showed up at Terese's house the same night, each one thinking that they had a date with Ana.

Ana's sudden outing seemed to have relieved some pressure between Rick and Johnny, because they'd both murmured jokes about Ana's past relationships and discussed how the reason she'd left so many boys heartbroken was going to be retold many times over at the church.

"How are you doing?" Riley finally asked.

Ana placed her hand on Riley's thigh but continued to stare out the window. "I don't know. Numb?"

"That bad?"

"I'll tell you tomorrow. My mom will call me and leave a voice message. Then Isabel will call but only because Mom asked her to. Then Sabrina will call to check in afterward. She hugged me tonight. But I knew she'd be fine with everything. Sometimes I think she is the only reason I come back to Lodi at all." She sighed. "I'm relieved, I guess. And yet waiting for the other shoe to drop."

"I liked your family. Johnny is kind of rough around the edges, but he's sweet with Sabrina. Rick and Isabel gave me some advice for surviving your mom's Christmas as if I were already invited. And I think your mom likes me."

"I knew she would. But she didn't talk to me at all after our conversation at church." Ana pulled her hand off Riley's leg. She sank back in her seat and covered her face with her hands.

"Maybe because you acted like you didn't want to be in the same room as her," Riley said. She noted Ana's murmur of dissent but continued anyway. "Maybe you weren't ready for this."

"What do you mean?"

Riley glanced at her. "We haven't been together that long."

"I never once thought about bringing Tom to meet my family and we were together for years. Not even after he proposed. I figured they would all meet at the wedding."

"So why bring me?"

Ana took several minutes to answer. "I finally feel like this is the real me. When I'm with you, I don't have to try to be anything. I just relax and…am."

"Where were you hiding today, then?"

"I don't think my family has ever let me be that person. I'm used to pretending with them, like I did with Tom." She sighed. "Maybe you're right. Maybe I wasn't ready."

* * *

Ana had started the morning off listening to messages from work and returning a stream of emails. She seemed upset by something that had happened in Atlanta, and Riley didn't want to interrupt her to say goodbye. She left a muffin on the table near her laptop and a note wishing her a good week in San Antonio. Ana was due to fly out that afternoon and wouldn't be back in Denver until Friday. Riley was exhausted from their late flight back from Lodi but managed to make it to work in time for her first appointment. She was distracted all day, though, thinking about Ana's family and whether they would call Ana as she had predicted. She went to the gym after work and only noticed a missed call from Ana after she'd finished the weight class.

Riley showered and called Ana from the car.

Ana answered on the first ring.

"How's San Antonio?"

"I'm not in San Antonio," Ana replied.

"Change of plans?" Riley asked. After a long silent pause, Riley continued, "What happened?"

"Are you on your way home?" Ana asked.

"I can be there in ten minutes. Why aren't you in San Antonio?"

"The trip was canceled. Can you just come home?"

Riley hung up and then stared at the phone for a moment. Ana's voice had been shaky, as if she'd been crying. Riley considered calling her back but started the car instead. She had planned to go to the grocery store after her workout. She knew there was nothing in the refrigerator and her stomach was already growling. She drove home, wondering what would have made Ana cancel the San Antonio trip.

Riley found Ana still at the kitchen table. The muffin was untouched on the napkin with the note Riley had left. Riley dropped her gym bag and went over to Ana. Her eyes were ringed with red, but she'd stopped crying at some point. She had a half-empty bottle of wine next to her. She was drinking out of a juice glass. Riley only had two wineglasses in the house—which Ana had bought at some point or another—and they were probably both in the dishwasher. There was a doodle on the back of an envelope with the word "Atlanta" and a slash across it. The slash was decorated with fancy swirls, and little stick figures with knives danced along the edge of it. The whole thing was too beautifully intricate to be left on the back of an envelope.

Riley poured some of the wine into the juice glass and took a sip. She'd gotten used to even the bitter stuff that Ana sometimes brought home, but she still preferred beer. Riley picked up the envelope and turned it over. It was her utilities bill. She set it down again and glanced at Ana. "So, I'm guessing that whatever happened in Atlanta was pretty bad."

"I got fired over it anyway."

"What? You're serious?"

Ana nodded.

"I'm sorry, Ana." Riley wanted to ask what had happened, but she held back the question. "Shit."

"Exactly." She paused and shook her head. "I am so done with that entire family and especially Bea. It is absolutely ridiculous to fire someone over something like this, a single, simple mistake, but that's the way Madam Bea works. And the whole family follows her lead."

Riley sat down next to Ana. "Bea fired you?"

"No. Tom did. Or he will tomorrow. But I know Bea is putting him up to it."

"Ouch."

"Yeah. I was on the phone with just about everyone in the damn company today. Tom called at noon to say that he was flying into Denver tomorrow. I'm meeting him at the airport to turn in my laptop. He didn't have to give me a day's notice. I think he was trying to be nice. He wanted me to have a chance to take off my personal files. They usually don't give you any warning. That's why I know I'm going to be fired tomorrow. All he said was that he was going to meet me at the airport and I had to bring my laptop. He didn't need to say the rest of it."

Riley wanted to ask about the Atlanta trip. Instead, she said, "One mistake?"

Ana nodded. "That's what keeps going round in my head. Along with every other curse word I know."

"I'll drive with you tomorrow, if you want. I can change my schedule around and block off some time."

"I can't believe he's going to be the one to fire me. And I know he didn't even try to stand up for me when Madam Bea sent down her ruling. He doesn't have that kind of backbone."

She paused and looked at Riley. "I won't be able to swing the winery. Tom hinted that he's thinking of pulling his money out of the deal. It's his own money, but he won't go against Bea. I'll lose the bank loan without his money as collateral."

Ana reached for the juice glass and took a sip of wine. "This one's terrible, isn't it? Sometimes I hate wine. Besides all that,

I'm not going to have any income coming in from the winery until this summer, at the earliest. Even if I still had his money backing everything, the loan payments will start before the winery is making any money and I'm not going to have my usual paycheck from Bea to keep everything afloat in the meantime.

"So maybe it would be for the best if I did lose the loan… At least I will have the money from the condo when that deal finally closes. The way my day is going, maybe I should say, *if* the deal closes."

"You have other clients besides Tom's family, right? Maybe you can shift to working more with the other clients. I can help you out over the next few months. I have money in savings." Riley stood up and went to fill a glass of water. She set it in front of Ana.

"I used to have other clients. Now I just have Tom's family. I've been so busy working with them that I had to let my other clients go." Ana paused. "You know what I really hate about all of this? Atlanta had nothing to do with wine. I was helping Bea manage a transaction with one of her other businesses. My screwup happened to be with one of her clients that she doesn't even like." Ana picked up the glass of water and then set it down without taking a sip. "I haven't eaten anything today."

Riley stood up and went to the refrigerator. She closed it a moment later. "Eggs or toast. Or both. That's all we have." Ana nodded and Riley took out the eggs and the bread. She cracked an egg and stared at the yolk in the center of the bowl for a long minute. Finally she said, "There's something I haven't told you."

Ana leaned back in her chair and closed her eyes. "This day can't get any worse, can it? You know, my sisters both called this morning. Each one said they were worried about me. I got their voice messages, but I haven't called them back. I knew I wouldn't be able to stop myself from swearing at them. Worried? Your sister is sleeping with a woman. Why does that worry you? As I predicted, my mom never called." Ana opened her eyes and stared at Riley. "Okay, tell me what you have to say. I just want to get this day finished."

Riley scrambled the eggs while the butter melted in the pan. She dropped two slices of bread into the toaster. "I've got as much as what Tom put down for your loan sitting in the bank in a savings account." Riley paused. She didn't look at Ana. "And my credit score is good. I can be your partner on the loan."

"I don't want you to put all of your savings into this. It's a sweet offer, but I'm not about to pull you down with me."

"Ana, that isn't all of my savings. I have that savings account plus two other CDs, each with more money than I make in a year." Riley met Ana's gaze. She continued, "And I've got more money invested in stocks. A lot more, actually."

"How much more?"

"A little over four million, last time I checked the numbers. But I reinvest the interest and don't really touch anything that isn't in my bank account."

"Wait, what? You have how much money in stocks?"

Riley waited for Ana to process her omission. It felt like a secret that she'd kept from her, and it was a relief to have finally said it out loud.

Ana continued, "You drive a ten-year-old car, have Target furniture in your house and the only expensive pieces of clothing you own are overpriced jackets, but you have over a hundred grand sitting in a bank? And four million invested in stocks?"

"You buy purses from designers in Italy because of the label, but you are going to get on my case for a high quality jacket? It's cold here."

"I'm not talking about the jacket. What the hell, Riley?"

"Anyway, I didn't buy the really expensive one. It was a Christmas present from my parents."

"And they are rich too, of course. Why didn't you tell me you had money, oh, I don't know, six months ago? How did I not know? You don't act like you have money."

"Well, how should I act? It's just money. It doesn't change how I'm going to live my life."

Ana shook her head. "Only someone with four million would even think of saying that. Damn it, Riley, why didn't you tell me? And why the hell are you working your ass off as a physical therapist?"

"I like the job. What would I do otherwise?"

"I guess this explains why it was no big deal for you to get the diamond replaced on my necklace. By the way, I noticed that you upgraded the chain. It came back a lot nicer than I left it. A chain like the one you gave me probably was over five hundred, wasn't it? I thought it was odd that you were being so nonchalant about it. Now I know." She shook her head.

"Look, I'm sorry I didn't tell you before. I didn't think it really mattered." Riley paused. There was no way of undoing what she'd said. "I'm only bringing this up because I want you to know that I can help. I don't see why you should be upset."

"I'm not upset. I just found out my girlfriend is rich. Why should I be upset?"

"Yeah, well, you sound pissed."

"I've had a hell of a day." Ana sighed. "Maybe I am pissed. But I'm not pissed at you."

Riley placed a slice of buttered toast on each plate and then scooped out the eggs. She set one plate in front of Ana, then sat down opposite her with her plate. Riley waited for Ana to start eating, but she only stared at the plate. Finally, Riley took a bite to appease her growling stomach.

"What the hell, Riley? How do you have that kind of money and not tell me?" She paused a moment and then added, "I've been calling you my girlfriend since Christmas. But I don't think I've ever heard you say it. Do you call me your girlfriend when I'm not around?"

Riley hadn't called Ana her girlfriend yet. She had plenty of reasons for this, but she didn't know how to admit any of these to Ana. "I haven't really talked about you to anyone here. My parents knew about you at Christmas. When my mom calls, she always asks about you. Now that I think about it, she calls you my girlfriend. But I haven't told anyone at work. Seeing as how I was with the boss's daughter for two years and everyone at work seems to be her friend, there doesn't seem to be an easy way for me to bring it up."

"Yeah, of course." Ana's voice was quiet. She picked up her fork and pushed at the eggs.

"I'd like to tell every damn person I meet," Riley admitted.

Ana looked up from her plate. "Why don't you?"

"I guess I worry that if I tell anyone, maybe I'll somehow break the spell. I don't want to say it out loud." Riley set her fork down. She took a sip of water, feeling unsure about admitting anything more. Ana continued staring at her, waiting.

Finally Riley said, "Sometimes when you are gone for several days I think about all the ways it could go—you might just not show back up again or maybe you'd email me a breakup letter. I don't know how these things work when so much of it is long distance. Mostly, I think you would just call and say it over the phone. I know this probably sounds pathetic, or desperate, or maybe even neurotic. All of these thoughts have crossed my mind."

"I took you to meet my family and you are thinking that I'm going to drop this just like that?"

"What if your family convinces you that being with a woman isn't for you? You wouldn't come out to them before. Why not? Or what if you realize that I'm not all that interesting when you are around me more than one day a week?"

"You sound like you've been listening to your ex again." Ana shook her head. "This is crazy. I'm an adult, Riley. My family isn't going to convince me of anything I don't want to be convinced of."

"Well, that's how I feel. You asked. So, no, I haven't called you my girlfriend yet."

"You need to start." Ana took a bite of her eggs and then set down the fork. "How exactly do you have four million dollars?"

"Trust fund. My grandparents set it up. Their money paid for my schooling and bought this condo. I've invested the rest. My brother wasted a big chunk of his money gambling right at the beginning. Now my parents manage his investments along with theirs. He gets a monthly stipend deposited in an account that he regularly empties. He drinks too much and likes expensive call girls. It's nothing for him to drop a couple thousand in one night. He's blown through two cars, both of which were more than a hundred thousand each. He totaled the first one when he was drunk and the other one he drove to Mexico and left there. He won't say anything more about what happened there. Now he's got another one. A black Mercedes convertible. I'm just waiting to hear what happens to that one..."

"So that's why you don't like my car? You think luxury cars are a waste of money?"

"I don't like your car in particular because it came from Tom."

"So it has nothing to do with luxury cars necessarily. It's just that you might still be a teeny bit jealous of my ex."

"I was until about a half hour ago. Now I don't feel one bit jealous."

"I guess that is one good thing to come out of today." Ana shook her head. "When were you going to get around to telling me you had money? After you decided that I was, in fact, your girlfriend?"

"Maybe."

"I can't believe you are a trust fund kid."

"I'm twenty-nine," Riley countered.

"I didn't mean 'kid.' It's just an expression." Ana started eating. "You know, I would have never guessed. If I hadn't lost my job and Tom was still going to let me use his money for the loan, I bet you would never have told me."

"It would have come up eventually. I thought about it, but the timing never seemed right. I figured you would think I was jealous of Tom if I told you that I could loan you the money for the winery."

"You *are* jealous of Tom. Were jealous, I should say."

Riley shrugged. "See?"

"I think you should replace your car. How about a nice Mercedes or BMW?" Ana's face cracked with a smile.

"No way."

"Maybe just a new Honda? Or at least a used one that was made in this decade? Consider the new safety features." Ana reached over their plates and took Riley's hand in hers. She squeezed Riley's hand. "I want to start this conversation over."

"Okay. Where should we start?"

"I want you to offer to help with the loan payments for the winery one more time. Then I'm going to say 'okay.' And 'thank you.'" Ana sighed. "Just for the next few months until we're open with a full schedule and only if I can't swing the payments on my own."

"Then I'll say 'you're welcome.'"

Ana picked up her toast and took a bite. "Maybe I should have eaten this breakfast twelve hours ago. I feel better already."

"I'll tell the next person I meet that you're my girlfriend."

"I want to hear it. And I want to present my business plan to you. Again. I want you to be sure you are making the right decision if you put your money down on this winery."

"And then, let me guess. You want to review my assets," Riley said, predicting Ana's thoughts.

"So, let's talk about your stock investments. Do you realize you have only invested in three different companies? Most people have a whole portfolio."

"I like the three that I picked." Riley pulled her shirt on over her head and glanced at Ana. She was sitting up in bed, naked, with Riley's laptop propped up on the pillows next to her. Riley buckled her belt and then picked out socks. Ana's bra hung from the knob on her sock drawer.

"You need to diversify. The way you have things set up is pretty risky. One company goes down and you haven't lost a couple thousand dollars, Riley. You've lost a million or more. When was the last time you looked closely at these numbers? You can't put all your eggs in one basket."

"Technically, there are three baskets, not one. I decided a while ago that I can't keep track of more than three companies."

"You don't have to," Ana argued. "That's why you have an investment firm managing the money for you."

"No. I want to manage my own money. And, yes, I've looked at my numbers lately. I check the numbers every day. I'm doing quite well, thank you very much."

Ana sighed. "I figured you were going to say that. All right, at least I tried. And I'm not sure that I'm done reviewing everything. Mind if I keep tabs on your three picks?"

"Not at all. But don't expect me to change my mind without a fight. Anything else?"

"When will you be home?"

Riley laced her shoes and eyed Ana. "Do you know that is the first time you have ever asked me that?"

Ana nodded. "It did sound a little weird. I'm not used to waiting around for anyone to come home."

"Call me after you meet with Tom?"

Ana closed the laptop. "You mean, call after I get fired."

"You sure you don't want me to drive with you to the airport?"

"No thanks. I'd like to cry alone. And then I will be done with crying over this whole thing. We've got a lot of work to do so I'm not even going to think about what happened in Atlanta or with Tom's family after I get back from the airport. I'm making you dinner tonight. When will you be home?" She repeated the question.

Riley leaned over the bed and kissed her. "I'll leave work when you call. You can call the front desk. Tell my receptionist that I need to get my ass home to my beautiful girlfriend."

Ana returned the kiss. "Don't tempt me."

* * *

Ana was inside the winery. Riley could see her through the panes of glass. She was directing the placement of wine bottles, surveying a tray of appetizers that the chef had brought out to her and casting periodic glances at her watch and the clipboard in her hands. The chef wasn't French, though Ana had hoped that she was when she'd seen the name on the résumé. Claire Rousseau was from Georgia, actually, and had a warm Southern accent that flew in the face of Ana's grand vision. Her creations, every recipe that she'd tested out on Ana and that Riley had shared, were amazing, however. She'd made even Riley consider the finer points of a merlot, juxtaposed with one of her dishes. Ana couldn't argue. More than the congeniality of any of the servers, Claire's artistry could convince guests to linger a while longer and to taste another wine or perhaps even have dessert.

The first week had gone smoothly, but tonight's official opening, complete with a reporter from the food section of the tiny local paper, seemed to have Ana on edge. Riley watched her a moment longer and then crossed the footbridge.

Sharon was inside with Deb, sitting at one of the tables with a view of the river. They had a basket of folded napkins between them and a much bigger pile still to fold. Sharon looked up and said, "Perfect timing. Your girlfriend needs a break. She's hollered at just about everyone in here."

Ana set down her clipboard. "I may have raised my voice."

"They can handle it," Riley said, hugging Ana.

"The band is running late. Claire had to go to the store for something last minute. She refused to let anyone else run the errand. I was going to have the linens folded, but it slipped my mind. Now I'm trading a bottle of wine to have Deb and Sharon fold for me."

"The place looks great."

Ana sighed. She stepped back from Riley and turned about slowly. "I didn't have time to touch up that spot above the door," she said, pointing to the back door leading out to the patio. "I forgot about that. Damn. Do you think it's too late to grab a brush?"

"Well, I'm sure the guy from the paper is going to pick right up on that spot if you don't touch it up," Riley teased. "Ana, they're here for the wine and the food. They are going to love this place. Relax."

"You're *telling* me to relax?" Ana shook her head.

"Yeah, I am. It's a warm night, the streets are crowded with tourists…"

Ana placed a finger on Riley's lips. "I've got a better idea. Why don't you *show* me instead." She clasped Riley's hand and then turned, pulling her toward the back hallway. They passed the kitchen and reached the storage room. The door was unlocked.

Boxes of wine were stacked from the floor to the ceiling. There was a lightbulb that hung from a beam with a chain cord, but Ana didn't reach for it. Instead, she pushed Riley up against the first row of boxes. Her palm pressed against Riley's chest, pinning her in place. She leaned close and their lips met.

* * *

Sunlight streamed in through the cottage window. Already too warm, Riley pushed back the sheet and pulled on a T-shirt and cargo pants. Ana was still sleeping, curled up on her side, and didn't shift when Riley opened the front door. It was before eight and the day already promised to be a hot one. Riley went to the main house and found Sharon making breakfast. Deb was flipping through the paper and munching on a piece of toast. They looked up and smiled when Riley pushed open the back door.

"I didn't expect to see either of you up this early," Sharon said.

"Ana's still sleeping. Is there another copy of the paper? I wanted to see if they had the winery's review in there yet."

Deb pointed to the side counter. "I grabbed two copies when I went out this morning. And no, I won't tell you what it says."

"I already know it says that my girlfriend rocked that grand opening."

Deb shrugged and Riley felt a moment of misgiving.

"'Girlfriend,' huh? Last time we talked, I didn't think you were ready to call her that." Sharon set two coffee cups and a carafe on a tray with toast and pointed at a bowl of fruit. "If you want to chop up your favorite fruit, go right ahead. Ana likes the peaches. When you two are ready for my frittatas, just let me know."

"I've been wanting to call Ana my girlfriend for a long time," Riley admitted. She picked out a peach, a mango and a handful of strawberries and began slicing. "But I had this fear that it wasn't going to last."

"So what changed?" Sharon asked.

Deb reached over and stole a strawberry from Riley's pile. She popped it in her mouth and smiled. "She's been calling you her girlfriend for months now, you know."

Riley nodded. She continued slicing the fruit, grabbing an extra peach when half of the first one was snagged by Sharon. When Deb reached for the other peach, Riley pointed the knife tip at her hand playfully.

"Your mom called to reserve a room in August," Sharon said. "They're only here for two nights?"

"Yeah, they're always too busy to stay anywhere long. I doubt that they will want to do any of the usual touristy things anyway. They're mainly coming to meet Ana. My mom liked her as soon as she heard Ana was into fancy jewelry."

Riley finished slicing the fruit and set half of it in a bowl in front of Deb, who smiled in return. The rest of the fruit, aside from the pieces that Sharon picked out as she walked by, she put in another bowl on the tray with the toast.

Sharon rolled the newspaper up and tucked it under Riley's arm. "Ana's nervous about meeting your folks."

"You think so?" Riley was surprised at this. Ana seemed so at ease in social gatherings that Riley couldn't imagine she'd be concerned about this introduction.

Sharon laughed. "Sometimes, Riley, you can be entirely clueless. You do know that she's head over heels for you, right?"

Riley shook her head. "Ana isn't the type to be head over heels for anyone." She thanked Sharon and headed back to the cottage with the tray of food. She passed a couple who were pulling back the hot tub cover and entered the cottage as Ana was coming out of the bathroom.

"Morning."

Ana nodded. She glanced at the tray that Riley had set on the dresser and eyed the newspaper before climbing back into bed. She pulled the sheet up to her waist. "I don't think I want to read it. Just tell me if it is good or bad."

"I haven't read it yet."

Ana sighed. She had put on one of Riley's T-shirts and her hair was pulled back in a low ponytail. "What if the review is terrible?"

"Blame it on the wine?"

"We make the wine, Riley."

Riley sat down on the bed and thumbed through the paper until she found the food section. The review had a picture of the front of the winery that Ana had a photographer take. It was a good shot, showing part of the footbridge and the new arched entryway above the new front door. She'd sent it to the newspaper along with the notice about the winery's grand opening.

"Well?" Ana asked.

"I still haven't read it yet."

Ana leaned over Riley's shoulder, but then sank back against the pillows. "I can't read it."

Riley stared at the picture a moment longer. The photographer had shot the picture from nearly the same place where Riley had stood when she'd watched Tom kiss Ana. It didn't seem that long ago that she had watched them together, and yet so much had happened since then.

Ana exhaled. "It's bad, isn't it?"

Riley glanced over her shoulder at Ana. "I was thinking about something else. Sorry. I'll read it now."

"What were you thinking about?"

Riley set the paper down and shifted back in the bed. She reached for Ana's hand and kissed it. "It really doesn't matter what the review says. The staff's friendly, the food's awesome, the wine's great and your renovations made the place. We had a big crowd last night, and everyone was excited about coming back. It's going to work. I just know it." Riley added, "Unless we get completely destroyed by a flood, that is."

"You made me get flood insurance, remember?"

Riley continued, "I'm really looking forward to seeing what happens next. With the wine shop—and with us."

"Right now I just want to know what's going to happen with the wine shop. Read the damn review."

Riley picked up the paper again and started to read. The article was short but entirely positive. The reviewer loved the wine. She'd had the Peach Sauvignon first, then the Mountain

Merlot that was made in the big barrels inside the shop. She'd sampled several of Claire's small plates and had given every dish a rave review. Riley smiled at Ana. "It's a great review. You have to read it."

"Really? It's good?"

"It's great." Riley set the paper in Ana's lap and leaned over and kissed her. "And—I love you."

Ana distractedly returned the kiss. She read the three paragraphs quickly and then clapped her hands together. "We nailed it. She loved everything!"

"Totally nailed it," Riley agreed. "And she didn't even notice that spot over the door that needed painting. Probably a good thing that I slipped her that hundred bucks, huh?"

Ana arched her eyebrow and swatted the paper at Riley's shoulder. "Don't even tease like that." Ana sighed. "My mom called last night. She left me a message. She remembered it was the winery's grand opening and she said she wished she could see it."

"You could send her a plane ticket," Riley suggested. Sabrina had had her baby in May, and Ana had a trip planned for the christening at the end of the month. Riley knew that Ana was in touch with Isabel as well. It seemed that whatever issues her family had initially with her dating a woman hadn't been enough to keep them from calling. Since the trip to Lodi, though, Riley hadn't heard Ana say anything about her mom.

"She won't fly," Ana returned. "But I think it's enough that she called."

Riley pulled Ana into an embrace. "Did I mention how much I love you?"

"Enough to pay off a newspaper reporter, apparently."

"Even more than that." Riley grinned.

"I love you too," Ana said, relaxing in Riley's arms. "And I want to spend the rest of the day with you. I'm not going anywhere near the winery today. Maybe we should climb that mountain you keep talking about."

"Pikes Peak? Are you serious?"

"You don't think I can?" Ana kissed her, this time without any distraction. "I think you underestimate me." She curled her arm to show off her flexed biceps. It was hard to make out the muscle bump and Ana knew it.

Riley kissed Ana's arm. "I'd love to go hiking with you."

"By the way, in case you're wondering, I already know what will happen with us."

"What's that? Do we get a happy ever after?" Riley joked.

"I don't really believe in those," Ana admitted. "But I think there's a good chance we're going to come close. Very, very close."

Bella Books, Inc.

Women. Books. Even Better Together.

P.O. Box 10543
Tallahassee, FL 32302

Phone: 800-729-4992
www.bellabooks.com